I0731383

A Country Mile
(Gifts of the Heart)

*A sweet, Latter-day Saint
contemporary romance*

by Lea Carter

Chapter 1

"Just let us know what you have and what you want," Merry leaned back against a beautifully restored mahogany armoire, "and we'll go a country mile for you." She carefully held the pose while she counted down—*five, four, three, two…*

"Cut!" Tony grinned as he straightened away from his camera. "Perfect!" He'd have to do a little tweaking to get the lighting right, despite his best efforts and equipment. But her voice hadn't broken *and* she'd remembered to smile the whole time. This clip, combined with the before-and-after photos she took of every project, was really going to dress up her business website.

"Yeah." She did her best to smile, but couldn't help asking one more time, "Are you sure that didn't sound too cheesy?" It was weird enough acting in front of Tony, whom she'd known since he spilled glitter all over her in kindergarten, but the camera's one unblinking eye made her positively jittery. Still full of nervous energy, she removed the hair monster that she'd used to tame her damp ginger-brown hair and clipped it to her jeans' front pocket. Deftly, she swept her hair back into a braid, securing it with a spare hair tie from her pocket.

Tony laughed as he eased his camera off the tripod. "I'm sure. It's great publicity, y'know?

Puts the name of your business out there, makes it easy for people to remember. Not to mention letting folks get a look at you. Face to the name, right?" Securing his camera, he began storing his lights and reflectors. A local photographer, he did it all, from filming quinceañeras to seventieth wedding anniversaries.

"Yeah." Merry maintained the plastic smile she'd perfected over the last three days of filming. Sure, she'd worn her favorite shirt—the one that camouflaged her flab without being shapeless—and had her hair down for the filming. She'd even worn mascara so that the full length of her eyelashes would show up, something Tony had enthusiastically supported. That didn't mean she was keen on the idea of thousands of strangers looking at her. The complete lack of control in the situation had knotted her stomach like a string of last year's Christmas lights.

On the other hand, if a thousand new people visited her website because of the video, well. That was the whole point. Tucking her hands into her jeans' pockets, she said, "Thanks again for helping me get my website updated to this century."

"Hey, no problem. Thanks for restoring my grandmother's armoire." He zipped his equipment bag. "Judy's going to go absolutely nuts!" When he'd approached Merry about getting her to fix it up as a gift for his wife, he hadn't been prepared for the estimated price tag.

After a hasty retreat and some furtive research confirmed she'd actually offered him the family and friends' discount, he'd started racking his brain for other gift ideas. Lucky for them both, Merry had the brilliant idea of trading her expertise for his.

Merry's mouth relaxed into a genuine smile. "It was my pleasure." And she meant it. She loved every bit of her job, from wheeling in the latest project to wrapping it in protective cloths and sending it on its way, ready to face the world again. "Maybe she can be my first video testimonial," she joked.

Unfortunately, Tony took her seriously. As they wrapped the armoire and loaded it onto his truck, his plans for videoing Judy's delight grew grander and grander until Merry was glad to wave goodbye. She dialed Judy as she swung the massive barn door shut. Tony had an embarrassing knack for guessing wrong when it came to gifts for his wife, so when he approached Merry, she'd discreetly reached out to Judy before offering to swap the armoire for the photos and video.

"Hey, Judy?" Merry grinned as the woman's excited voice reached her. "Yes, he's on his way. But," she cleared her throat, "I sort of gave him an idea. He's…going to video you being surprised." Relief washed over her as Judy's laugh sounded in her ear, followed instantly by promises to be convincing. "You've seriously been practicing?"

Merry shook her head even as she armed her security system. The sun wasn't quite behind the tree line in the far pasture, but she was worn out. And since she worked for herself, closing time was when she felt like it.

"No, I haven't forgotten. You were extremely convincing as Mary Poppins in high school," Merry agreed. "If anybody can do this, it's you. Have fun!" Ending the call, she looked down to see why her left hand was hurting. "Mystery solved," she muttered as she released her death-grip on the edge of the worktable. Texting Judy wouldn't have been as stressful, but calling had its good points. Like getting the job done quickly and with less risk of misunderstandings.

Shrugging, she crossed the room and climbed the stairs. The scents of oranges and baked bread—along with faint notes of the sweet grass hay that was stored here during her childhood—greeted her as she opened the door to her loft home, effectively banishing any lingering stress. Tucking her keys into her pocket, she stepped out of her shoes and padded across the hardwood floor she'd installed herself. Terrible as losing her grandparents had been, inheriting this place ten years ago was quite possibly the best thing that ever happened to her.

Lifting the bread pan out of the machine, she shook the loaf onto the granite counter, where she draped a towel over it so it would steam itself while it cooled.

Snagging an orange from the bowl on the island, she began peeling it on her way to the glass double doors.

From there, she could see out over the verandah to where a tractor moved in the south fields. The forecast was predicting rain for tomorrow, so Sam, the man she leased her pastures to, might be out there all night baling hay for winter.

Shifting a little, she looked to her right and could see the new barn he'd put up, as well as the front lawn of the old farmhouse where her father and his seven siblings were raised. Three of Sam's five children were chasing fireflies and she couldn't help laughing at their dramatic efforts. Though she couldn't hear it, she knew the instant the squeaky backdoor of the farmhouse opened. Heads swung toward it and shoulders slumped as the children obediently trooped inside for baths and jammies. Bedtime always came early on school nights.

Hard to believe Halloween was in a few days.

Popping the last orange slice into her mouth, Merry savored the explosion of flavor. Tony's filming took them straight through her usual suppertime, so she should be starving. Meandering back to the bread, she sliced off a heel and slathered it with peanut butter. Added a tall glass of chilled milk with a sigh. The older she got, the less interest she took in fancy foods.

Which was another way of saying that at the ripe old age of thirty-seven, she was getting bored.

Folding her arms, she offered a prayer of gratitude, addressed her stress over the video, and asked a blessing on the food.

She could see most of what she was thankful for when she opened her eyes. The wide-open floorplan showed living room and kitchen at a glance. A comfy, extra-long couch stood near the door, its back suitably draped with soft, colorful blankets, and opposite a modest flat-screen TV. She'd built the shelves and closet that ran along to the right of the door with her own hands.

A single piece of plush carpet remnant stretched from the far wall to what she figured as the kitchen boundary. That was also where the flooring switched to sensible linoleum. A walnut island with a stainless steel double basin sink was positioned near the stove and fridge. The same dark wood continued around the edges of the room. Having a personal loathing of below-waist cupboards, she'd gone with a drawers-only approach under the counter, supplemented with shoulder-height cupboards and a closet off to one side that she'd designed specifically for pots, pans, and those once-a-year appliances.

To the left of the double doors was her version of a pantry, reinforced wooden shelves stacked high with canned goods. It followed the wall to where it ended opposite her washer and dryer set, which sometimes doubled as a handy sorting surface when she came home loaded after a box sale or the like.

Her stomach satisfied, she rinsed the glass and set it in her half-size dishwasher. Memories of her friends' disbelief at the one economy-sized item she'd chosen made her chuckle. Living alone, she didn't dirty enough dishes for a full-sized dishwasher. And she'd rather run it twice after a party than do dishes by hand routinely.

Frowning, she checked the time on the huge old wall clock. It was only six. There were still two hours until she was due for movie night at her friend, Noella's. Her fingers tapped out a rhythm on the counter as she considered her choices. She didn't have quite enough time to start her latest project, a massive old dining room table with soft spots in the middle and a badly scarred leg.

However. There was one ongoing project that took as big or as little a chunk of time as she had.

Going back downstairs, she headed straight for a table on the far side of the room. Settling herself on the padded stool by the table, Merry opened a long, flat box to reveal a set of expensive carving tools. They'd arrived with the wood for the job and still took her breath away.

Gently, she moved a soft cloth to expose twenty smallish pieces of red teak wood.

From inside a carefully padded, silk-lined box, eight completed ebony spider monkeys grinned at her from individual slots. A pair of regal black panthers occupied the center of the row above the monkeys, the male panther's teeth bared menacingly. On either side of them, pairs of South American predators were frozen in various hostile poses, perfect matches for the images her customer had provided along with both kinds of wood. The last sixteen slots sat temporarily empty, waiting for her to finish carving the red teak half of the chess set.

Merry selected a tool and turned her attention to the squirrel monkey she'd left half-finished in order to get the armoire done on Tony's schedule. Painstakingly, she carved out the monkey's mischievous lips and pronounced eyes. Exposed slender fingers wrapped around a slim branch, already partially stripped of its bark.

She gasped and glared at her phone when it began to vibrate.

She didn't recognize the number. Or even the area code. So why did she feel prompted to answer it? It was true that people didn't always change their cell number when they moved, which could explain the strange area code. Of course, she could always listen to the message…assuming the robo-caller left one.

But this felt different. She fidgeted with the tool she was still holding, groaned, and took the call.

"Hello?"

"Hello!" A deep voice cheerfully responded.

"Is this Sister McKinney?"

Her frown deepened. What in the…? "Yes, this is she." Why was someone from church calling?

"This is Brother Tyrel Scott from church," the voice identified itself. "How are you today?"

Merry very carefully set the tool down. She despised small talk with strangers—and even if they belonged to the same church. Until she could at least put a face with the voice, he was a stranger.

"Fine." The monosyllabic response was the best she could muster on short notice. In the past, she would've used an ice water tone to boot. Discourage him as best as she could as quickly as possible so she could get off the phone. Since she was trying to be less prickly, though, today she took a deep breath and got to her feet to walk off some of her anxious energy. Politely asked, "How are you?"

"Great! Thanks for asking!" His chuckle thrummed through her, jangling already taut nerves. "Now, to make a long story short, we've got a family moving into the area tomorrow and rumor has it that you've got a pickup truck."

Merry stopped pacing so suddenly she almost fell over. *Her truck?* She'd gotten worked up over a call to borrow her truck? For a move-in that she already knew about? Shoot, she'd spent a couple of hours over at the house that week, helping clean it. Still. She couldn't exactly control her fear of the unexpected.

"What time do you need it?" she asked, skipping over the part where he actually asked for permission to use it. Finishing other peoples' thoughts was something she did too often, really.

"Oh, um…" Tyrel cleared his throat. "We're meeting over there at ten tomorrow morning, but it's about a thirty-minute drive from the church. What I'd like to do, if it's okay with you, is come over around nine tomorrow morning and trade my car for your truck. That way you'll have access to a vehicle in case the project takes longer than expected."

Merry arched an eyebrow. Pleasant voice, direct, and thoughtful. She could almost enjoy this conversation if she just knew who he was. Surely they'd bumped into each other or someone had pointed him out? But she drew a blank.

"That would work," she agreed. "Thank you." While it was highly unlikely that she'd need his car, she appreciated the gesture. It would've been just as easy for him to bring a second driver and take both vehicles to help with the move.

"Wonderful! And *thank you*." He stressed the last two words. "I hated to ask you last minute like this, but one of the trucks we were counting on broke down this morning."

She opened her mouth to reassure him, to tell him it was no trouble or some other half-true platitude. But it was a little bit of trouble, if only because of the phone call. So that wouldn't be accurate.

Biting her lip, she redirected her thoughts from herself and went a different route.

"It must be hard to put something like this together."

His answering chuckle didn't seem nearly as abrasive as the first one.

"Every time I think I have it corralled, it jumps!"

Despite herself, she laughed with him. It wasn't just the funny mental image of a group of pickup trucks leaping a barbed wire fence, either. Milk cows had been part of her childhood, including one particularly persnickety Angus that led them on many a lengthy chase until it was finally decided she'd be just as useful—and a whole lot less trouble—in the freezer.

"Anyhow," he paused briefly. "Thanks again. See you in the morning."

"You're welcome." He ended the call and she was left staring at her phone, waiting.

Usually she felt relieved when a call ended. Especially unexpected calls from people she didn't know personally.

"Weird." Tucking the phone into her pocket, she put her tools away, dusted the table and squirrel monkey with a shop brush, then covered it all with the cloth again.

Bouncing the shop brush's bristles lightly on the surface of another table to remove any dust and wood chips it might've picked up, she dusted off the front of her clothes. As she threaded her way through tables and equipment toward the side door, she automatically checked each piece of equipment to make sure they were secure.

Her hand hovered over the coat she kept hanging by the door, then she shrugged. October in the Ozarks could get nippy after dark, but so far it hadn't been all that bad.

On her way to her truck, she idly pulled up a church app on her phone. Searched for Brother Tyrel Scott in her ward directory. Odds were slim to none that he'd have uploaded a photo to go along with his contact information. She certainly hadn't. She…nearly dropped her keys. *Whew!* Piercing blue eyes stared at her out of a ruggedly handsome face. Almost more startling than his good looks was that he was in an Air Force uniform. Tapping on the photo, she enlarged it and squinted at his insignia—a brace of silver bars. Just like Captain Faye Turner on *Pool of Stars.* Hmmm.

Giving herself a good shake, she put her phone away. Yanking her truck door open, she climbed in and buckled up. Her cell phone began playing "The First Noel," making her jump in surprise. Fishing it back out with two fingers, she accepted the call and brought the phone to her ear.

"Noella, hi."

"Merry!" A flood of Acadian French followed, propelled along by Noella's anxiety.

"Too fast!" Merry shoved the English words into the conversation. "I can't listen that fast, Noella!" She'd learned a little French from one of her companions while on a proselyting mission for the Church of Jesus Christ of Latter-day Saints, and enjoyed trying to learn more by talking with Noella. She simply didn't speak the language well enough to keep up with this breakneck pace. "Now you said something was missing," she switched to French as Noella began muttering something under her breath. "Did someone break into your house? Are you alright?"

"Yes, yes, fine," Noella responded, still in French but much more calmly. Changing to English, she explained, "There has been no break-in. I am missing the ingredients."

"Ingredients?" Merry choked back a laugh. Noella was *very* passionate about food and honestly, nobody liked to be laughed at. "Um, what are you out of?"

"Cinnamon," Noella almost wailed. "I use it all up making the filling."

"Cinnamon?" Merry pivoted toward her door. "I have plenty of cinnamon. I'll be there in a minute, okay?" The sound of a doorbell echoed in her ear. Noella's doorbell.

"No, no!" Noella definitely did wail this time. "They are here! They are here and the pastries are not ready!"

"It's okay, it's okay," Merry soothed as she bounded up the stairs to the loft. "It's probably

Grace, right? She likes to be early." Shouldering the door open, she raced to her cupboards and pocketed the cinnamon. Hopefully, ground cinnamon would be good enough. "Ask her about the puppies she delivered last week. That'll keep her busy until I get there."

"Yes! Yes, I will."

Merry pulled the phone away from her ear. Yep, Noella had ended the call as abruptly as it had begun. Chuckling, she stuffed her phone back in her pocket and hurried back to her truck, her melancholy officially banished. It was good to be contributing something tangible to the evening. Hauling herself into the cab, she headed toward Noella's house.

Chapter 2

Thirty minutes later, Merry accepted a tray of piping hot les oreilles de cochon pastries—which translated into the charming 'pig's ear' pastries—from Noelle and added it to the stack. There wasn't exactly enough room for Noella's love of cooking in her tiny kitchen, so they were improvising as usual.

Grace volunteered to wash dishes while Noella swirled the dough in hot oil to create the shape they were named for. It was the politest way Grace knew to turn her back on her hostess, the 'cute French girl' as Alec Fitzsimmons had called Noella earlier. Oh, he made Grace so mad sometimes! It was bad enough that he was oblivious to how she felt about him. Did he have to notice other women out loud to her?

Merry bravely tackled decorating the finished pastries with the also-handmade sweet syrup, making sure to leave three of them nut-free because of Harmony's mild tree nut allergy. Speaking of which...

"Has anyone heard from Harmony?" she asked in French, shooting a worried look at the oven clock.

"She was planning to come when I talked to her on Wednesday." Grace shook her head, sending soft waves of her red hair swishing over her shoulders. She'd taken French while getting her undergraduate degree and was thrilled at the chance to speak it. "Sometimes I worry about her."

"*You* worry about her?" Noella spared Grace a glance. "If you hold still for more than five seconds, you will fall asleep on your feet!"

Grace blushed a little. "There was an emergency last night," she protested. The local vet, she was at the mercy of stuff and things for the entire county.

"And Harmony's been stretched kind of thin lately," Merry filled in, stumbling a little over the translation. "That can happen when you work for yourself."

"Et voila!" Noella lifted the last pastry clear of the oil and transferred it to a paper towel-lined tray. She'd already turned the stovetop off, so now she carefully lifted the pot to a backburner where there was less danger of it getting knocked over. "Time for the movie!"

Merry looked at the clock again. Noella was right. The agreement was that they'd wait half an hour for anyone who couldn't make it on time. After that, you were just late and had to take the consequences. Even if that meant you only got to watch the end of a mystery. Stepping aside to let Noella access the treats, Merry accepted a plated pastry and took a seat in the living room.

"What're we watching tonight?" Grace asked, seating herself beside Merry. She hoped it was funny. Distracting. No unrequited love.

"*Murder at the Opera*," Noella announced, producing a case with a flourish.

"Hmm." Merry chewed her first bite of pastry. Her ears pricked up at the familiar sound of a loud, rolling bass—getting louder. "Harmony's coming."

"So I hear," laughed Grace. Popping out of her seat, she hurried to the door. Waited, then opened it when Harmony's car radio turned off.

"Hello, hello!" Harmony was halfway out of her coat before she made it all the way inside. "What're we watching?"

"*Murder at the Opera*," chorused Merry and Grace, grinning at each other.

"With English subtitles?" Harmony looked at them over her shoulder as she hung her coat up.

"With English speaking," Noella announced, her finger hovering over the play button.

"English speaking?" Harmony echoed as she kicked off her shoes. She didn't mind subtitles, but this was a pleasant surprise. "Wow, tonight must be special!" Taking off her hat, she shook her chestnut brown hair free. "Sorry I'm late. Had a flat." She shrugged dismissively, not quite ready to discuss the handsome—if grumpy—man who'd helped her out.

"You get the floor," Merry told her as she came around the end of the couch.

"I see that," Harmony laughed. "Oh thanks, Grace." Harmony beamed at her friend, who was offering her a plate with a delicious-looking treat.

Spying the nuts on the other desserts, she discreetly inspected her own. The girls were careful of her allergy, but she held herself responsible. Thankfully, she'd never had worse than a bad rash, but held firmly to the belief that an ounce of prevention was worth a pound of cure. Plopping down where she could lean against the couch, she bit into her pastry.

"Wow." Harmony gave Noella a thumbs-up. "This is great!" The spices were a little strong for her taste. And she wasn't sure flavored fry-bread was actually better than plain with butter and honey…but there was nothing to be gained by voicing her dissenting thoughts. Noella would still like what she liked and the recipe wouldn't change.

Once they were all settled, Noella started the show again. *A Sharp Soprano*, the first installment of the *Murder at the Opera* series, was a lighthearted, mostly plausible yarn about a woman whose persistent nosiness helped solve two baffling murders—and the good luck that kept her from becoming victim number three. It also turned out to be the first in a five-movie series.

"Guess we know what we're watching next time you host," Grace chuckled as she collected plates.

"Absolutely!" Noella agreed enthusiastically. "But if you think I'm waiting four weeks to watch the rest of them, you're nuts."

Merry laughed with the others and high-fived Noella. "Nice idiom!" Though Noella spoke English quite well, they all enjoyed teaching her new phrases.

She hung around a while longer, savoring her time with her friends. Petite, honey-blond Noella was the youngest of the group and a fairly recent transplant from Prince Edward Island. Willowy Grace, the friend of a lifetime, and the most easy-going member of the group, in direct contradiction to her fiery red hair. Vivacious Harmony, running so hard to keep up with herself that few people could keep up with her; luckily for their little group, she also happened to be a die-hard silver screen fan.

"Alright, well," Merry nodded at the clock on the wall, "if I don't get home on time, I'll miss my appointment with the sandman." Grace, caught mid-yawn, started to laugh. Merry hid a worried frown. When Grace laughed that easily, she was too tired. Like the time at girls' camp where she couldn't find her shoes to wear to the bathroom in the middle of the night. Merry had woken up to find her giggling while she put on every sock she'd brought, one after another. Most of them on her right foot.

"Mmm, the sandman." Harmony grinned, stretched by arching her back like a cat, then bounced to her feet. "Y'know, he's never once gotten my order right?"

"Never?" Noella grinned. "No dreams about

handsome, single billionaires for you?" They all laughed at that.

Merry stepped into her shoes and hugged Noella, who'd come to stand by the door. "Thanks for having us over," she smiled. As she stepped out into the darkness, worry hit her full force. Should she say something? If she gave Grace a lift and Harmony drove Grace's work truck, she could bring Harmony back here to pick up her car, a tough little hatchback. Of course, she'd be traveling the same direction as Grace for the first few miles, but then Grace would turn north and she'd head south. She could follow Grace, just in case something went wrong?

Anxiety—a phantom mass of cold, cooked spaghetti noodles in the pit of her stomach— wriggled happily and spread a little further through her torso as the other girls came out to their cars. Exhaling shakily, Merry pasted a smile on her face and hugged Harmony, whose bear hug squeezed some of the tension out of her.

When it was time to hug Grace, she encouraged, "You'll be careful on the drive home, right?"

"Of the deer?" Grace nodded gravely. "They've been bad this year. Especially out on the long, empty stretches of highway."

Merry didn't feel much better as she watched Grace cross the yard and open her truck door, but what else could she do? Grace was a full-grown, highly competent woman. And Merry knew her own tendency to over-think things.

"Text me when you get home, alright?" Grace called. "Both of you." She pointed at Merry and Harmony.

"Will do!" Harmony agreed immediately. She appreciated having someone spare her an extra thought.

"Will do," Merry echoed, relief flooding through her and beating back the 'spaghetti' monster. She'd text Grace, who'd text her back, and she wouldn't have to lie awake worrying about her friend. Who was more like family, with all the time they'd spent together growing up. The three-year gap between them felt like the Grand Canyon in her early teens, but now she hardly remembered it.

Offering a final wave to Noella, Merry climbed into her own truck. "Let's go home, girl," she murmured as she turned the key in the ignition. Easing onto the street, she meandered away until her rearview mirror showed Harmony's car turning left out of Noella's driveway. Lowering her passenger side window a bit, she hummed along with an old song on the radio. In an unusual bit of luck, the radio station kept up a steady stream of similar, hummable songs all the way home.

As always, it was a relief to walk into her own home and take off her shoes. Starting the washer as she passed it, she texted Grace on her way up the stairs to her bedroom. Paused in the doorway to fully enjoy the sensation of her bare feet sinking into the plush carpet.

Smiled when her phone buzzed with Grace's response.

[Glad you're home safely! See you Sunday!]

After typing out a reply and hitting send, Merry crossed the room to an apparently unused section of pearly-white wall that stood to the left of her nearly room-width window seat. No shelves, no decorations, not even a doorknob indicating a peaked-roof closet.

Undeterred by its obvious uselessness, Merry brought both hands up and pressed on the wall. There was a faint *click* as the paneling popped free of its restraints to swing open. Smiling, she slipped inside her expertly sound-proofed recording booth, triggering a motion-sensor floodlight. Inside, a small array of instruments greeted her—guitars, a violin, a short row of handmade ocarinas, a low D Irish whistle, and an inexpensive drum set.

Tugging the door shut behind her, she turned on her electronic keyboard. It didn't sound quite as sweet as a genuine piano, but she'd never figured out how to get a piano inside the six by ten recording booth. Not comfortably, and certainly not without having to explain it to whoever helped her lug the piano up all forty-four steps from the ground floor. It didn't matter, to be honest. She wasn't a diva performing for the queen of…anyplace. Setting a 'lights only' timer for an hour, she settled onto the keyboard bench. Stretched her fingers and rolled her shoulders to loosen them.

Hymns were her go-to for warmups. "Before Thee, Lord, I Bow My Head." "Did You Think to Pray?" "Come, O Thou King of Kings." A tear escaped as she sang the last verse of "I Stand All Amazed."

Calm and relaxed, Merry turned her attention to a new tune that had been circling around in her mind for the last few days. Starting with the base melody, she slowly added harmony. Fiddled with the dynamics until she discerned the piece's natural volumes. Over and over it she went until she was satisfied with how it sounded.

Just in time, too. If she yawned any wider, her jaw was going to unhinge itself!

Slipping on an inexpensive set of headphones, she plugged the keyboard into her computer so the music notation software could capture the completed song.

As always, she ended her day by kneeling at her bed for prayer. As always, it was a joy to finally crawl onto her bed and let the last of the day's tension seep out as she sank into the thick foam topper. It was still too warm on her third floor for a blanket, so she fell asleep on top of soft, navy blue sheets.

A new dawn was lighting the room when she woke. Yawning, she dressed for the day. Having completely forgotten about her appointment, she chose a comfy, grass-green tunic-length shirt and a pair of well-worn jeans. Ran a comb through dark ginger waves.

Unplugging her phone from the charger, she went downstairs for a leisurely breakfast of over-easy eggs, whole wheat toast, and fresh-squeezed orange juice. Something nagged at the back of her mind as she ate, but a quick review of her work schedule showed nothing pressing for the day, so she dismissed it.

Halfway through her scripture study, her phone began to ring. "What…oh!" The pieces finally clicked in her brain and she groaned aloud. "Tyrel?" she answered, already digging herself out of her spot on the couch. "Hey, I'll be right out."

Outside, a somewhat perplexed Tyrel looked down at the phone in his hand, confirming that she'd hung up without letting him get more than a word in edgewise. Shrugging, he stuffed his phone back in his pocket and began twirling his keyring on one finger, one eye on the side door. He'd started to pull into the driveway of the house nearby before remembering that someone had mentioned Merry lived in a made-over barn. He'd heard of people doing that, but this was the first time he'd ever seen one.

A wry chuckle escaped him as he reviewed his own adult housing history. Broom closet apartments, when he wasn't living on an Air Force base. There hadn't been much time for sleeping, let alone anything that resembled a life.

Which was a major part of why he'd decided to take a crack at civilian life a couple of years ago.

Hadn't done him much good, though. Sighing, he massaged the bridge of his nose. Sure, sure, he'd never have to worry about money again now that he'd licensed his air filtration patents to the government. A full six months later, and he was still barely making it as a human being. Wasn't having a social life supposed to be easy?

"Morning."

Startled, he looked up. A woman had appeared on the second story verandah and was looking down at him. He'd never been as grateful for perfect vision as he as was at that moment, taking in every detail of her as she stood, framed against the golden-blue sky. The breeze caught her loose, dark hair and swept it to one side, leaving him wishing he could reach out and smooth it for her. Intelligent hazel eyes looked down at him from above high cheekbones, a perfectly turned nose, and a generous mouth.

"Sorry," the mouth said, snapping him out of his perusal before he got any further. "I forgot you were coming. Can you catch?" She held something up, waited for his response.

"Sure." He caught her keys with his left hand. "Can you catch?" He grinned and held up his own set of keys.

"Oh, no thanks." Merry shrugged and wrapped her arms around herself. Should've at least put a blanket around her shoulders. Or stepped into some shoes. Either choice would've contributed to a comfortable temperature.

"Where do you want me to put them?" he persisted. He got a chance to finish his observation while waiting for her response, right down to the bare toes peeking at him. The thought of her up there barefoot was enough to make him feel ten degrees colder than he reasonably should.

"By the windshield wipers is fine." Merry caught a handful of her mane of hair as it tried to blow in front of her face. Seriously. From now on, putting her hair up was going to have to be more of a priority in the mornings!

"Okay." Tyrel agreed. The forecast was for cold but dry, perfect moving day weather. "I'll be back sometime this afternoon."

"Great." Merry watched him wave jauntily and gave a short nod back. She wanted to be friendly…she just didn't see the point. Even if his ring finger was bare—which she hadn't been able to confirm, doggone it—he wasn't her type. He seemed to smile easily, had broad shoulders, and his thick black hair was just long enough to make a woman want to run her fingers through it. Nope. Definitely not her type.

Turning on her heel, she went back inside. After failing for five consecutive minutes to refocus on the New Testament, she got up to tidy the kitchen instead. Not quite ready to start her real workday, she opened a spiral notebook labeled 'BUDGET' and flipped to the last couple of pages. Now. What should she call her newest composition?

The music was relatively easy compared with writing the lyrics, but this morning she preferred struggling for words to match the music to daydreaming about a man she couldn't ha…um, didn't want. As was usually the case, however, the lyrics finally began to come once she hit on the song's mood.

It's so hard, makin' friends. So hard knowing it's bound to end…

Pen on paper and a little humming were the only sounds until, reluctantly, she stopped for lunch at eleven-thirty. She could've ignored the hunger for quite a while longer, but she'd agreed to have the table back before Thanksgiving and needed to get at it.

She made a face at herself as she reached the mirror by the living room door, where she stopped to turn on her automated vacuum-mop. A tuna sandwich later, she headed downstairs to tackle the table.

Eight feet by three feet, it stood a solid waist-high. The turned table legs might once have been elegant, but the years—and youngsters—hadn't been kind.

"Hey, you." She trailed a hand on the tabletop as she walked around it, murmuring half to herself and half to it, as if to reassure it. "Looks like you'll need some new boards."

Tracing a burned spot, she shook her head. "We can take care of that," she promised it. Squatting near the scarred leg, she explored the depth and length of the scars with sensitive fingertips. Tested the underframe for soundness. "Yeah, you'll be all right. You just need a little work."

Patting the item once more, she put her hair up in a short braid and pulled on a shop apron. First came the unglamorous disassembly. Warped boards spat splinters as she worked them free, making her grateful for her safety equipment. Pulling replacement boards from her stock, she measured and cut them before running them through her planer to smooth their surfaces.

As she worked, the dust rustled through the collection hoses, a huge improvement over her first year there, when wearing a dust mask had been a mandatory discomfort. Unfortunately, they were still mandatory at times. While using her belt sander, for example, which did a terrible job at dust collection.

Someday, she was going to upgrade to an RCJ 7715. For now, though, the sander she had would do well enough. A little heavy-duty sandpaper took care of the failing finish—as well as the burn marks and water stains that littered the tabletop.

"Okay." Putting the belt sander away, Merry shook out her arm muscles. "Well, that was fun. Now for the hard part."

Time faded to some distant part of her mind

while she continued with an electric palm sander, removing the old finish from smaller, more easily damaged sections. Eventually, she flexed cramped fingers and crawled out from under the table to unwind the sander's cord.

Having found a mirror to be an equally necessary discomfort, she'd hung one near the oversized clock by her office door. Now, as she reached back to untie the apron, she stopped to laugh at what she saw. Here and there the original green of her shirt peeked out through the wood dust—but for the most part, she looked like a deranged snowwoman. Her hair had escaped its neat braid and rearranged itself scarecrow-style, poking out wherever and in whichever direction it chose.

"I know, I know," she told her stomach as it growled fiercely at her reflection. "I think she looks a little scary, too. I'll bet she looks better after a shower and some supper, though." Hard to believe it was already after four in the afternoon. And she hadn't a clue what to have for said supper.

She discussed it with her reflection while going over her clothes with a soft-bristled bench brush. "Let's see. A casserole would take too long. Sandwiches are quick but…not that satisfying." As the dust began to settle she took off the dust mask, tossed it into a wastebasket, and started up the stairs.

"I could heat a tinfoil dinner," she mused as

she flicked off the workshop light and stepped into her living room.

Later, as she wrapped wet hair in a lightweight towel, she glared at her freshly scrubbed face. "You are so hard to please," she grumbled at herself. "If you keep this up, you're going to have to eat out or go hungry." There were only a half-dozen restaurants close enough to bother with when she felt like this. That would narrow her choices, at least.

Climbing into her favorite gray, knit culottes and tossing on a faded t-shirt, she very determinedly went back out into the kitchen. She was staying *in* tonight. Jerking open a cupboard door, she yelped in surprise as a bag of egg noodles dive-bombed her. Tentatively, she tapped the brittle bag, which astonishingly hadn't burst open on contact with the countertop. Hmm. Maybe…

Five minutes later, she had canned chicken, half a bag of frozen peas, and a head of lettuce on the island. She didn't exactly believe that a watched pot never boils, but she had plenty of other things to do while she waited to put the egg noodles in. Draining and rinsing the chicken, she emptied two cans worth into a large plastic bowl. Dumped in the peas.

The water had gone from savage hissing to the rumbling of a rolling boil, so she lifted the lid and poured in the noodles. That left her with plenty of time to rinse and tear enough lettuce for a green salad. She was moving at full steam when her phone rang.

"Hi." She switched to speakerphone so she could keep working.

"Hi!" Tyrel's voice filled her kitchen, making her shrink back a little. "Sorry I'm late."

She blinked at the phone, temporarily at a loss for his meaning. "Oh, the truck!" She forced a laugh. "Not a problem. I spent all day working on a new project." She might even be too tired to overanalyze. Maybe.

"Yeah? They were telling me today that you do furniture restoration and even some remodeling?"

"That's right." She nodded at the phone, then laughed silently at herself for doing it. "Keeps me pretty busy."

"I'd love to see what you're working on."

Her knife hesitated over the hard-boiled egg she was about to cut. Should she pass up a potential customer? After all, why else would he ask to see a project he knew nothing about? On the other hand... She looked at the noodles and half-finished salad. Set the knife down. Put one hand sadly over her stomach.

"Sure thing. I'll be down in just a minute." Ending the call, she draped a kitchen towel over the salad-in-progress. Turning off the stove, she emptied the pot into the strainer she'd placed in the sink. In turn, she emptied the strainer into the bowl with the chicken and peas. Popping open a jar of Alfredo sauce, she poured the whole thing in with the noodles, and stirred it all together. Lidding the bowl, she set it on the counter near the stove, where she hoped it would stay warm until she got back.

The mirror near the door reminded her she was still wearing a light towel on her head and she hastily hung it on one of the empty coat hooks while she slipped some shoes on.

Chapter 3

Outside, Tyrel divided his attention between the verandah and the side door this time, just in case. He was inordinately pleased with himself for wrangling some time with the ward's mysterious carpenter. 'Mysterious' was his word. He liked it better than 'odd,' which someone had hesitantly used to describe her earlier. She'd grown up in the area, but nobody in the moving group seemed to be able to tell him much about her. Of course, that group was about eighty-five percent male; and most of them were already married with no interest in the 'local spinster,' as someone indelicately joked.

Not that he was thinking of marriage. That was waaaay out in his future somewhere.

No, he'd been careful to phrase his questions as naturally as possible, starting with how glad he was for the loan of her truck and… His thoughts ground to a halt as she poked her head out the door. Her hair was still down, but this time it was curling around her face and shoulders with abandon. She'd replaced the vibrant green shirt from earlier with a tee that he couldn't quite read at that distance.

"C'mon in," she invited, waving him over.

"Thanks." He deliberately didn't offer her keys as he moved past her into the shop. And stopped to whistle. "Nice setup!"

A row of deep shelves lined the wall directly opposite him, the ends of boards hanging out of most of the slots. A radial arm saw and table saw were positioned right beside the shelves, followed by a planer and a jointer near the perpendicular wall. Pipes lead from each machine to a larger overhead conduit, for dust collection he presumed. The drill press stood in the corner under the stairs to his left, near what looked like a spacious cabinet. A gluing station stood empty to his right, and four good-sized worktables stood in the middle of the room, each ready with a bench vice on one corner and a stool for convenience.

"Thanks." Merry shut the door and leaned against it while he drooled over her equipment. His reaction was flattering, in a way.

"Wow." As he completed his visual turn about the room, his gaze stopped on the table, which was almost directly in front of him. "Is that white ash?" he asked. Rapping it lightly with his knuckles, he found that it was solid wood. "You hardly ever see that anymore." The wood dust on and around the table was so fresh that he could smell it, telling him that this was most definitely what she'd spent the day working on.

"I know." She was a little surprised that he did, though. "Most people favor oak for some reason."

"Right?" He grimaced at a memory. "I wanted to make a new front door for my house when I was in high school. The coach passed on the sketches and everything, but put his foot down when I suggested using white ash. Told me the school wasn't going to pay extra to re-sharpen the tools just so I could have a fancy front door." He shrugged. "Made me use oak." Looking around at her, he found that he was able to read what was left of the graphic on her tee now. Once upon a time, it had probably been a blushing ear of corn with the words, 'Aw, shucks' just to the left of its head. There might even have been a dialogue bubble around the words at some point.

"I guess he had a point," she agreed, following his gaze down to her graphic tee. She'd already forgotten which one she was wearing. She used to joke that if she ever had to fill out her own missing person's report, she'd have to leave the bit about her outfit blank.

He jerked his gaze back up to her face. Opened his mouth to explain that he hadn't been ogling her—not that she wasn't… Shut his mouth before he could insert his foot up to his knee.

"Nice tee," he observed tersely. He liked the shin-length shorts she was wearing, too. Capris, he thought they were called? Modesty was key, and he knew a lot of women who struggled to find clothes that covered them the way they wanted. Not only that, she looked comfortable. A step up from sweatpants, give or take.

"Yeah." Relieved, she tugged at the hem to smooth it. "Hand-me-down." Ugh, why had she said that? In all her thirty-seven years, she'd never quite mastered the art of thinking before she spoke.

The corners of his mouth quirked up. "I heard you're from a big family. Nine, isn't it?" The size of her family had come up while he was helping to carry a particularly heavy sleeper sofa, so he couldn't quite remember. "Must be nice. It was just me and my grandparents growing up." Wondering why he'd shared that with her, he stuffed his hands into his pockets.

"It can be nice," Merry admitted quietly, his remark having shifted her perspective on the subject considerably. She loved her family—that would never change. Sometimes she wished she lived a little further away, but to be without them entirely? Perish the thought.

The sound of a stomach rumbling broke the comfortable silence, making them both grimace.

"Wait, was that you?" he asked, one hand still protectively over his stomach.

"Maybe," she hedged, though of course it had been. "Don't you know?" Interesting that she already felt like she could tease him. He wasn't nearly as scary now that she'd met him in person.

He wrinkled his brow thoughtfully. "I mean, it could've been me..." He broke off and clenched his stomach muscles, but it was too late. His stomach had officially growled.

Unable to help herself, Merry burst out laughing. It was all too ridiculous. Too much like talking with one of her brothers.

"That's an easy fix. C'mon." Waving for him to follow her, she headed over to the stairs. "Turns out you're just in time for supper." *Wow.* She must be having a good 'people' day—or she just couldn't let him leave hungry. If her mother ever found out, she'd never let her hear the end of it.

"You don't have to feed me," Tyrel protested, hurrying after her. As they climbed the stairs, he couldn't ignore the sinking feeling that he'd somehow activated her mothering instinct. That might not have been so bad if he wasn't looking for someone to date.

"It's no problem. Here, there's room for your shoes," she pointed at the rug where she left hers. "I was in the middle of making supper when you called." She started to turn away, then stopped, puzzled as to why he just stood there.

He shrugged apologetically. "Would it, um, be alright if I kept my shoes on?"

"I'd rather you didn't." She upgraded herself from puzzled to bewildered. It was a simple request. Saved her floors a ton of wear and tear.

"Well, see, I would, but…" He lifted his left leg. "Getting my prosthetic foot in and out of shoes is a real hassle." He waited to see how she'd react. Would she ask a ton of questions? Would she act like it was some massively impressive feat to be an amputee? Would she make the most cringe-worthy request—asking to try it on?

"Your…" She blinked. "Oh." Folded her arms across her chest to protect herself from the waves of self-incrimination that washed over her. She hadn't known. He wouldn't be mad, would he? "I didn't know." Ugh, this was why she shouldn't let her guard down. Pain. Every. Time.

"No reason you should've." He smiled, hoping to put her at ease. "So it's okay, then, if I…" He lowered his left leg so it was touching the floor again.

"Yeah." She prayed for help to not get stuck in a mental loop, replaying the awkward moment over and over. "No problem." Prying a hand loose from where it gripped the opposite arm, she gestured for him to follow her. "Food's this way." Pivoting, she went back to where she'd been working.

Taking a deep breath, he marched over to the empty sink and washed his hands. "How can I help?" She'd taken the news about his leg relatively well, further piquing his interest in dating her. Now he just had to find a way out of her 'he's a hungry little boy' box.

Merry looked up and suddenly her good intentions were sidetracked by a dizzying awareness of her guest.

"Careful!" His hand shot out, catching her by the wrist before she could bring the knife down on her hand. Deftly, he removed the knife from unresisting fingers. "How about I slice the hard-boiled eggs?" he offered with a disarming grin.

"Sure." Wiping her fingers on a towel, Merry made a beeline for the bowl of noodles. Her back to him now, she pressed her palms against the cold counter and tried for a steadying breath. When was the last time a man had been up there? Not counting her brothers? She bit her lip. Or Sam, who was married and totally off-limits. Yeah. This was a first. Which was probably why his fresh, woodsy cologne seemed to follow her as she carried the bowl to the far corner of the island and set it down. She'd noticed it when she let him in downstairs, but it seemed ten times as alluring here in her living space.

"What's next?" he asked, adding the egg slices to what she'd already prepared. And obviously she'd done it without injuring herself. So what had changed between then and just now when she'd nearly taken a finger off? Good grief, the woman worked with sharp objects all day long in her woodshop. What could've rattled her so badly? He shot her a curious glance. She hadn't responded to his question. Or asked any about his amputation, for that matter.

"There are some plates in that cupboard," she pointed. Producing silverware from an island drawer, she started setting two places across from each other. By the time she got back with the glasses, however, he'd rearranged things so they would both be sitting at the corner. Gritting her teeth at his presumption, she handed him the glasses and opened the fridge for the last few items.

"You did all the work," he observed as he slid onto one of the two stools. "Shall I say the prayer?" Her curt nod added to his growing suspicion that she regretted her decision in inviting him up. Off-balance and without quite thinking it through, he offered her his hand to hold. Tried not to be offended when she stared at it like it was some kind of a trap.

Merry knew many families who held hands during prayer, so she understood there was nothing personal in his gesture. *Nothing* personal. Her hand shook a little anyway as she lowered it into his. A peculiar sense of peace washed over her as they bowed their heads and his mild, baritone voice humbly thanked God for their blessings.

"Amen," she agreed. Un-lidding the bowl was a good excuse to retrieve her hand and she did so. "Hope you like pasta." She slid a serving spoon into the bowl and passed it to him first. Only to find that he had his hands full with the salad bowl!

"I love pasta." Tyrel hastily moved to set the salad bowl down and reached for the pasta with his other hand.

Their eyes met and he nearly dropped both bowls. He hadn't said anything profound in his prayer—hadn't even mentioned her beyond expressing gratitude for her generosity, sharing first her truck and now her food—and yet the change in her was night and day. The anxiety clouding her hazel eyes was gone, leaving them clear and full of warmth. He could stare into those eyes forever.

"What?" The gorgeous eyes blinked, breaking the spell.

His mouth suddenly dry, he cleared his throat. Had he said that out loud?? "Nothing. I…" He looked at the bowls they were holding. "I like salad, too," he finished lamely.

"So I see." She pushed the bowl of pasta toward him. "Better eat this while it's hot." She managed a small smile.

"Smells amazing." Grinning back at her, he dished up some pasta, though he didn't take as much as he would've liked. He had to leave some for her, didn't he? They'd taken a break for pizza around noon, then promptly worked it off. Unable to wait while she served herself, he forked some from his plate into his mouth.

"Any good?" she asked, uncertain what the expression on his face meant.

"Delicious!" he asserted, loading more onto his fork. The Alfredo sauce coated his tongue with a rich, creamy flavor that complimented the buttery taste of the egg noodles. If he wasn't careful, he was going to do a fairly good imitation of a steam shovel, trying to get as much of the pasta into his mouth as quickly as possible. Tamping down on his enthusiasm, he took a smaller bite.

"Hunger's the best sauce." She delivered the borrowed quip with a half-smile and shrug.

"No, I mean it." He drank half a glass of water in a gulp and went back to eating. "What's in this?"

Merry dropped her gaze and chewed slowly while she tried to decide how much to divulge. A peek into her recycle bin would tell most of her secrets, but she didn't intend for that to happen.

"Sorry. Secret recipe."

"I'll bet!" His plate emptied, he eyed the bowl hopefully and laughed when she nudged it toward him. "The only thing that could possibly make this meal any better would be garlic bread."

"That's easy." Getting up, she pulled a half a bag of garlic bread from her fridge. "I forgot I had this," she explained as she arranged some pieces on a microwaveable plate.

"Store bought? That hardly seems good enough to go with your pasta." His eyes narrowed at the way she choked on nothing and abruptly turned her back on him. *No way.* He took another bite of the pasta, chewing it more slowly and trying to identify tastes. After two years in the mission field and ten in the Air Force, if there was an easy way to make a dish like this, he'd know about it.

"Yeah, well." Merry started the microwave and did her best not to laugh. Her box and bag pasta was too good for store bought garlic bread? If he only knew. "It's the best I can do at the moment."

He watched her flip a lock of nearly dry hair back over her shoulder and was surprised to see a glint of red. Her hair was getting lighter as it dried and, though she was still very definitely brunette, he began noticing red highlights on the crest of every ripple as it fell down her back.

"Hope you saved some pasta for me." She turned to go back to the table. Caught him staring at her. Again. What was with him, anyway? "Here." She set the plate on a hot pad holder between them.

"Thanks." *Uh-oh.* She was upset again. Her lips had thinned and she refused to look at him while she resumed eating her pasta. Okay, the lady did *not* like being stared at. And who could blame her? So, time to lighten the mood. "Something's puzzling me." He waited until she looked over at him. "What're the pickles for?"

Shoot. She'd forgotten all about the pickles. Should she tell him? Would he tease her like her brothers did? She went back to that last thought. Actually. That wouldn't be so bad. She'd rather be teased by him than stared at. "They're for the salad." Finishing off her pasta, she reached for the dish of lettuce.

His eyebrows shot halfway up his forehead before he could stop them. "Oh?" He tried for a neutral tone. Failed miserably.

Merry sprinkled her lettuce liberally with shredded cheese, spooned on some hard-boiled egg, and reached for the pickle jar. "They add a nice crunch." Picking up the same sharp knife she'd started on the eggs with, she expertly sliced the dill pickle into four spears. "Want some?"

Was she…was she daring him? Tyrel assessed her too-sweet tone, the sly twist of her lips. Oh yeah. He was without a doubt being dared. It didn't fit with any of her other behavior so far. Nevertheless, he felt a need to rise to the challenge.

"Absolutely!" He grabbed the tongs and added lettuce to his plate, then took a handful of cheese like she had. He'd had every other imaginable kind of hard-boiled egg, so he helped himself to some of those, too. It took him about thirty seconds to slide his plate under her still-outstretched hand.

Uncertainly, Merry chunked one of the dill pickle spears onto his salad. "Would you…would you like some of the juice, too?" She didn't know what to make of him at that point. Had she finally found someone else who enjoyed a dill-flavored vinaigrette?

He eyed his salad, then examined her perfectly serious face. "Sure." This time he managed to keep his doubts out of his voice.

"Help yourself." Confused that he'd taken the dare, Merry chunked a spear's worth of pickle onto her own salad. Taking up her fork, she peeked at him through a curtain of lashes. Eyes widening, she watched him lift the entire pickle jar and drizzle juice over his salad like he might've syrup on a pancake. Somehow he managed to set the jar down without losing a drop. Impressive!

Tyrel stirred his salad briefly. Glanced at her and saw that she hadn't waited. Alright then… Deliberately he captured a piece of the pickle along with some lettuce and hard-boiled egg. Popped it into his mouth. Dill flavor hit his taste buds like a ten-ton truck, then gave way to the smooth egg texture and crisp, watery iceberg lettuce.

"Hey." He swallowed and began refilling his fork. "That's good!"

"Sorry to disappoint you," she mocked lightly.

He laughed aloud at that. "What can I say? Maybe offering gross food is a guy thing?"

"Sounds about right." Forgetting for the moment that he was still an unknown quantity, she rolled her eyes. "My brothers were always competing with each other where food was concerned. Who could eat the most. Who could eat the grossest."

"Who could eat the most of the grossest?" he interjected, again thinking back to high school days. Thankfully, most of that sort of foolishness hadn't survived basic training.

"Ugh, yes." Her nose wrinkled in disgust. "I still can't eat pineapple and I wasn't even the one putting…"

"Whoa! No gory details, please." He held up

a hand to stop her. "I love pineapple and I don't want it ruined."

"You *like* pineapple? As in, you eat it voluntarily?" She did her best to sound appalled.

"Um, most people do," he fired back. "Especially on pizza."

"Not on my pizza, thank ya kindly," she retorted. "Canadian bacon all the way!"

He paused for a drink of water and filed that bit of information away for later. Attention to detail was his forte. "So how'd you get started on woodworking?" he changed the subject.

She shoved the last few pieces of lettuce together and scooped them up with her fork. "Sort of fell into it, I guess." On guard again, she wondered how much she truly wanted to tell him about her private life. About the precious hours she'd spent tagging along after her grandpa learning how things worked.

It was one thing to laugh about similar memories with him like they'd been doing. Venturing any deeper could cost her a lot of self-esteem points when he got bored and moved on to more interesting friends. The way people almost always did.

"Sounds painful." He focused on what was left of his own salad when his joke fell flat. In fact, the whole mood of the evening had fallen flatter than a pancake. One second she was laughing, the next she treated him like a stranger. Well, no, that wasn't quite it. He *was* a stranger, technically. Who wanted to become a friend—and maybe more—but was getting crazy mixed signals in the process.

"Not a lifelong dream, then?" he tried again.

"Nope." She stood up to put her dishes in the dishwasher. Her 'lifelong dream' wasn't anything spectacular or even original. Just a solid expectation that one day she'd grow up, fall in love, get married, and have kids. Who knew that such a simple dream could be so presumptuous? So achingly unattainable?

Her silence worried him more than her curt response. Shoveling the last of his salad into his mouth, he collected his dishes and added them to the dishwasher. Saw her painfully straight face and felt an urgent need to break the stony silence.

"So…" He backed away from her and gestured generally at the room. "I'm guessing you did all the remodeling yourself."

"That would've taken forever." She shrugged and leaned back against the counter. "I had to hire Ed Wilcox to install the wiring and the plumbing anyway, so I paid him to help with the stairs as well."

Tyrel looked at the ceiling above him, realizing for the first time that there wasn't room in the remodeled barn's floor plan for a bedroom on this level, which meant there must be a third level above him. He could feel her watching him from her unsmiling face as he fumbled for another topic of conversation.

"Well," he said as brightly as he could, "thanks for supper."

"You're welcome." She forced the obligatory response through stiff lips. It wasn't that she didn't mean it. It was just that she felt like some cosmic parasite had drained the energy right out of her. She simply couldn't…*people* anymore tonight.

"You probably want me to get out of your hair," he paused to shake off the wish that he was speaking literally. Her hair looked so soft and smelled so *good* he'd been distracted by it the whole time. And she didn't say a word, just went on watching him. She looked so…sad.

"See you at church." The usually jaunty expression came out gently, almost like he was promising her.

She nodded her head fractionally and he left.

Chapter 4

Merry reached out to shut off her alarm the next morning, but her hand hit empty air. Half-asleep, she started to sit up, thinking she'd knocked her phone onto the floor while she tossed and turned during the night.

"Whoaaaa!" Feeling herself starting to slide, Merry twisted, trying to keep her place on the bed…and landed on her side on the floor. "Ohhh. Ouch." The alarm continued beeping while she drug herself into a sitting position. For a few seconds, she just leaned back against the bed, trying to orient herself.

There was no pillow on the floor beside her that she could see. In fact—unless her room had rearranged itself during the night, there should've been a small end table within reach. A wall. She ran her fingers through her hair and started to laugh.

Getting up, she put her hands on her hips and surveyed the mess she'd made of her bed. It took some serious talent to dislodge a fitted sheet, but she'd done it. Rubbing her bruised hip, she sighed and began setting things to rights. One pillow was on the floor on the far side of the bed. The other was jammed between the bed and the wall. Eventually, she even found her phone and shut it off.

A cold shower woke her up a bit more, but she

~ 49 ~

was still groggy enough that she almost burned her eggs. Somehow she managed to eat most of her breakfast between the yawns, though she didn't care for the overcooked yolks that were supposed to have been over-easy.

The worst part was that every time her eyes drifted closed, she saw his gorgeous blue eyes. His pure blue eyes, as clear as a summer morning. Except…except when she didn't know how to respond. When she shut down. When she tried to shut him down. That hadn't been easy, either. He had a good sense of humor. Her lips tried to curve up as she remembered his efforts to engage her. She couldn't let him, though. He was just passing through, on his way to someone who enjoyed small talk, laughed easily, and had endless energy.

She caught her breath as pain lanced through her chest at the thought. Her hands shook a little as she picked up her keys. That was weird. It usually didn't hurt to lose a friend she'd never had. At least, not this badly. Stepping out onto the verandah, she locked the door behind her and absent-mindedly threw the lever that opened a trapdoor to a slowly descending ladder. She was so preoccupied that she didn't even register the dark four-door sitting in the driveway beside her truck.

Tyrel looked up at the sound of a door closing. His jaw dropped at the sight of Merry riding a ladder as it slowly lowered itself from where it must've been stored under the length of the verandah. Her long-sleeved ivory-colored shirt gracefully curved around her form, while the toes of a sensible pair of shoes peeked almost shyly out from under the hem of her plain black skirt. Her gaze must've been more or less on those shoes because she didn't see him until she was nearly at ground level.

"Morning." He gave her his best smile. It wilted a little under her wide-eyed dismay, quick though she was to hide it.

"Morning." *He's not supposed to be here.* Her morning unexpectedly disrupted, Merry gripped her keys hard enough that they dug into her palm. The resulting pain helped divide her emotions, making them marginally easier to manage. "Need to borrow my truck again?" Not a bad quip under the circumstances.

Tyrel winced. "Not exactly. I," he cleared his throat, embarrassed, "forgot to gas it up last night." Gestured toward his car. "Came to give you a ride to church."

Merry couldn't help looking toward Sam's van, as if it might somehow hold the solution to her predicament. She remembered in time that their youngest, a cuddly six-month-old boy, had claimed the last available spot. She might've tried calling one of the girls for a ride, but… When they asked, how could she explain her reluctance to accept Tyrel's offer?

As attractive as he'd been yesterday in his off-white tee and jeans, his muscles more or less on display, today he was positively dashing—in a comfortable, understated way. It was a toss-up as to which was a purer black, his suit or his wavy, oh-so-tempting hair. His white dress shirt accentuated his tan while his red-and-indigo striped tie made his eyes seem even more startling in their blueness.

Tyrel experienced a vague sense of disappointment when she just nodded and started moving toward the passenger door. He had to hurry to get there in time to open it for her, then walk back around to slide into the driver's seat. The pain in his left leg, still sore from yesterday's prolonged workout, eased off slightly as he seated himself.

"Well." He carefully maneuvered his car so that he was facing the street. "I guess this isn't so bad." She looked at him through narrowed eyes, prompting a hasty, "I mean, I didn't plan this. But if I had, it would've been kind of clever. Don't you think?"

Merry sat there for several seconds, hands clasped tightly in her lap, while she tried to figure out how to respond to that. Naturally, she was glad that he hadn't intentionally sabotaged her Sunday morning. On the other hand, she wasn't at all impressed with someone who didn't take care of what they borrowed. Of course, she was no exception to the rule that everyone makes mistakes. Like the time that she…

With some difficulty, she reigned her thoughts in before they could get any further from what he'd originally asked. "I suppose so."

She had to bite her tongue to keep herself from expounding in near-pedantic detail the fact that this hadn't been intentional and so was not clever at all. Sad experience had eventually taught her that people didn't appreciate that level of clarity. Just like they didn't want to hear every story she knew that *their* stories reminded her of. Conversation truly was an art form, and she was no artist.

Ouch. Disappointed at her complete lack of response to his attempt at flirting, Tyrel tapped his thumb on the steering wheel, at a loss for what to try next. He'd never had this much trouble talking to anyone. It was like trying to swim up Niagara Falls. Sure, there'd been an old sergeant who stuck to one-word answers. But there was taciturn and there was deliberately killing a conversation. This felt like the latter. And what bothered him most was the question of why. *Why* was she making it so hard?

"Guess it'll be getting cold soon," he ventured. "I've never spent a winter in the Ozarks. I guess it get can get pretty bad?"

"The ice storms are the worst," she agreed halfheartedly. "Sometimes the ice piles on so thick it takes out the power lines."

He whistled softly. "That sounds rough. What do people do for groceries, things like that?"

"It's too dangerous to drive while it's icy, so when a big storm is predicted, there's usually a run on the stores."

"I'll bet," he nodded knowingly. Lots of times he'd seen reports about that on TV, comparing empty shelves with overflowing shopping carts as people tried to stock up on everything in a single trip. "Good thing we learned to keep some food storage and emergency supplies on hand."

"Yeah."

Silence descended again, thick and heavy as peanut butter. It made his tongue stick to the roof of his mouth.

"I enjoyed studying for Sunday school this week," he gave it a final try as the church came into view. "Sad to say, I haven't taken the time to go through the New Testament since high school." He looked at her out of the corner of his eye, but she was staring straight ahead. "The Apostles had their work cut out for them." Despite everything, he was sorry to see the church coming into view. He wanted to get to know her and when it'd hit him that he hadn't filled her tank, he'd thought this would be perfect. New morning, fresh start. He'd had no idea…

"Yes, they did." Merry leaned back against the seat a little. The church was just up ahead. Only a few more minutes. "Those few from the House of Israel who accepted Christ as their Savior still struggled to let go of the day-to-day practices of the Law of Moses. And the Gentiles who accepted Him found themselves more or less out of sync with the world around them. No longer part of the religions they'd grown up in and certainly not literal descendants of Abraham."

What just happened? Tyrel signaled and turned into the church parking lot on autopilot.

"It was all made harder," he agreed, "by the communication limitations. I mean, can you imagine waiting for weeks or months for a letter to arrive from the prophet? Especially when it's all brand new to everyone?"

Merry shook her head fervently, unwittingly filling the air with the scent of her shampoo. "I honestly don't know how any of them kept the faith in the face of the confusion that Paul and the others worked so hard to dispel."

Tyrel parked and jumped out to open her door for her. The gospel! She liked to talk about the gospel! Okay, so it wasn't typical ice breaker chitchat, but so what? She wasn't a typical woman.

Merry wasn't quite sure what to do with the warmth in Tyrel's eyes. Bizarrely, it seemed to be directed toward her. Except it couldn't be. She hadn't done anything to warrant it. Grimly, she pushed the idea away and marched into the building.

"Thanks for the lift." She paused in the foyer, surrounded by half a dozen families that were in various stages of arrival. "I'll get a ride home with one of my siblings." She stuck out her hand, relieved that she was able to let him off the hook.

"Oh." Tyrel frowned at her hand. "Are you sure? I wouldn't mind taking you home."

Merry's smile started slipping and she allowed her hand to return to her side. Why was he making this so difficult?

"That won't be necessary," she started to assure him.

"I mean it," he interrupted, worried that she thought he was just being polite. "Do you have a meeting afterward? I could wait, it's no problem."

"No." Merry lifted her shoulders. "I don't have any meetings."

Tyrel hesitated. She sounded almost sorry that she didn't have an excuse for not riding back with him. As much as he hated to admit it, it was starting to look like she just didn't like his company. It wasn't a first, exactly. It just hadn't happened in a while. Granted, he hadn't tried very hard for the last three years. Too busy with his patent and the legalities of licensing it for use, etc.

"Either way." He managed a smile despite his disappointment. "I'll be here when meetings are over, so just let me know, okay?"

She nodded mutely and watched him stride away.

"Wow." Noella liked English slang and she'd

never had a better opportunity to use this word. Linking her arm through Merry's surprisingly stiff arm, she asked, "Who was that?" Naturally, she switched to French to thwart any potential eavesdroppers. People were alike the world around, she'd decided. Some were good, some were bad, and most were inherently curious.

"I am so glad to see you!" Merry gripped her friend's hand, delighted at her good luck. "Can you give me a ride home after church today?" Registering Noella's startled expression she hurried to explain, "I couldn't drive myself this morning because I…didn't have enough gas." She stumbled a little over the explanation, deciding mid-sentence that this wasn't the time to go into detail. "I got a ride in, but I could *really* use a ride home."

"I wish I could," Noella began to apologize. "I have agreed to take the sister missionaries out on appointments for the rest of the afternoon. Of course," she half-shrugged and started leading Merry into the chapel, "I am sure you would be most welcome to come along?"

Merry's heart sank. "I'd love to. Unfortunately, if I go out with you, I'll miss supper at my parents' this evening."

"Oh, yes!" Noelle nodded. "I forgot about that."

"It's okay," Merry promised. "I'll just ride with one of my sisters."

"Ah, but you have not forgotten about the

meeting on Tuesday?" Noella spoke quickly, softly. "You will help with the set design?" After listening to several people complain about how bored they were with the annual charity Christmas play—the exact same play every year for the last ten years—she planned to present the community theater group with a new play at their next meeting. They hadn't taken any of her suggestions as yet, so this time she was coming prepared to volunteer her friends.

"Yes, of course." Merry smiled, amused despite everything else. "I'll be there."

They parted quietly, as befitted the reverent nature of the chapel they'd just entered. Merry turned toward the pews where her family usually sat. And swallowed hard. Like Sam, most of her family members filled their vehicles with their own children. Or with a siblings' children, if they were swapping for a few hours. Heidi, her sister that had a daughter in college and a son on a mission, was missing.

Slipping in behind her parents, Merry kissed their cheeks and whispered, "Where's Heidi?"

"Good morning to you, too," her father teased quietly.

Her mother patted her hand and murmured back, "They're off visiting at another ward today."

"Oh." She was running out of options. Noella couldn't, Heidi wasn't there… Grace? She looked around but didn't see her friend. As the only vet for miles, Grace had little to no control over her schedule and was frequently called on to work Sundays.

Harmony? No, she didn't even see Harmony. The phantom spaghetti monster was back, slithering out from her stomach, spreading the miserable chill of failure through her entire body. What was left? Walking home?

"Who was that handsome young man you came in with?"

Merry's head jerked around in surprise. "What?" She couldn't have heard her mother correctly.

Just then, the pianist began the prelude music and an even more pronounced hush fell over the congregation.

Taking a deep breath, Merry exhaled as much tension as she could and filed the rest away for later. She only got to take the sacrament once a week and she wanted to concentrate. The opening hymn, "I Need Thee Every Hour," helped her gather her focus on her reason for coming to church. To worship.

After the sacrament was passed and the young men had rejoined their families, an older couple stood up to speak. They both talked about the important role of prayer in their lives, sharing examples and testifying that Heavenly Father hears and answers prayers.

"We're used to things happening right away," the brother stated with a chuckle. "Frozen pizza.

Instant messaging. Things like that. Well, prayer doesn't always work that way. It can take a little time and effort on our part. Sometimes more than we figured on. Maybe a whole lot more." He finished by reading Ecclesiastes 3:1-2.

To every thing there is a season, and a time to every purpose under the heaven:

A time to be born, and a time to die; a time to plant, and a time to pluck up that which is planted…

Merry couldn't explain the peace that started in her heart and worked its way outward. She rarely missed her daily prayers. Quite honestly, there was nobody that she kept in touch with better than her Heavenly Father. So she probably shouldn't have been surprised that, by the end of the meeting, her peace was mostly restored to her.

She even felt up to contributing in Sunday school, where they discussed 1st and 2nd Thessalonians. Where, for some reason, 1st Thessalonians 5:21 fairly jumped out at her— "Prove all things; hold fast that which is good."

She turned that verse over and over in her mind as the lesson went on, trying to understand why it had caught her attention. She highlighted and bookmarked it on her phone for further pondering, then bowed her head for closing prayer.

Having forgotten all about her situation, she got all the way to her feet before she saw Tyrel approaching from the back of the room. *Prove all things; hold fast that which is good,* leapt to mind as if in large, bold letters.

"Oh, hello." Tyrel was on his way to check in with Merry when the woman seated in front of her suddenly stood up and offered him her hand. "I'm Merry's mom, but you can call me Elaine."

Merry closed her eyes tightly. She loved her mom. She truly did. Occasionally she was embarrassed by her, too, but that went with the territory.

"Hi." Tyrel smiled a little uncertainly at her. She certainly looked like Merry. The same nose and chin. Same thick hair, though hers was a much lighter brown. Her mouth, though similarly shaped, lacked the tightness of Merry's. And her hazel-brown eyes were alight with good humor. "I'm Tyrel Scott," he introduced himself.

"Oh, Brother Scott." Tyrel found his hand gripped firmly by a man he assumed was Merry's father. "I'm Brother McKinney. Sorry I couldn't make it out to the moving project yesterday. I was all set to go when…"

"Don't you listen to him," Elaine interrupted, directing a mock scowl at her husband. "Andy had surgery on his back and he's not to lift anything heavier than a pillow."

Tyrel tuned out their friendly squabble and tuned into Merry, who was still standing by her pew. 'Stricken' was the word that came to mind as he studied her face. At least this time, he thought he understood. He'd never had a mother to be exasperated with—not that he remembered anyway—but he'd heard plenty of stories about blind dates, inflated expectations, and jumping to conclusions from those who did.

"Now, I'm sure you're right, Sister McKinney," he interjected smoothly. "There are no shortcuts to recovering from surgery." That bit of wisdom he'd picked up from his grandmother, who'd often had the same conversation with her father that the McKinney's were having right now. "But there's nothing to apologize for, Brother McKinney. A couple of your sons were able to help out for a bit, and quite frankly, it was your daughter who saved the day. Yes," he smiled at Merry, belatedly noticing how the color was fading from her cheeks. "Without her truck, it would've taken us twice as long."

"She's got a great truck for moving." Andy nodded. "Big enough for furniture but still small enough that you don't need the whole road to maneuver."

"Exactly." A smile fixed on his face, Tyrel knew he'd somehow bungled again. All he'd meant to do was explain why he'd come over, to…defuse any expectations that might leap ahead of where Merry was comfortable with.

"It was nothing." Merry shoved her emotions into a box to be dealt with later.

"Young man." Elaine looked sternly at Tyrel, whom she sensed had been about to excuse himself. "What're you doing for supper this evening?"

Tyrel knew two things instantly. First, he was about to receive a 'royal invitation' to their house for supper—meaning an invitation he wouldn't be able to politely refuse. Second, Merry would rather die than have him accept. She couldn't get any paler, but the flash of emotion in her eyes just now qualified as raw panic.

"For supper?" Offering up a prayer for help, Tyrel decided not to fight the inevitable. "Oh, nothing special. I…"

"Good!" Elaine beamed at him, winked at Merry. "You're coming to our house for supper. Merry can give you directions. We start at six." She stepped past him, figuratively dragging her husband along behind her. "Be prompt! We wouldn't want the food to get cold."

Tyrel just nodded his acquiescence and kept smiling until they were out of sight. Shoving his hands into his slacks' pockets, he turned a miserable gaze on Merry.

"Hey, she wasn't going to let me get out of that one," he told her bluntly.

Surprised, Merry blinked. Exhaled slowly. "You're right about that," she conceded eventually. "I could use a ride, if you're still offering." She was surprised again when his frown became a smile.

Prove all things; hold fast that which is good. Why couldn't she get that verse out of her head?

"I'd like that." He didn't try to start a conversation right then. It was enough to know she wasn't mad at him. He got as far as pulling out of the parking lot before he ventured, "I should probably give you a ride tonight, too. You've got enough gas to get to the filling station where I meant to stop last night, but not much further."

She chuckled. "That won't be necessary. They're my neighbors."

"Hey, that's great!" He stopped for a red light and turned to face her. "I've got an idea. It's a little after one now. Why don't you come over to my place for lunch? Then we can hang out for a few hours and be at your parents' in plenty of time for supper."

Merry tightened her grip on her keys. More than anything else, she wanted to go home, put on her pjs, and crawl into bed. She was…done. More so than usual, thanks to her sleepless night. Done peopling. People were the worst part of going to church. The surface-level questions. The expectation that she smile to make other people comfortable. Never knowing who was going to do what when and powerless to change that.

Prove all things; hold fast that which is good. What did that even mean?!

"I…wouldn't be very good company," she demurred, hoping he'd take the hint.

"At least let me make you lunch," he persisted. "I'll take you right home afterward if that's what you want."

Merry closed her eyes wearily. She *wanted* to go home right now!

The light turned green and he reluctantly returned his attention to driving without a response from her.

Chapter 5

"I'll make Canadian bacon pizza." Tyrel decided he was on the right track when she opened one eye to look at him. "And we can have ice cream floats afterward."

Merry's taste buds perked, intrigued by the menu. "*You*'ll make the pizza?"

His lips quirked up in amusement. "While you sit back and watch."

She hesitated, still hearing the siren call of her pillow. But not quite as loudly. "Okay."

Inordinately pleased with himself, Tyrel checked his mirrors and made a U-turn. "One homemade, piping hot Canadian bacon pizza, coming up!"

Tired as she was, Merry was undeniably curious to see where he lived. The duplex where he pulled in and parked was as nondescript as his dark, four-door car. What had once been a cream-colored stucco was now a dingy beige. The three steps up to the door boasted a handrail that was too short to be effective for anyone of average height and wobbled under the slight pressure of her hand.

The inside of the apartment was much darker than she'd expected, primarily due to the fake wood paneling that covered three of the four walls. The carpet was a rough, low-pile affair that might have been cream-colored once upon a time. A gray couch leaned against the wall to her right, while directly ahead of her was a short hallway that led to an open door. The kitchen was off the hallway, also to the right, with a small island breaking up the open floor plan. If she had to guess, she'd say the off-center island, with its wall that extended from floor to ceiling, was the architect's solution to adding support for the roof.

What stood out the most to her was how spic and span everything was. She hadn't planned a white glove inspection, but it seemed likely that his apartment would've passed with flying colors. Habit, maybe, after years in the military? Every breath brought the scents of cleanser and laundry detergent and…him. More than cologne, it was that underlying something unique to each person.

"Have a seat." Smiling, he took her coat and indicated the couch. "I've been meaning to get some chairs, but you're my first guest so I guess we'll just have to make do." Hanging their winter things in his closet, he swapped his suit jacket for an apron.

"Thanks." Skirting the shin-knocker of a coffee table, Merry eased herself onto the couch. Instead of the soggy-wood firmness she'd expected, she was delighted to find that the cushions and back had just the right amount of give.

"How do you like your crust?" he called as he pulled the bowl of dough out of the fridge. "Thin? Thick?" He grinned at her over the island. "Hand-tossed?" he teased. What he'd have done if she'd agreed, he didn't know. Luckily, she didn't make him eat his words.

She laughed and shook her head. "Regular is fine."

"Regular crust it is." Whipping out a rolling pin, he floured his surface and set to work. "Tomato sauce all right?"

"Yes, thank you." Merry did her best to stifle a yawn and wound up covering it with her hand.

"Excellent." Transferring the dough to the pizza pan, Tyrel smeared it with a layer of tomato sauce. "Extra cheesy?" he double-checked while he shook some dried oregano onto the sauce.

"Great." Merry's eyes were drifting closed and there didn't seem to be a thing she could do about it. It was a little surreal, sitting there, hearing and answering questions without being fully awake. It reminded her of some of her teaching appointments toward the end of her mission. She'd been...so...tired. People just...wore her...out.

"Can I interest you in spinach as a topping?" Tyrel doled out the last of the Canadian bacon while he waited for her to respond. Looked up. Caught his breath. Awake, Merry seemed to vacillate between cold and sad. Well, and determined. Asleep, she...she was serene. Wiping his hands, Tyrel silently crossed the room to where she'd slumped against the wing of his couch.

The fine lines on her forehead had smoothed completely out. Her shoulders were completely relaxed. The determined set to her mouth had been replaced by the disarming vulnerability of slightly parted lips.

Rubbing the back of his neck, Tyrel tried to think things through. If he left her like that for any length of time, her head rocked sideways and back at a peculiar angle, she was going to get a terrible kink in the neck. It seemed cruel to try to wake her. She might insist on staying awake, no matter how firmly he told her that the pizza would keep or that he didn't mind or... Yes, based on his short acquaintance with her, he was confident she'd be very obstinate on the subject.

Which left him with the third option—that of trying to reposition her without waking her. Without getting decked if he *did* wake her. A single woman used to living alone was probably going to punch first and ask questions later. Perfectly logical.

He blew out a breath and unbuttoned his shirt cuffs so they wouldn't hinder his movements. Lifted the coffee table out of the way. Hesitated.

"Merry?" She stirred, but only just. He leaned closer. Touched her shoulder. "Merry?" Nothing. Hmm. Offering a quick prayer for their mutual safety, he bent to his task. Something prompted him to keep talking and he did. "I need to move you, Merry," he murmured as he put one arm behind her back and one under her knees. "Don't hit me, okay?" Straightening, he made a quarter turn to his right. Awkwardly nudged a couch pillow into position with one knee. "I'm going to lay you down right here on the couch," he explained his actions. "You'll sleep better there, I'm sure."

Taking the blanket from the back of the couch, he spread it over her, then set her shoes on the floor. Rising, he said another prayer, grateful that it had worked out so well. "I'm sorry, Merry," he apologized sincerely. "I had no idea you were so tired."

Loosening his tie, he walked back to the kitchen, where he covered the pizza. Getting his scriptures from his bedroom, he returned to the front room and hesitated. Raked his fingers through his hair in frustration. Yep. He was definitely going to have to get some chairs if he decided to stay there. It was Halloween next week, and his six-month lease would end just before Christmas.

Funny, it seemed like a good idea when he signed the lease. Sort of a test period in this new town with its new people. An experiment. He hadn't known what he was looking for in life. Just that he hadn't found it living at the lab. Or in the Air Force barracks. Or in the cramped apartment that he'd paid way too much rent for. So after several heartfelt prayers, he'd sold everything he didn't want to pack and moved here. A rural area that was completely different from anywhere he'd lived up to that point—but still close enough to an airport that he could fly out to see his grandparents as often as he chose.

His grandparents! He smacked himself on the forehead. He hadn't called them yet that week! Silently, he stole down the hall to his bedroom, where he left the door open a crack and pulled out his cell phone.

Merry wasn't sure what woke her. A noise? A noise she didn't recognize. Which was just weird. Sure the old barn made some peculiar sounds, but she thought she knew them all by now. A smile played across her lips. One thing she would never miss about life in the big city was having neighbors on four sides—above, below, and two out of four walls. Apartments. Yuck.

Yawning, she scrubbed a hand over her face. Wriggled her shoulders in an attempt to nestle down and go back to sleep. Buuuut when she put her hand back down, it flopped into something. Something too soft for a wall. And yet, it was something solid…where there shouldn't have been anything.

Prying her eyes open, Merry squinted at the room around her. Ran her hand along the coarse, vertical surface beneath it. Found a button. A couch? Whose couch? Where was she?

Sitting up sharply, Merry threw off the blanket. And stopped. Nothing was making sense, so she took a deep breath and tried to remember. It was…Sunday. She swung her feet to the floor. The lumps under her feet turned out to be her shoes, which she promptly slipped on. The room was still unfamiliar, yet the more awake she came, the more strongly she felt that, wherever she was, there was nothing to be afraid of.

At last, she spotted a set of scriptures on the oddly positioned low table beside the couch. Read the embossed letters on their cover. Dropped her flaming face into her hands. Perfect. She'd let Tyrel talk her into joining him for lunch, then fell asleep. That was new. Strange, though. She remembered the drive here. Remembered him asking her about toppings. Didn't remember lying down, though.

Her cheeks heated again as she came to the conclusion that he must've moved her. Must've picked her up, all one hundred-ninety pounds of her dead weight, and moved her. At five feet six inches, she carried her weight well, a gift she'd inherited from her mother. Nobody ever believed that she weighed that much. Not that she ran around telling people if she could help it. Tyrel was the first man to gain firsthand knowledge of it, though.

Wait. Where was Tyrel? The humiliation scorched deeper into her soul as she wondered if he'd gotten bored waiting for her to wake up and decided to take a walk or something. Rising, she peered into the kitchen. The stove clock told her that it was a few minutes after two-thirty. So…she hadn't been asleep as long as she'd thought. Forty minutes, forty-five at the outside?

"I will, Grandma." She looked up sharply as the sound of Tyrel's voice came floating down the hallway. "Maybe next year, you and Grandpa can come visit me. No," he laughed. "Not during the winter. I know you don't like the cold."

Merry slowly seated herself, her thoughts running a dozen different ways at once. Okay. She'd found Tyrel. He hadn't taken off, he'd called his grandparents. Both of whom were apparently still living. That was nice. But they didn't like the cold. And while winter in the Ozarks wasn't overly predictable, freezing temperatures were non-negotiable. Sometimes they even had ice storms where the streets…

She ruthlessly shut down the thought paths that weren't directly related to the here and now. Massaged the bridge of her nose. There was nothing for it. If she wanted a ride home, she'd have to stay long enough to choke down some pizza, endure his ribbing, and…go through it all over again when they went to her parents' for supper. Or she could move. Cadmia wasn't the only city in the world, after all.

She was reaching for her phone to call Grace—to beg for a ride if she had to—when she heard footsteps.

"No, and it's driving me crazy," Tyrel's voice said. "I don't even know how to begin." His low chuckle preceded him into the room, where he stopped, looked her in the eye, and smiled. "Hey, Grandma, I'm glad I caught you, but I have to go now." He listened briefly, nodding even though she couldn't possibly have seen the action. "I'm having someone over for lunch and they just got here."

Merry's tension level went up when he winked at her.

"Yeah, I'll call you soon. Love you." Ending the call, Tyrel set his phone on the counter. "Hope you're hungry." He tossed the words over his shoulder as he entered the kitchen, a low-risk conversational foray. Setting the pizza in the oven, he started the timer. Turned to face her.

"I'm sorry…" They broke off. Stared at each other.

Merry bit her lip, torn between her shock at his apology and the rather ridiculous hope that she could get ahead of the afternoon's torture. At least, it had seemed ridiculous. Her mind was already racing along, exploring potential reasons why he would feel the need to apologize to her. *Prove all things; hold fast that which is good.*

Taking a deep breath, Tyrel moved around the island and started for the coffee table. And knew the instant she noticed that he'd changed out of his silicone prosthetic to his running blade.

Her slight intake of breath. Widened eyes. He kept walking, waiting for her to say whatever she was going to say. Assuming she was planning to say anything.

He sat down beside her, crossing his prosthetic over his right ankle. "I need to apologize for insisting on having you over. I know I wanted to spend some time with you, but," he turned his hands palms up, "I should've respected your first answer."

"Thank you." Merry braced her hands on the couch. "I'm sorry I fell asleep on you. I mean. Like that. While you were talking to me." She didn't know what to say after that. Or do. 'I wanted to spend some time with you' didn't sound like a fair-weather friend. It sounded…serious. She wasn't ready to look him in the eyes, and if she lowered her gaze, it might look like she was staring at his prosthetic. Deciding that might be the safer topic, she risked asking, "So. What happened to your leg?"

Tyrel blew out a breath. "There was a forklift accident. I, um…" He stopped to clear his throat. Talking about his amputation would be a lot less difficult if he didn't also have to deal with the flashbacks. And yet, it never occurred to him not to tell her the full story. It was almost as if he *needed* to share it with her. "While I was in the Air Force, I was assigned to help coordinate at a construction site." He shrugged, but nothing was going to make the memories easier. "It was busy, y'know? Big equipment, people everywhere, and a couple of forklifts buzzing around."

Her embarrassment forgotten, Merry studied his face as he talked. Heard the growing tightness of his voice. Noticed the way his hands had begun to tremble. She didn't want to interrupt, but she couldn't let him tell the story alone. Timidly, she reached out.

"One of the forklift drivers suffered a heart attack. The accelerator on his lift got jammed forward." He looked down as her fingers settled lightly on his. Kept looking at their joined hands as he continued. "It was traveling at over twenty miles per hour—and still accelerating—when I finally saw it. We all started to run, but me, well, I managed to trip on a piece of loose trash." He paused to take a steadying breath. Talking about the accident stirred up unpleasant memories of slipping in and out of consciousness while he was being rescued. The scents of hot asphalt and blood.

His hand was cold under hers and Merry tightened her grip. His nostrils flared and his brow wrinkled as if he'd smelled something unpleasant. A memory?

"The impact shattered both bones above my ankle." He shook his head. "The surgeon in charge said there was nothing they could've done to save it, so they saved me instead."

She blinked, but a tear had already slipped past her defenses. Embarrassed, she swiped at it with her free hand.

"Did you get to ride in an ambulance?" she blurted, then cringed.

Tyrel barked a laugh, taken completely by surprise. "Yeah, I did." He took another breath, a deep breath this time, taking in the smells that currently surrounded him. The pizza. His cologne. Merry. It helped ground him in the present. "Honestly? It wasn't as much fun as I'd imagined."

The oven timer started going off and he stood. "I'll be back in a sec," he promised, reluctantly releasing her hand. "Then you can tell me what you're sorry for."

"Oh, that." Her laugh sounded panicked even to her own ears. How could she apologize for being overweight? *Should* she apologize? She hadn't asked him to move her. He hadn't said anything about it, either. Aaand he was already returning, laden down with pizza. This was an incredibly tiny apartment. "Can I help?" she asked, suddenly spotting glasses and a bottle of soda on the island.

"I've got it." He made sure to smile at her as he set the sliced pizza on the coffee table. Usually, when people asked about how he'd lost his leg, he stuck with the short version. Especially on a first date—which this wasn't, not exactly. Anyway. She'd taken the more-detailed version well, relatively speaking, but how would he know for sure? And why did he care so much? "Hope you like root beer."

"Absolutely!" Merry tried for a cheery tone. At the very least she owed him a little enthusiasm, after falling asleep on his couch mid-conversation.

"Here you go." He handed her a glass of root beer, then set a stack of napkins on the table.

"Plenty of room on the couch," she offered when she saw him sizing up a chunk of floor. While it wasn't as long as her couch, there was certainly room for them both.

"Thanks." Tyrel smiled. She seemed a little on edge and he hadn't wanted to crowd her.

"I guess it's my turn," she volunteered once he was seated. She started to fold her arms, then saw his proffered hand. Hesitantly slipped her hand into his, self-conscious about the callouses on her fingers and palm.

Peace welled up inside Tyrel as Merry gave a simple prayer. Peace and so much more. He'd dated before. It was a necessary evil, so to speak, for someone in their culture who wanted to get married. He'd learned a lot in the process, too. Some about women; mostly about himself. Unlike the stereotypical male, he didn't have a 'type.' Blonds, brunettes, redheads, and women who changed their hair color as often as he changed his socks. They were all people, with individual strengths and vulnerabilities.

As he lifted his head to look at Merry after the prayer, he saw a woman with thick, dark hair and mesmerizing fiery highlights. The faintest of down-turned lines around her sensitive mouth and expressive, green-flecked hazel eyes lent a sad air to an otherwise appealing face. He liked the way she carried herself, had liked it from the first time he saw her. He'd appreciated her reverent, knowledgeable remarks at church.

Merry couldn't breathe. Her hand was still in Tyrel's and he was looking at her so… intently. As if he was evaluating her somehow. For something. It made her distinctly uncomfortable.

She tugged on her hand and he released it immediately.

Chapter 6

"Sorry." Tyrel gave himself a hard mental shake. Tried a boyish grin. "Now, tell me this isn't the best pizza you've ever had." Over the next forty-five minutes, he went out of his way to keep things lighthearted. They discussed the pizza. Agreed to disagree about whether root beer was better than orange-flavored soda. Found that they both enjoyed a variety of music. "Okay, you've *never* heard of Rondo Veneziano?"

"No more than you'd heard of Gordon MacRae," she retorted lightly. She had a hunch he was overplaying his dismay at her 'ignorance' of one of his favorite groups. Truth be told, he seemed to be trying too hard in general. He hadn't let the conversational ball rest once since she'd taken her hand back.

"I guess you know what this means." Tyrel wiped his mouth and fingers on a napkin. "We're going to have to get together again."

She nearly choked on the last sip of her root beer. *At least he didn't say date*, she reasoned, trying to calm herself. Because an impromptu luncheon after church wasn't her idea of a first date. Not even when the man did the food prep.

"Oh?"

Tyrel leaned forward and began stacking things together to hide his frown. What exactly did this woman want? Besides good food, charming conversation, and a handsome companion? And…*why* was it so important to him? Why was he so determined to date her?

"I mean, yeah." She nodded, sensing his displeasure with her response. "We could do that. It…it might be a while before I have free time, though." A really, really long while. Like, after she'd recovered from this weird whatever it was, and his intensity and she just wanted to go home where it was comfortable and…

"Because of work?" He regretted the clipped way his question came out, but it was too late to fix it.

"Yeah." Merry sagged back against the couch as he stalked off to the kitchen. "Sure," she added, whisper-soft. This was one of many reasons she hated hanging out. She was always done long before everyone else. Ready to leave. To go home, where she could hold still and be quiet. Why was that such a foreign concept to her peers?

Even the weekly—most weeks—movie nights were sometimes more than she could handle. At least at those, though, she could count on most of the discussion being about movies; or the lives of the women she'd learned to trust and risk getting attached to.

While in the kitchen, Tyrel spotted a quote he'd stuck to his fridge with a magnet.

"Tied to this misconception is the erroneous belief that all members of the Church should look, talk, and be alike. The Lord did not people the earth with a vibrant orchestra of personalities only to value the piccolos of the world. Every instrument is precious and adds to the complex beauty of the symphony. All of Heavenly Father's children are different in some degree, yet each has his own beautiful sound that adds depth and richness to the whole." Elder Joseph B. Wirthlin, April 2008.

Slowly, he put things away and wiped down his counter. Turning to wipe down the island, he got a good look at Merry. A roundhouse kick to the face couldn't have hit him any harder than the sight of her slumped shoulders and lightless expression. He didn't begin to understand her, but he hated the idea that he'd had anything to do with her obvious melancholy. Dropping the cleaning rag into the sink, he said a prayer and re-entered the front room.

"Please take me home now."

"Yes. Yes, right now." Her quiet words wrenched his heart. "Um, as soon as I change my leg." He turned toward his bedroom, then turned back.

"I'm an idiot." He met her startled eyes and plunged ahead. "I ignored your needs. Twice." He grimaced. "So I completely understand if you don't want to see me again. But if you decide to give me another chance, I promise I will pay better attention. If you say you're not up for something, I'll wait. If you want to go home, I'll take you home. If you want me to stop talking, I'll…"

"Stop talking." Merry watched him as he abruptly closed his mouth. Sighed. "I can't give you a definitive answer right now." That two-dollar word was an undeniable sign that she was much too tired to make such a big decision. To even figure out what he was asking. "But, we'll be seeing each other at my parents' in a few hours. I'll try to have an answer by then."

"No rush." Tyrel nodded sharply, determined that he meant it. He quickly changed back to his walking leg, then escorted her out to his car.

Merry spent most of the ride to her home waiting for him to say something. To comment on the sugar maples, which were just starting to turn brilliant reds and yellows. To ask if she liked this or that. Instead, she was treated to a blissful silence. She glanced at him once. Found him watching her with an anxious expression on his face. By the time he'd parked and come around to open her door for her—which she thought she might be able to get used to—she'd scrounged up some energy.

Enough that when it became obvious he intended to escort her to her door, she managed to say, "Thank you for the pizza." His eyes brightened and his mouth opened instantly. "Thank you," she repeated quickly.

Tyrel closed his mouth. Walked a few more

steps while he digested the fact that she was just being polite, not giving him the go-ahead to plan anything.

"I'm glad you liked it," he said as she inserted her key. They smiled at each other and she slipped inside. The door clicked shut behind her.

Frowning, Tyrel started toward his car. When he reached it, he shoved his hands in his pockets and kept going. Maybe walking would clear his head.

From her upstairs window, a bewildered Merry watched him. She'd expected him to go, but not on foot. More confused than ever, she went over to her couch and knelt down. In one of her less-organized prayers, Merry recounted her day and asked what, exactly, she was supposed to do with Tyrel? As weary as she was, the gloomy thoughts that surged up got a good hold on her before she rallied herself against them. Wiping tears from her face, she continued praying until she felt a measure of peace.

Finally crawling onto the couch, still in her church clothes, she tugged a blanket over herself and closed her eyes. Sleep came quickly, relieving the stress she'd been under since Tyrel had appeared on her doorstep that morning. All too soon, however, her rest was interrupted. Invaded, rather, by a ringtone.

Merry cracked one eye and looked around for her phone. It wasn't on the table by the couch. Opening her other eye, she examined the floor beside the couch. Nope, not there. "Silver," from *Treasure Planet*, stopped playing while she was rubbing the rest of the sleep out of her eyes. Resumed playing mid-yawn.

Aha! Her phone had slipped beneath her while she slept. Rescuing it from where it had gotten wedged between two cushions, Merry answered it before her sister could call her a third time.

"Hello?" She wrinkled her nose at the croaking sound she made.

"Merry? Are you alright?" Heidi, her sister, sounded like she was wrinkling her nose.

Merry cleared her throat and got up to unwind herself from the blanket. "Yeah, fine. What's up?"

"Oh, okay, you sound better now. For a second there, I thought you'd swallowed a frog."

Merry rolled her eyes at the old family expression for a sore throat. "Nope, just," she yawned, "just woke up."

"Must be nice to be able to set your own hours." Heidi sounded faintly exasperated now. "You've got about twenty minutes to hightail it over here before we start supper without you."

Merry hesitated, tempted to stay right where she was. Of course, if she did, she'd have to deal with Heidi in person, because she'd come barging over to check on her.

"I'll be there." Hanging up, Merry plugged her phone in and meandered to the end of the hall. Clothes that she hadn't gotten around to carrying upstairs were neatly stacked on top of the dryer. Selecting a fresh t-shirt and some jeans, she changed and ran a comb through her hair.

Stepping into a pair of sneakers, she left the same way she had that morning, riding the ladder down from the verandah. Originally, it'd been intended as a fire escape. During testing, however, she'd discovered that she genuinely enjoyed it, so now she used it whenever possible.

Tyrel's car was still parked beside her truck, but she didn't see him anywhere. *Odd.* Tucking her hands into the pockets of her light jacket, she headed out into the field that separated her grandparents' home—her home, she reminded herself—from her parents'. She could barely see over the round bales of hay that littered the field and knew that she'd have to borrow a flashlight to make it back across in the dark in one piece.

It was so quiet crossing the field that she was able to hear the noise from her parents before she was halfway there. Chelsea, a teenage niece, was chanting an old jump rope rhyme, which probably meant she'd organized the others for a game. She was a natural-born leader that way. Lately she'd started coming in with the adults for after-dinner conversation, though. Like everything else, she was growing and changing.

Sure enough, as soon as the yard came into view, Merry was able to see the tops of two heads and one more that bobbed rhythmically into and out of sight. She also saw Tyrel on the porch with Toby, one of her brothers. They were talking. Her legs kept moving, propelling her closer and closer, but her lungs had stopped at half-full. That was actually kind of lucky because when they stopped as she finished exhaling, it was much more difficult to goad them into working again.

Dropping her gaze so that she was watching her feet, Merry concentrated. Compelled her rebellious lungs to finish expelling all the air they held. Sucked in a gasping lungful. Repeated the process.

"There she is!" From his place on the porch, Toby clapped his hands and hollered at the gaggle of kids. "Supper in five! Get inside and get your hands washed!"

Taking that as an admonition to herself for keeping everyone waiting, Merry hurried in along with the children. Swinging one of the smaller ones up over the steps, she managed to keep from making eye contact with Tyrel.

"Hey, sis." Toby's hand came down on her shoulder. He had an uncanny knack for bringing attention to her when she least wanted it. "You almost missed supper." He grinned mischievously at her. "You should've ridden over with your boyfriend." Before she could get open her mouth to correct him, Toby'd slipped past her and gone inside to finish his self-appointed job of 'corralling' the kids.

Daring a glance at Tyrel to see how he'd taken the erroneous remark, Merry saw the creases on his forehead even in the failing light. He held out his hand to her and, much to her surprise, she moved forward to take it.

"Are you alright?" he asked mildly. "You look a little pale."

Merry shrugged. "I'm fine." Or she would be, once his fingers weren't resting lightly on her wrist. How did other women cope with holding hands?

The color creeping up in her cheeks only served to puzzle him further. "Are you sure? Because…" He was interrupted when someone poked their head through the open door.

"Come on, you two." Heidi was almost disappointed to see how far apart the two of them were standing. To hear her mom tell it, they were practically engaged. Granted, Mom could exaggerate with the best of them. And even read things into situations that weren't there, as Heidi's own dating experience had taught her. "The kids are getting restless!"

Merry jerked her hand free, hoping desperately that her sister hadn't seen it. It would just be too hard to explain that they weren't holding hands. Not like that, anyway.

"Here we come." Tyrel grinned at Heidi over Merry's shoulder. "I can't wait to taste your mom's chili."

Merry's pulse jumped when his hand settled

on the small of her back. It was in an appropriate place, so she didn't exactly squirm away from him, but she did hustle to put a little distance between them.

Tyrel did his best to keep a smile on his face as Merry moved away, ostensibly to assist her mother. Who didn't need any help, from what he could see. Was it just his imagination or had Merry flinched away from his touch a moment ago?

Overall, the McKinney's were a noisy, happy bunch, chatting about grades, braces, the weather, and everything under the sun as they consumed chili, green beans, cornbread, and a gallon or two of milk. Tyrel quickly got involved in a conversation with Chad, another of Merry's brothers, about the space program.

"Hold up," Chad interrupted, narrowing his eyes. "Did you just say you've actually been to DSS?"

"That's right," Tyrel nodded. "I was assigned to work there while I was in the military." Monitoring for deep space signals might not be the most exciting job in the world, but maintaining the equipment kept him plenty busy while he was there.

Chad took another bite of chili, then one of cornbread. He was on his third helping but didn't seem to notice that everyone else had finished. He chewed, swallowed, and looked sideways at Tyrel, who was highly amused at the other man's not-so-subtle build-up.

"Ty." Embarrassed by what she knew was coming, Merry blurted out a shortened version of Tyrel's name.

His head snapped around to where Merry sat, a scant four feet away from him, still on the other side of the table.

"Could you give me a hand?" she requested, getting up abruptly.

He rose without and followed her without hesitation, leaving Chad with his mouth hanging open.

Once they were in the kitchen, she stopped to lean against a counter. Brushed a hand across her eyes and laughed shakily. "I never realized what a blessing a kitchen door could be."

Tyrel leaned closer to catch what she said, then eyed the door that had swung shut behind them. Her brothers hardly seemed the protective type, but he'd noticed her father watching him closely ever since he arrived early, alone, and on foot. His lips twitched in a moment of wry amusement at what Andy, as he'd been instructed to call the man, would think of Merry's having fallen asleep on his couch earlier.

"There's no point telling me you're all right this time," he informed her as gently as he could. "What did you bring me in here to say?"

She hesitated, no longer sure of that herself. He probably wouldn't have cared about Chad's question. Sighing heavily, she folded her arms across her chest.

As if he needed more of a reminder that she was closed off. Tyrel slowly closed the distance between them, noting the increased tension in her shoulders and face as he did so.

"Best guess? Chad's a conspiracy theorist. He was planning to ask me if I'd met any of the aliens who work in the government or," he dismissed the matter with a wave of his hand, "something equally ridiculous."

"Yeah." Merry nodded. It sounded silly, hearing him say it in the quiet of the kitchen. In the other room, with over a dozen voices pounding away at her, the idea of Chad bringing up one of his cockamamie ideas had seemed painfully embarrassing.

"Well, you don't have to worry." Smoothly, Tyrel changed position so that he was leaning against the counter beside her, being careful not to touch her. "I didn't have that kind of clearance." He looked sideways and down at her—she was a couple of inches shorter than he was—and dropped a sly wink. The laugh that bubbled up out of her was the sweetest sound he'd ever heard.

"Sorry, I guess I made a big deal out of nothing." And yet, she didn't feel like finding a rock to crawl under. Tyrel wasn't just not upset. He didn't seem the least bit phased.

Tyrel shrugged. "Hey, at least I can hear myself think in here." He locked eyes with her unintentionally. "That's…something."

Taken aback, Merry stared up at him. At the rate she was being drawn into his sky blue eyes, she was going to reach escape velocity in nothing flat. She already felt like she was floating.

"I mean, I like your family and all that." He let his eyes rove over her face, delighting in the pale freckles he discovered scattered across the bridge of her nose. "I just appreciate peace and quiet, too." For the first time, he got the impression he was making progress with this lovely, enigmatic woman.

"Me, too," she confessed. She had no idea what she'd done to make him smile, but it warmed her, touched a walled-off spot inside her.

"You, too?" Heidi had entered the kitchen unnoticed, and now she was the one with the folded arms.

Merry jerked visibly, her hands coming down to her sides with such force that she slammed the side of one of them into the counter. Stifling an outcry of pain, she bit her lip.

"What?" Merry echoed, blinking rapidly.

Tyrel watched her reaction with a great deal of interest. Sure, the thought of kissing her had flitted through his mind, but he hadn't let it linger. It was way too soon to be thinking about that—not to mention he wasn't sure they would ever reach that point. So, what about her sister surprising them set her on such a hard edge? Perhaps the idea had crossed her mind as well?

That was an interesting thought. He filed it away for later and flashed a grin at Heidi.

"You, too, what?" Heidi repeated a tad testily.

"Did you know that I moved here six months ago?" Tyrel smiled engagingly. "And I still haven't finished unpacking." The skillful use of misdirection served more than magicians.

Heidi opened her mouth, then closed it. She was pretty sure that had nothing to do with whatever they'd been talking about, but what could she do about it?

"Sad, isn't it?" Tyrel dropped a few more words into the silence, then captured Merry's hand. "C'mon," he invited. "I want to thank your mom for supper before we go."

Merry allowed him to lead her past Heidi and was confused when he released her hand. She'd wanted her hand back, but hadn't expected him to just let go like that. Somehow, he switched positions so that he was behind her, and once again his hand rested lightly on the small of her back.

Chapter 7

Mere minutes later, Tyrel had thanked her mother, shaken hands with her father, and excused himself with the explanation that he had an early appointment the next morning. Almost before she was ready, Merry found herself stepping out onto the back porch with him.

She paused to watch the sunset paint the sky vivid reds and pinks. A soft breeze tickled her cheek with escaped tendrils of hair, carrying with it the scents of freshly churned earth and exhaust from the fields. A bird sang somewhere in the distance while a chorus of crickets chirped near the garage. She almost relaxed.

"Thanks for walking me back." Tyrel smiled. "I have a funny feeling I'd have gotten lost."

"Between here and my place?" Merry frowned, unsure if he was joking or not. "That would've taken a fair bit of talent," she said, keeping her tone as light as possible. "The road's that way," she pointed to her right, "and there's a fence on the left—if you go far enough." Ooops. She probably should've kept that last observation to herself.

"All the same," Tyrel looked a little uneasily at the expansive hayfield, "I'll be glad for your company." He thought he'd adapted pretty well to life in a small town, but this would be a first.

"Sure." Merry didn't know exactly what to say

to that. She looked forward to reaching the solitude of her own home again, though. Kind of nice to have an excuse for leaving early since she was struggling tonight.

Feeling his fingers reaching for hers, she pulled her hand away and stuffed it into her pocket. What was it with him and holding hands?

"Does," he drew the word out, "that mean you've decided not to give me another chance?" His confidence that she'd decided exactly that evaporated when she moved her hand out of reach. She walked on without answering and he frowned. "Or…was tonight my last chance and I just blew it?" He mentally reviewed the evening for any grievous mistakes but came up empty. Their moment in the kitchen hadn't amounted to anything much. Anyway, he thought she'd enjoyed it.

Merry kept walking, struggling to find the right answer. She'd decided his invitation from earlier was strictly casual. Friendly. She blew out a breath. A long time ago, she'd been friends with a man. She'd secretly hoped it would turn into something more, but never pushed the issue. When she'd announced her plan to move back to the Ozarks, he hadn't objected. Or offered to come with. Or even bothered to keep in touch. They could hardly continue hanging out with over thirteen hundred miles between them, could they?

She realized then that Tyrel had stopped talking. "We can be friends," she said at last. She'd just have to stay ahead of her attraction to him. It wouldn't be easy, even after she'd noticed at church that his shoulders weren't all that broad when compared with the farm boys she'd grown up with. Something about bucking hay and splitting logs really made a man fill out. On the other hand, none of them had his wavy black hair or... Hang on a second, whose side was she on?! She shook her head to dislodge that train of thought.

"Great." Tyrel took her by the elbow and brought her to a stop. She refused to look at him. "Is that all?"

"Is what all?" she asked, a catch in her voice belying her flippant retort.

What am I doing? Tyrel asked himself again, searching her suddenly blank face for clues. He found Merry McKinney physically attractive, but her personality seemed totally wrong for him. So far, getting to know her was like...trying to hug a cactus. Still. He'd done a lot of praying while he walked that afternoon and kept getting the same answer, no matter how he phrased the question. There was something special here, even if he couldn't see it.

"Maybe I'm getting ahead of myself here, but I'm not some gawky teenager trying to figure out how to date. I'm looking for an eternal companion." Much to his dismay, her eyes filled with tears. Good grief, now what?

Merry bit her lip savagely, but it was too late. Once she started crying, especially when she was already tired and off-balance, she was doomed. It wouldn't be a pretty cry, either. No glistening tears or genteel whimpers for her. Twisting free of his hold on her arm, she resumed trudging toward her house. The steady exercise might at least help regulate her breathing.

"Hey." Tyrel hurried to catch up, nearly breaking an ankle in a rut in the process. "What's wrong? Merry." He spun her to face him, holding onto her by both shoulders this time. "What *is* it?" He hated the desperate note in his voice, but he had no idea what was going on.

She struggled against his grip, but short of actual violence he seemed determined to hold onto her. Well fine. He wanted to know? He deserved to find out.

"You want to know," she stopped to suck in a breath, "what's wrong? I'm what's wrong." His left eyebrow went up and his mouth started to open. "*I'm* what's wrong," she insisted. "I was the girl the 'gawky' teenage boys never asked out." She glared at him, cut to the quick by his innocent assumption that everyone dated in their teens. "I was the young woman who spent four years as the perennial wallflower at college." She tried to jerk away, but his grip hadn't loosened. Tears streaming down her cheeks, she ranted on. "I finally flunked out of the church's young single adult program and guess what? Seven years later I've still never…never even…"

But the pain was too much. She lived with it

every day, the conviction that something was so desperately wrong with her that no man had ever looked her way. Not even casually—and mercy dates didn't count. When she kept busy enough, which was most of the time, she didn't think about it.

Tyrel stepped in and wrapped his arms around her, holding her up while she dissolved into tears. Each sob tore at the assumptions he'd accumulated over the years of his life. Things he'd taken for granted simply didn't apply here. In his arms, he held a woman completely without experience. And because of that, she believed the absolute worst about herself. That she was unloved. That she was…unlovable. He was both shocked and troubled by this revelation.

"Shhh," he murmured, pressing his cheek to the top of her head. "I've got you." Her windbreaker was soft under his fingers and she was soft in his arms as her convulsive sobs rocked them both.

Merry desperately wanted to stop crying. An outburst like this inevitably resulted in a raging headache, the kind that clung to her even after a night's rest and sucked the will right out of her.

Unfortunately, it wasn't that easy. She'd just have to cry until she was done.

Except…tonight was different. Every gasp for air brought in a fragrant dose, part fresh air and soil, part Tyrel and his cologne. His chest was a lot firmer than the soft bed she usually curled up on when old devil gloom sank its fangs into her. And now, as her crying quieted, she found that she could hear his heart beating. Steadily. A little faster than she might've expected…

Oh, she'd probably scared the wits right out of him, breaking down like this. Yes, that was it. Yay. One more humiliating memory to haunt her when she was down.

Tyrel kept praying as he held her, praying to know what to do. There would be no shortcuts in this relationship. She wouldn't know what she liked or didn't like, and there were bound to be rough patches on what could be a long, uphill trip to the temple. Yet this was a journey his soul yearned to take.

"Merry?"

She pressed her face harder into his chest, afraid to let him see what a mess she was. She'd seen it before and had no desire to see it again. Puffy eyelids, red, runny nose… Could the night get any worse? She felt fingers under her chin and knew without a doubt that it could!

"Merry," he repeated, gently forcing her chin up. "Oh, sweetheart." He wiped her damp cheeks. "C'mon."

Dazed, Merry let him lead her through the field to where his car sat waiting for him. Except he didn't go to his car. Come to think of it, he hadn't abandoned her in the field, either. Or let her run away to hide. What was going on? She sniffled as quietly as she could while she tried to make sense of it.

"Let me have your keys," he prompted as they approached the side door to her shop. Of all the nights to be without a handkerchief or a tissue or even a leftover napkin hiding out in a pocket! "I noticed a couple of doors over here yesterday. Is one of them a bathroom?" He took the keys from her trembling fingers and watched her nod. "Okay." He opened the door and shooed her inside. "Wash your face, and then we need to talk."

Merry couldn't figure out what was left to be said, but she was too wiped out to argue, so she cooperated as far as splashing some cold water on her aching eyes. When she was feeling a little better, she dried her face and hands on one of the clean shop rags she kept in there, then peeked out to see him standing in front of the table.

He turned to face her when she came out and she cringed as a place on his chest glistened under the glaring shop lights. "Sorry about your shirt," she mumbled.

"My shirt?" Tyrel glanced at the soggy spot and shook his head. "It's not important. *You're* important." It had taken a ton of bricks to fall on him, but he finally knew why he was willing to try so hard with Merry. She was worth the effort. Now he just had to convince her. He held up a hand to keep her from interrupting. "You're important to me, Merry."

Her response was to massage the bridge of her nose.

"Headache?" he guessed.

"Naturally." There was no heat in her tone. It was a flat statement of fact.

"Can I help?"

She opened one eye to peer at him. "I don't..." She swallowed the rest of the flippant response and tried again. "I don't know how you could."

"Sit down." He pointed at the stool nearest her. "My grandmother used to get pretty bad headaches." He moved up behind her. "I was the only person she trusted to give her a massage."

"I don't think that's a good idea." She was halfway off the stool before she finished speaking and he still managed to catch her by the shoulders.

"Consider it a home remedy," he suggested, releasing her almost as quickly as he'd taken hold of her. He'd never gone in for the so-called caveman approach. Tonight, however, he'd already held her, albeit briefly, against her will— twice. "In fact." He walked around so that he was facing her. "Let me show you what I mean. I'll start with your hands."

"If I didn't know better," she muttered grumpily as she slid back onto the stool, "I'd think you just wanted to hold hands." Was it weird that she thought they sort of already had held hands? Nobody else counted prayers, she was ninety-nine percent certain. At least, nobody who wasn't a lovesick kid. Scowling, she shoved her hand toward him.

"Oh, we'll get around to that." Despite her scowl, he flashed her a friendly grin as he put his palm to hers and spread her fingers. He admired the callouses on her hands and what they told him about her love of woodworking. "That's what I want to talk to you about. But I need you to tell me if this hurts, okay?" One by one, he lifted her fingers away from his palm until he reached her thumb. She hadn't said a word, which worried him a little. "This is usually where things get serious," he warned.

Merry hissed in pained surprise as he moved her thumb away from her fingers. "Felt that," she announced needlessly.

Tyrel chuckled. "We're on the right track, then." For the next few minutes, he kneaded the muscles around the base of her thumb. Stretched it again. "Better?" When she nodded, he set her hand on her knee and picked up the other one. Repeated the process.

"Thank you." Merry had relaxed quite a bit during his ministrations, which robbed the headache of some of its potency. Regrettably, curiosity got the better of her, causing her to blurt out, "Why are you still here? Why aren't you halfway to the county line, running scared?"

Tyrel gave her other hand back and pulled up

a stool for himself. "Is that what people usually do?"

Merry looked to the left, then down. Massaged the bridge of her nose again. "Yeah. And with a lot less provocation." She watched his eyebrows draw in and braced herself for an outpouring of well-meant pity.

"For the record, what I'm about to say is highly unorthodox." He paused and wondered where that turn of phrase had come from. Maybe she was rubbing off on him already. "In the past, I've always tried to express my feelings through actions. So, the more I liked someone, the bigger the date. The…fancier the restaurant. That sort of thing. It was a kind of defense mechanism, I guess. I never committed to anything, but it made me feel like I was holding up my end of the relationship." He waved the subject away and looked her in the eyes. "However—obviously—none of those relationships ever amounted to anything." Yeah, that wasn't awkward at all. Well so what? Awkward or not, he'd come too far to back down now.

"Ty, I…" She tried to interrupt, but failed. The phantom spaghetti monster in her stomach was shivering like it was about to have triplets.

"What I'm trying to say is that I think you need to know I'm done playing games. Done playing hide-and-go-seek with love." The words came out in a rush and he took a moment to recover from them. "If you're up to a serious relationship, I'd like to take you out for dinner this week," he finished with a hopeful smile.

The words hung in the air between them, filling Merry with hope and dread. "I…" Suddenly a thought occurred to her and her lips twitched upward. Of all the peculiar happenings in the last forty-eight hours, what were the odds that she would be asked on her first official date the week of Halloween? Better than April Fool's Day, she supposed.

Her lips and her spirits drooped as she pondered the odds that this could be some sick joke. Sort of the big brother of what used to happen to her in grade school, when people would be nice to her just long enough to get ammunition for making fun of her later.

Tyrel watched in growing dismay as emotions raced across her face. He was debating something when her eyes suddenly locked on his. He'd endured white glove inspections during his time in the military and voluntarily participated in temple worthiness interviews with his bishop every two years. This, though…this was an entirely different kind of soul-searching. Without even knowing what she was seeking, he promptly worried that he wouldn't measure up.

"And what did you mean when you said we'd get around to holding hands?" She'd decided that very, very few things were worth the amount of trouble he'd already gone to on her behalf. Not that it made any sense, just that he was probably (impossibly) in earnest.

Startled, Tyrel didn't answer immediately. Thinking back on the number of kisses he'd participated in over the years, he was suddenly embarrassed. Most of them had been casual, given and received without much thought from either participant.

"I just meant that, given time and sufficient mutual interest, we'd eventually hold hands," he answered lamely.

Merry felt herself blushing. She was still reeling from his direct approach, among other things. *Serious relationship… Eternal companion…* He hadn't actually asked her to marry him, thank goodness. Nevertheless, it was a lot for her to take in. It directly contradicted her mindset for the last twenty-one years, which was enough to set her world on its ear. So, while she appreciated his honesty, and wished she could reciprocate…

"I don't know what to say," she admitted at last. "I have to think about this first."

A wonderful peace settled over Tyrel, making it possible for him to sincerely say, "I'm glad. I think I'd have been worried if you had an easy answer to such tough questions." Rising, he wrapped his arms around her in a brotherly hug. "That's to help ward off any mid-night doubts," he told her as he straightened away.

He was halfway to the door before Merry remembered. "Oh! Wednesday's the ward trunk-or-treat. I…was planning to go to that." His first answer was that wonderful smile of his.

"I'll pick you up at six-thirty." He winked. He left then, securing the door behind him. "Whoa."

As they knelt by their beds that night, Tyrel and Merry both prayed for wisdom and courage.

Chapter 8

Dawn found Merry ensconced in her recording booth with her completed song, "Alone Again." Inspiration had woken her in the middle of the night, providing a final verse that changed the tone of the entire composition. Made it lighter, optimistic even. It also provided a distraction from Tyrel's blunt speech the night before, which had been on repeat even in her dreams.

Setting aside her drumsticks, she turned to her computer and queued up the best of the recordings she'd made that morning. Carefully, she mixed the guitar and keyboard tracks, which she'd recorded earlier, in with the percussion. Finally satisfied with the results, she adjusted the settings to record a vocal track.

As her microphone warmed up, she silently acknowledged to herself that this was the hardest part. Even here, where there were no cameras. No narrowed eyes or snide remarks. Here, the only criticisms were echoes of years past. She was free to explore her musical aspirations. To express herself.

She chuckled softly. Express herself? Though she'd run through the lyrics with each recording, she hadn't managed to make it through once without needing to clear her throat. Well. Ninth time was the charm?

"It's so hard," she sang softly. Tears pricked her eyes and stung her nose, making her stop again. She restarted the instrumental track that was playing in her headphones. Tried again, this time with more air. "It's so hard, makin' friends. So hard knowing it's bound to end."

She held her breath after the last note faded away, then stopped the recording. That might've been the hardest part, but the *worst* part was still ahead. Now she had to listen to it.

It took another two tries before she hesitantly decided there was no point in making a fourth recording. The technical quality of her singing might improve, but the feeling and warmth in her voice would dwindle.

Leaning back in her chair, she worked with the vocal and instrumental tracks, balancing the volumes so that the lyrics came through clearly without drowning out the instruments. Her stomach grumbled as she logged onto her website, making her laugh.

Helen Montgomery, her alter ego, smiled at her from her artist page as she uploaded the finished track for digital purchase. Amazing what a red wig, glasses, and a little makeup could do to alter one's appearance. It was a good thing, too. She'd nearly fainted a month ago when she'd heard one of her songs at a local store. It turned out that a younger employee had figured out how to sync her phone to the store's speaker system and was 'sharing' her personal playlist that way.

Said employee also shared her glowing personal opinion of the artist and her other songs. All of which Merry had overheard while waiting in the checkout line.

She'd promptly earned herself the stink-eye from both participants by asking if it was ethical for a personal playlist to be used that way. Thank goodness she'd been at the store's one and only self-check, or she'd probably have gotten home with cracked eggs and bruised fruit! Would she never learn to hold her tongue?

Shaking her head, she got up and closed the door to the booth behind her. Her hunger drove her to the kitchen next, where she made a hasty meal of scrambled eggs and pears with toast. Today was the day she was going to tackle the scarred table leg.

She kept busy after that, resolutely refusing to check her phone for messages. From anyone. At all. Tyrel got to her anyway, though.

"Ms. McKinney?" A young man called to her from the doorway. "Delivery for Ms. McKinney?"

Merry switched off the lathe and shoved her safety glassed up into her hair. "That's me. Whatcha got?" Weird. She wasn't expecting anything. She was halfway to him before she saw the padded envelope he was holding.

"They don't tell me what's in 'em, just where they go." He grinned, revealing clear braces. "Sign here?"

"Um." She glanced at the padded envelope in his hands, but there wasn't a return address. Accepting the proffered tablet, she was surprised to see the logo for a local mailing company on the form. "I didn't know you guys delivered anything smaller than fridges," she admitted as she signed and dated.

"Neither did I," he laughed. "This is a pretty special package." Trading her the envelope for the tablet, he gave her a nod. "Have a good evening!"

Surprised, she checked the time on her clock. Yeah, four-forty-five was evening. And that explained the cramping feeling in her back muscles. Taking the legs off the table had been hard work, but re-turning them to the same specifications was an exacting process.

Dropping her safety glasses into place, she turned the lathe back on and finished the fourth leg. Setting it beside the others for tomorrow, she hung up her work apron. Resolutely, she ignored the envelope long enough to sweep the wood chips and curls from the lathe work into a dust collection terminal.

That was as far as she got, though, before curiosity overcame her. Curiosity and the pain sticking needles in her trapezius muscles. She tore the envelope open as she climbed the stairs. Slid a CD and a note into her palm. She had to blink a couple of times to be sure she was seeing what she thought she was seeing—the CD cover featured robots wearing renaissance costumes. Not only that, they appeared to be playing a violin and a cello while taking a ride on a glistening, golden gondola.

Shaking her head, she opened the note.

One of my favorite CDs. Hope you enjoy it! Tyrel

Rats. She'd been successfully not thinking of him. Her cheeks warmed as she set the note on the kitchen island, then hurried upstairs to run a hot bath. It took a little digging, but she did find a small CD player stashed in the attic. Popping the CD in, she let it play while she added lavender-scented Epsom salts to her oversized tub. Much to her relief, she quite liked the instrumental music that sparkled out of the player.

Refreshed and invigorated by both the CD and her bath, she heated up the last of the chicken pasta from Saturday. Picked up her phone for the first time since she'd finished her scripture study that morning. Started scrolling through her notifications. Choked on the pasta.

As part of setting herself up as Helen Montgomery, she'd signed up to be alerted in the extremely unlikely event that she ever became a hot search engine term. Tonight, it seemed she made it!

Helen Montgomery's latest soulful lyrics will change how you treat your friends! predicted one headline.

I've never been so happy to be sad! boasted another in a twist on the lyrics themselves.

The pasta grew cold as Merry kept reading. She

She was trending on social media! Ouch. Not all of it was positive. A good twenty percent of the comments expressed disappointment in stinging—and occasionally witty—words. Another third wasn't interested in amateur singers and wanted to know where they could get the song performed by their favorite artist. The rest of the comments were profusely complimentary…to the point of making her squirm.

Dazed, she took a bite of pasta. Grimaced and shoved the plate back in the microwave. Froze in place when her phone began vibrating. This was it. Helen Montgomery had been found out. She was about to live her own worst nightmare.

The phantom spaghetti monster slid down her legs, making them heavy, so heavy she could barely lift them to turn around. It wriggled and thrashed throughout her stomach area until the few bites she had eaten threatened to abandon her the hard way.

She had a hard time getting a grip on the vibrating phone, but she finally got it flipped over. The tension left her in a whoosh of expelled air and she sagged against the island.

"Hello?"

"Hey. Are you okay?" Concern filled Tyrel's warm voice, spawning a swarm of butterflies in her stomach.

"What? Oh." Her attempt at a casual laugh sounded shrill. She winced. Lying was obviously out. "I'm…fine, really I am. I just…found something out and…" In a way, the butterflies were worse than the phantom spaghetti monster, which hadn't yet learned how to do backflips. Emphasis on the *yet* if Tyrel didn't move on soon. It was one thing for him to declare that he was ready for a serious relationship. She wasn't at all sure about herself.

"Merry?" His voice had a soft chuckle to it now. "Your microwave is going off."

"Yeah, I," she ran a hand over her face. "I was reheating the last of the pasta."

"The chicken pasta?" She could almost hear him drooling. "You never did give me that recipe."

This time her laugh sounded more normal. "I seem to recall mentioning that it was a secret." Opening the microwave, she lifted the plate out and sat down to try again.

"Well, if that's how you're going to be," he teased, "I just won't tell you what costume I've decided to wear for the trunk-or-treat." Trick-or-treating in the church parking lot was much safer than hitting random houses these days.

She shrugged and swallowed the small bite of pasta she'd been chewing. Lowered the phone so the microphone was near her mouth again. "Suit yourself." She'd seen plenty of epic couple costume fails in her life. No need to be part of one. Especially not when just thinking about being the other half of Ty's couple made her heart miss a beat. "How was work?"

"Work?"

"Yeah," she said when he didn't venture past that word. "That thing people do to make money?"

"Money, right."

"You remember money." She was starting to wonder.

"Sure do. I, um…y'know, I don't have a job. Not the way that most people think of jobs, anyway."

She frowned at the phone. *What's that supposed to mean?*

"I was a mechanical engineer in the Air Force. When I got my discharge earlier this year, I took a good look at my life."

"Wow, I…I knew you were in the military, but I didn't realize you'd left it so recently. That's a big change." *Congratulations on the understatement of the year!*

"It was time. I enlisted right after I got home from my mission. It was a great twelve years, don't get me wrong. I just got to the point where money wasn't my biggest need."

"I see."

A soft chuckle came through. "That would be a first."

"Pardon?" She wished he were there so she could see his face.

"Sorry, I just…" He blew out a breath. "The few people I've told, they've all needed convincing."

"Convincing?" She gestured with her fork. "Like, how? By showing them you're capable of doing basic math?"

He hooted. "Something like that. Now it's my turn to ask questions. What did you think of the CD?"

"CD?" Merry could almost hear him trying to outwait her as she chewed. She swallowed another bite, the shock of her unexpected fame having faded for now. If she was being honest, the fame itself would recede just as quickly. Blow over by morning, most likely.

"The one you signed for?" he coaxed at last.

"Oh. Oh, *that* CD." She grinned, feeling that she'd won some sort of victory by making him clarify.

"Glad you liked it." Warm amusement filled his tone.

"I always like good music," she agreed cheekily. A thought struck her then and she ventured to ask, "I suppose you've looked up Gordon MacRae already?"

"I have," he admitted. "Downloaded an entire album this morning."

"And…what did you think?" She almost hated to ask. She loved the silver-throated Gordon MacRae and was worried that Tyrel hadn't.

"I thought I'd save it for the drive on Wednesday."

Merry silently scraped together the last bite of

pasta while she thought that over. It wasn't a long trip. Fifteen minutes from her home to the church, depending on incidentals. So, thirty minutes in a cramped space with a handsome man whose cologne befuddled her from two feet away in a hayfield. While Gordon MacRae sang love songs in the background.

Leaving the pasta, she rose and began pacing. "I might have to meet you there." Her voice squeaked a little and she grimaced.

"Oh? Why?"

Faced with a blunt question, she scowled. One reason she was a terrible liar was that she didn't believe in it. On the other hand, what kind of a straight answer could she give him? The disappointment she thought she heard in his voice didn't help any.

"I, um… Errands. I've got some errands." She paced some more. She had a to-do list as long as her tape measure, but even she didn't believe that as an excuse. In her case, the truth tended to come out in full sentences. Or at least without fillers noises like 'um.' Because she wasn't having to invent it as she went.

"Oh." Awkward silence. "I'd be happy to chauffeur you around town. We could have an early supper or…something."

She rubbed the ache in her forehead. He didn't have to be this nice about it!

"Right," she snorted. "Traipse around town in costume." Her hand flew up to cover her mouth and she tensed for his rebuttal.

He laughed easily. "Hadn't thought about that."

"Sure." She rammed her hip into the corner of her island and bit back a yelp of pain. Convenient timing, in a way. The pain snagged all of her available attention, keeping it from running amuck with thoughts of how she could apologize to him. If an apology was needed. She couldn't tell from his reaction.

"Well, no worries. We can listen to Gordon MacRae another time."

In other words, she'd only delayed the inevitable. "Right." She frowned. Apparently, she fell back on single-syllable words when she was trying not to say what she was thinking.

"Unless you'd rather not? Listen, I mean. To music. With me."

"It's not…" She winced. "I mean, it isn't… I…" She stopped. Even if she had the words to explain, would she have the courage to use them?

Because I might like it too much. Nope. No, she couldn't say that.

"You *don't* not want to listen to music with me?"

She rubbed her forehead again. "Something like that," she mumbled.

"It's a start," he chuckled. "We'll talk later, okay?"

"Yeah." Setting her phone down, she rolled her eyes at herself. How idiotic was this? She badgered his life story out of him, then couldn't explain a simple thing like why she couldn't ride with him? Okay, so it wasn't that simple. She hadn't even been able to come up with a suitable excuse!

Stuffing the last bite of pasta into her mouth, she loaded her things in the dishwasher. It was going to be a painfully long forty-some hours before the trunk-or-treat.

The question was, would it be long enough?

How could she want marriage and a family so badly that it hurt—and still be scared to death of getting close to someone? Scared to death of depending on someone else to be there, every time, just for her? Of being totally committed to that same someone? Of…holding hands?

The words of James 1:5-6 came to mind:

If any of you lack wisdom, let him ask of God, that giveth to all men liberally, and upbraideth not; and it shall be given him.

But let him ask in faith, nothing wavering. For he that wavereth is like a wave of the sea driven with the wind and tossed.

Dropping to her knees beside the couch, Merry took her distress to her Heavenly Father.

Her fears of the unknown didn't evaporate. But she was humming "Sweet Hour of Prayer" when she rose, her heart much more at peace.

Shoving everything else out of her mind, she started setting up for her family home evening, a program started by the church decades ago. One night a week devoted to strengthening one's family in the gospel.

Sometimes it hurt to have it solo, true. Sometimes she was invited to join her family members or—rarely—Sam's family. No matter how kind they were, though, she always felt like an intruder. And members of the church were too spread out around here to form singles groups, so most of the time she did what she always did and kept to herself.

Tonight her plans were simple. Opening the scripture app on her phone, she brought up the last general conference and started the audio playing. Then she retrieved a few dozen clean quart jars from a storage closet. Along with several recipes she'd printed from food storage sites.

She carefully attached a copy of the complete recipe to every jar she filled with ingredients and soon the boxes on the island contained jars of various savory meals. Hamburger stew. Scalloped potatoes. Breakfast taquitos. Chicken noodle soup. And, of course, some tasty dessert choices.

The two hour session of general conference finished before she could, so she packed things back up for next week. This was the first year she'd done this, and she still hadn't figured out how she was going to wrap them against her nephews' curiosity. Bubble wrap under the decorative paper, perhaps?

Closing the door on the incomplete Christmas project, she curled up on the couch and pulled up her digital movie collection. Since Gordon MacRae was on her mind, she chose to watch *Desert Song*. Comedy, action, romance, horses… The reviews online might be mixed, but she loved ninety-eight percent of it.

A silky tenor voice filled the room as Gordon's character sang of longed-for love.

Like any sane woman, Kathryn's character joined in singing "One Alone," their first duet. The storyline kept Kathryn in the dark about the dashing hero's mild-mannered alter ego almost until the credits rolled, yet that made the last kiss seem so much sweeter than the others.

Sighing, Merry put the remote away and folded her arms across her chest. Kathryn's character, Margo, was used to being pursued. That was something Merry had no personal experience with. Should she just assume that whatever Tyrel did going forward was his way of 'pursuing' her? The CD had been a complete surprise. Did he like surprises? She didn't. Not as a rule, anyway.

Was it supposed to be perfect, then? A whirlwind of attraction void of mistakes?

The thought made her snort aloud. That might work fine in a world of scripts and retakes. Real people made real mistakes. She needed to be prepared for that. Without allowing herself to create a self-fulfilling crash-and-burn prophecy.

Sighing, she climbed the stairs to her room. Adulting was hard.

Chapter 9

By lunchtime the next day, Merry had finished sanding the table and reattached the legs. Switching to goggles, she used her air compressor to 'dust' the table. After allowing the first layer of dust to settle over a short lunch, she repeated the process to be sure she got as much dust out of the grain as possible before moving on to the varnishing stage.

For the next several hours, she alternated between applying a high gloss varnish to the table and emptying the contents of her dust collector into her wood pellet mill. The behavior of Mother Nature's minions pointed toward a harsh winter. The squirrels were racing to collect nuts, each of them sporting thick coats of fur. She hadn't seen a purple martin for weeks. And the wind rattling the wind spinners in Sam's yard was blowing toward the east, bringing a storm.

She was sending the last batch of pellets up to the verandah via her electric winch system when a refrigerated truck stopped in her driveway. Large, black letters spelled out FRESH in a rustic font, positioned just above a stove as if they were made of the steam rising from the pot. The ice cream trucks of her childhood, they delivered frozen food throughout the Midwest. Except she hadn't placed an order with them in months.

"Hey Merry!" Jason, the driver, hollered to

her as he climbed down. "Special delivery for you!" His straw-colored hair stuck out over his ears as usual, making him look rather like a gangly scarecrow.

Now what? she wondered.

Letting the lift box dock, she activated the hydraulic tipping function and waited until the bag of pellets had slid out onto the rest of the pile. Once the box was on its way back down, she headed over to where Jason was consulting his work tablet.

"You having a party?" he asked as he lifted out three Canadian bacon pizzas.

"Not that I know of." She shivered a little in the cold seeping out from his storage. The outdoor temperature was dropping with the sun and she didn't envy him his job. Thank goodness the company provided insulated uniforms for when things got bitter.

"Well you sure could with all this food," he observed cheerfully.

Merry's eyes widened as he tugged out a box of caramel chocolate ice cream bars, summer dreamsicle pops, one of their drool-worthy Dutch apple pies, and two containers of dark chocolate mint ice cream. In short, while she didn't have a favorite dessert, per se, someone had done an excellent job of selecting her top four.

"Looks like someone's trying to fatten me up for Thanksgiving," she muttered, shooting a suspicious glare in the direction of her mother.

Her sweet tooth gave her enough trouble without outside help!

Jason laughed and double-checked his list. "It ain't your mom," he informed her cheekily. This was a rare experience for him. Merry kept to herself far too much, in his opinion.

"What?" Merry's stomach dropped as another thought occurred to her. This could be the world's cruelest breakup ever. She started blinking rapidly against the tears welling up in her eyes.

Hey, I've been thinking it over and you're too heavy so I changed my mind. Didn't want to leave you empty-handed, so here! Eat yourself into a new dress size.

"I ain't supposed to know what's in these gift messages," Jason chuckled, oblivious to her heartbreak, "but they hand 'em to us straight from the printer. Unfolded and all. Impossible not to at least catch a glimpse, if you take my meanin'." Handing her his tablet for her digital signature, he pulled a single sheet of paper out of the driver's door pocket and waved it at her. Years of working a regular delivery route had taught him to enjoy a bit of gossip, and he had every intention of wheedling a name out of her before he left. "Somebody's sweet on you, Miss Merry."

Merry's self-control exploded, flinging great globs of high-energy feelings all over the place. As messes went, this one rivaled last year's pumpkin patch vandalism, where three high school freshmen decided it would be fun to pack pumpkins with leftover fireworks.

"Jason Taylor," she fumed, scribbling her name with her finger, "I've hated that nickname since grade school and you know it."

He blinked. "I didn't…"

"What?" She snatched the paper from him, wadded it up, and stuffed it in her pocket before she could give in to her raging curiosity. "You didn't think? What else is new?!" Thrusting the tablet into the poor man's hands, she picked up her items and stalked off.

Stepping into the lift box, she awkwardly jabbed the start button and left a slack-jawed Jason staring after her. Stumbled over the bags of pellets waiting for her on the verandah as she exited the box, which only added fuel to her emotional fire.

Embarrassed and mad and happy and scared and excited all at once, she slammed doors while she put the food away, then wished she hadn't. She loved her standalone freezer and wanted it to last forever.

"Sorry," she apologized, running her hand over the sleek silver door. "This isn't your fault." Resting her forehead against the freezer door, she took a few calming breaths. "It's…nobody's fault, I guess. I'll have to tell Jason that the next time I see him." She didn't always handle surprises well. Especially not high-stakes surprises.

Opening the freezer again, she took the time

to sort the food onto the appropriate shelves. Feeling a little better, she went back downstairs to cover the mill and lock up before heading into town for Noella's meeting.

Forgotten, the gift message rode silently along in her pocket until she arrived and tried to put her keys in beside it. She was in the process of smoothing out the paper to read it when a very perky Noella swooped in and caught her by the arm. It required all of her focus to catch even half of what the excited woman was saying in French, so she reluctantly folded the paper and tucked it back into her pocket.

"This time they will listen, I am sure of it!" Noella finished gleefully. She'd tried so many times to get the community theater group to try something different. "Yes?"

"You've got my vote," Merry half-answered. She trusted Noella's experience—the younger woman had been performing at local gatherings called ceilidhs on Prince Edward Island since she was six. And it was a good bet that any difficulties in her plan could be ironed out with a little help from the other theater members. "Hurry, go get a seat."

The local theater group was small enough to qualify as tiny, in Merry's opinion. But they'd gained a powerhouse of energy and enthusiasm when Noella volunteered to help with this year's traditional charity performance. All she needed was a direction to run.

Merry didn't pay much attention to the first ten minutes of the meeting, which covered old business and strayed into what sounded like a very old argument. Her attempt to read the gift message during that time was rewarded with disgruntled looks from those around her—because crackly paper was obviously just the rudest thing!

Just then, the chairwoman opened things up for a discussion of that year's charity play. Her nostrils flared slightly at Noella's instantly waving hand.

"The chair recognizes Ms. Cormier."

Merry frowned. Eight months on the committee and they still weren't using Noella's first name? Even worse were the stilted tones used by the older woman. Merry leaned forward, suddenly worried. Noella made her suggestion in a typically animated manner, though she took great care to enunciate each word clearly. The other people at the table asked a few questions. On the surface, everyone was playing nicely, as they say. Except that they were being too casual. Too easily won over.

"All in favor of Ms. Cormier taking the lead on this project?" Mrs. Arnold called for the vote.

Merry stood up, but she was too late. Half of them hadn't finished saying 'aye' before the other half had gotten up and started walking away.

"Good luck," smirked Mrs. Arnold, tucking her gavel into her oversized purse. "You'll need it."

Noella's smile faltered. She looked at the now-empty table. Turned back to ask Mrs. Arnold a question. And found her sauntering away.

"Hey." Merry put her hand lightly on Noella's shoulder. "Let's take a walk, okay?"

"What just happened?" Noella asked in French.

"I think you got set up." Slipping an arm around Noella's shoulder, Merry led her away from prying eyes. "How many times did you say you've been outvoted on what play to do?"

"Every time." Noella shrugged, obviously undeterred. "Last time, I thought they were considering it, but it was late and the chairwoman, she closed the meeting before we could vote."

"Ah. And when they came back, they voted for the play she wanted." Merry gave Noella's shoulders a light squeeze. "I'm sorry, kiddo. I think you're on your own here."

"But…but how?" Noella sputtered. "They agreed to the play. They *all* agreed. You heard it!"

"I heard them agree that *you* were in charge of putting on the play," Merry corrected, tugging her jacket more tightly around her. She might have to use her pellet stove tonight. "And, eh," she couldn't translate 'adjourned' quickly enough so she substituted, "closed the meeting. Nobody agreed to do *the work.*"

"You only see your side of things! I look

through a window, but you just see a mirror…"
A teenager wearing hot pink earbuds wandered past them, nearly derailing Merry's line of thought as she sang along with "Broken Windows," one of Merry's original compositions.

Noella muttered to herself all the way to the bakery that Merry was steering them toward, then threw up her hands. "Very well. If that is how they want to do things…"

Merry opened her mouth to agree that yielding was a tough choice but the right one and…

"Then I will show them how it is done!"

After a brief, pleasant interaction with a mutual acquaintance of theirs, Noella concentrated fiercely as she drafted her battle plan over fresh cookies and hot chocolate.

Merry's head was spinning by the time they paid their check. The one point she managed to isolate was that she'd been volunteered to be in charge of set design and construction. And props. Some of them. She thought.

Where Noella planned to find more help was anybody's guess. The cast, the stage crew…

She was still puzzling over the muddle when she popped a pizza into the oven at home and pulled the message out of her pocket one more time. Smoothed it. Turned to stare out the window at the driving rain.

Somebody's sweet on you. Jason's words echoed in her mind.

She bit her lip. It was perfectly natural for her to have the same attack of nerves that a teenage girl would get. Wasn't it? It ought to be. This was her first note. *Their* first note.

Not her first crush, though. No, she'd crushed on dozens of fictional characters over the years. All handsome, strong, and impeccably good.

Different temperaments, sizes, occupations, yet with one critical trait in common—they'd all been perfectly safe, because her heart was never in any real danger. Unlike now.

Exhaling, she picked it up and opened it.

"Can I interest you in a trade? My pizza recipe for your pasta recipe? Let's discuss it over supper."

A burst of laughter escaped her. This was Jason's idea of…what, exactly? A love note? He'd certainly made her think that's what it was. She'd expected… Shoot, what had she expected? What would she have written in a communication like this, where the secretary or delivery man could see it?

Lifting the perfectly browned pizza out of the oven, she circled back to the question of what was normal. Generally speaking, the media presented relationships according to a simple formula. Well, as long as they weren't created for a TV show or the like. Those relationships were drawn out and tortured for the fan's entertainment. She snickered and wrapped the rest of the pizza for later. Good thing she wasn't on a TV show.

Which meant that real-life normal was whatever worked best for her and Tyrel? Like gifting CDs and frozen food before their first official date. She bit into a chocolate caramel ice cream bar and her eyes drifted closed. Really tasty frozen food!

Her eyes popped back open. Uh-oh. Gifts were typically exchanged. Throwing her free hand up in the air, she started pacing. Manners were perfectly straightforward in theory. Holding doors for people whose hands were full. Taking a cell phone call outside of the movie theater. If someone offered their hand, you shook it.

Simple. Until money or pride or misconceptions got mixed up in it. And this situation involved all three. Did Tyrel think giving presents was the man's job? He had mentioned hiding behind extravagance the other night. Hmm. No, that didn't fit. Okay, the frozen food set him back around sixty bucks. Roughly the price of a dinner for two at a mid-range restaurant.

She clapped her hand over her mouth. She shouldn't have eaten the pizza solo! Oh, she was an idiot!

How to fix it? There had to be a way! Wait! She could reciprocate! Not with frozen food specifically, but she could get him a gift. Give it to him at the trunk-or-treat.

Like…what, though? He'd already gone and gotten himself an album of Gordon MacRae music. She knew absolutely nothing of his tastes or interests beyond that. He'd gotten excited about the white ash table downstairs, but that didn't help. Even if she had the materials and time to build one for him, where would he put it in his small duplex?

She continued pacing as ideas—each crazier than the last—swirled in her head. Unlike real-life boyfriends, fictional boyfriends were extremely low maintenance. And yes, she was starting to think of Ty that way.

Sighing, she walked back over to the island to answer her phone, which had begun playing a children's hymn, "Tell Me the Stories of Jesus."

"Hi, Mom."

"Merry, is everything alright? I've been watching you pace for the last twenty minutes!"

"I'm… It's fine, Mom. Everything's fine." Merry squeezed her eyes shut. Edged away from the glass doors.

"Are you sure?" Elaine was never so happy as when surrounded by family, so by Tuesday night she could be a little bored. "You didn't have a fight with Tyrel, did you? I saw you take off as soon as the delivery truck left and…"

"What?" Merry's senses went on high alert. *No way…* "What would the delivery truck have to do with Tyrel?" she probed.

"Why, everything." Elaine paused, then continued, sounding a little less sure of herself. "At least, I assumed it did. He specifically asked me what your favorites were while he was helping me set the table on Sunday."

Merry turned her back to the double doors and reached up to massage her temples. Her brain was screaming *Traitor!* at her mother even as her heart shivered like a giddy puppy at the thought of Tyrel going to the effort of asking about what she liked. Sure, it was a risky play.

For years, her mother had been convinced that she loved sweet potatoes despite the number of times she'd waved them off at family gatherings. No big deal, she didn't expect her mother to keep up with every detail of her life. But Tyrel had lucked out this time, for sure.

And hang on—*two* could play at this game. Crossing her fingers for luck, Merry managed a light laugh.

"I was wondering how he knew what to get me."

"Oh, so…it was from him!" Elaine tittered happily. "I knew it was, I just knew it! We talked some on Sunday and I recommended Fresh. I may have mentioned a few of your special favorites."

Aha! Okay, now for the tricky part. Getting the information she needed without tipping her own hand. Assuming she could get another word in edgewise.

"He's such a fine young man. Unusual name,

I'll admit. I keep wanting to call him Tyler." Elaine kept talking without even pausing for breath. "I understand he had some trouble in school on account of his name, but he seems quite resigned to it now. Children can be so mean."

Thinking back to her own school days, Merry could only nod in silent agreement.

"Well." She hastily dropped the word into the brief pause. "Thanks for calling to check on me."

"Oh." Elaine's voice warmed. "Of course dear. You're sure you're alright?" Effortlessly, she swung back to the original purpose of her call.

"I am. In fact, I'm better than alright now. Love you."

"And we love you, too." Out of habit, Elaine included her husband in the declaration of affection.

"Sleep well, okay?" Merry agreed to have a glass of milk before bed, then ended the call. While she drank the milk, she struggled to compose a 'thank you' text to Tyrel.

She was in the middle of updating her bookkeeping when her phone buzzed. As she texted back and forth with Tyrel, she realized again how little she knew about him.

Her ignorance aside, she successfully agreed to have him over to watch a movie—at which point she would apologize for opening…um, *eating* his gift without him.

Chapter 10

She got up early the next morning to take care of the table first thing. As long as she'd trapped herself into running errands that day, there was an auction house nearby that had some tempting items. Someday, she'd like to have a dedicated service for hunting down rare pieces and refurbishing them on commission. Someday.

After a warm lunch, she started the hour drive to Holloway House where, behind unassuming doors, lay a treasure trove of antique items. She brought her simple costume along just in case.

Upon arrival, she headed straight for the furniture gallery, where she immediately fell in love with a solid walnut cabinet secretary. It stood a mere six inches shorter than her—and while they'd dusted it off, that was all. The doors sagged. A style was badly cracked. The leather writing surface needed to be replaced. The list went on, but Merry was confident she could restore it. And resell it to a former client who recently mentioned a desire to own such a 'magnificent writing desk.'

She must've been the only carpenter there, because the bidding was tepid at best. Merry made the high bid three thousand and held her breath until the gavel came down. She couldn't have done it without her music royalties, but found herself gleefully signing paperwork while they loaded the desk for her.

More or less on autopilot, Merry checked the transport straps and climbed into her truck. If she put another coat on the table tonight, that would free her up to start on this project. She was still making plans when she pulled into her drive and backed her truck up to her shop.

Only as she shut off the engine did she fully become aware of the dark car parked in the deepening shadows next door at Sam's. The statistics were against it, but the twist in her gut made her think it must be Tyrel's car. Which might explain why she wasn't surprised to see him leaving Sam's house a few minutes later as she closed the lift gate on her truck. And the way the spaghetti monster started climbing into her throat.

"Hey." Tyrel grinned at her. "You're back early."

"You were checking on me?"

"What? No, I…"

She turned her back on him and started wheeling the desk inside. Gasped when it rocked under her hands. *And Tyrel's!*

"Watch it!" she snapped, her good mood mutating into fear-fueled irritation.

Tyrel sprang back, startled. "Sorry, I…"

She held up a hand to stop him. Left it up as she fought for control. She no sooner isolated an emotion than it slipped away from her, back into the tangle. *Ugh. It was so hard!*

Perplexed, Tyrel stared at her uplifted hand. It measured roughly seven inches from the base of her palm to the tip of her second finger, but it—and her glare—held him off as effectively as a ten-foot-tall castle wall with a monster-infested moat. Even a real knight in shining armor would've thought twice before tackling that combination. Except…they couldn't just stand there, locked in a staring contest all night.

"How can I help?"

Merry gritted her teeth. "Don't."

"Okay." Tyrel slipped his hands into his pockets. "I'll wait right here." Her head tilted to the side and her eyes narrowed. "Scout's honor," he promised.

Merry blinked up at him. "Okay." Turning her attention back to her prize, she maneuvered it safely inside. Rested her head against it, eyes closed. Sometimes, her emotions were like an exothermic reaction. Tonight, his well-intentioned attempt to help had been the catalyst and she'd nearly blown up at him.

And over what? A three thousand dollar investment? 'It's only money,' crossed her mind, but it was so much more than that. She'd gone on quite a flight of fancy during her drive back, using the successful restoration and sale of this poor little desk as the foundation of a future where she did specialty orders only.

Straightening, she patted the item gently. As wonderful as that would be, it wasn't worth ruining her first and only chance at love. Why couldn't people be more like furniture? Predictable. Forgiving. Ah. Forgiving.

Her head hung a bit as she returned to Tyrel. "I'm sorry for snapping at you. That piece is…very important to me and for a second, I thought it was going to tip over. I overreacted."

Tyrel's first instinct was to wave it away or say, 'no big deal.' However, it was obviously a *very* big deal to her. "You're used to doing things yourself," he said slowly, feeling his way forward word by word. "I shouldn't have crashed in on you like that."

"I didn't expect you," her throat tightened, "to understand."

Tyrel felt the corners of his mouth turning up and went with it. "We've got a lot to learn about each other, Merry McKinney. That's what dating is for."

"Sounds painful." She found herself smiling back at him, though her nerves were still a little raw. She hated it when she didn't handle things well. It reminded her of how different she was. A social freak.

"Yeah." Surprised, he laughed. "It really can be." Taking in her wide eyes and startled expression, he hastily clarified, "It's not a requirement or anything. Dating should be fun."

"Hey." She caught one of the hands he'd been talking with. "It's okay. I don't know a lot of people who don't think socializing isn't the best thing since…" She hunted in her mind for something more modern than 'sliced bread.'

"Since Canadian bacon pizza?" Tyrel asked softly, a hint of tease in his voice.

"Yeah. About that." She wrinkled her nose. So much for her plan to wait. "I started eating one of the pizzas before I read your note. Sorry." He laughed and caught her up in a hug that squeezed the air right out of her lungs.

"Was it good?" he asked, setting her back down. She nodded, dazed. "Then everything's perfect." Noticing the time on her giant clock, he whistled softly. "We'd better get a move on, though, or we're going to miss the chili cook-off!"

"Oh, they always start that late," she promised. "We'll be in plenty of time. Although." She hesitated. She might regret this, but… "It does seem silly to take two vehicles."

Tyrel shifted position so that he was standing at a softer angle than the 'head-to-head' stance. She seemed open right now and he didn't want to do anything to change that. Aside from asking, "I got the sense that I'd somehow upset you the other night."

Merry bit her lip so hard that she winced. "I…um…" Embarrassed, she dropped her gaze and tucked a loose strand of hair behind her ear. Struggled vainly to find words. Words to tell him she was afraid of the unknown, like how she'd react to holding hands. Words to tell him to let it go. *Any* words.

"I could download another album," he blurted. He'd had every intention of letting her respond. Until the blasted silence got to him and he'd realized how hard it was for her.

"What? Um, why?" Confused, Merry jammed her hands into her pockets. She hated feeling vulnerable.

"Because it's too early." He ran a hand through his hair. "For some people, I mean. The great yearly debate, y'know?"

She didn't. Crumb. She didn't have a clue what he was talking about. Noise ordinances, maybe? The kind that said no loud music between this PM and that AM? No. That didn't make sense in context.

"For Christmas music," he clarified when she didn't respond. "It's barely Halloween."

"*Christmas* music?" He hadn't found and purchased *Gordon MacRae Sings Knee-Weakening Love Songs*? He wanted to listen to Christmas music?! "No, it's never too early for Christmas music!"

"It's not?" It was Tyrel's turn to be confused. "Then what was bothering you?"

"I'll tell you later." *If I have to.* Merry pointed at her truck. "Right now I better change." For the first time, she stopped to consider what he was wearing—long-sleeve olive green shirt, khaki pants, and tan hiking boots. "Is that your costume?"

"It's most of it. The jacket's in my car." Pulling out his keys, he suggested, "I'll bring my car over while you change, okay?"

"Deal." Hustling to her truck, Merry lifted out her costume and ducked into her windowless office to change. Only as she slid her arms into her jacket did she begin to question how Tyrel would react to her outfit. It was perfectly modest—right down to her military surplus black combat boots—just peculiar. As her sister reminded her each year.

The headlights from Tyrel's car gave her plenty of light to work with as she closed things up. And plenty of light for Tyrel to see her by. Taking a deep breath, she started for the passenger side. The door opened and as she slid in, she found Tyrel grinning at her.

"Gretum harmoc," he greeted her in the Maz alien dialect.

Her jaw dropped. His 'jacket' transformed his outfit into a full-on Maz desert uniform from the show *Pool of Stars*!

"Mer ka q'ing!" she returned.

"I'm…afraid your Maz is better than mine." His brows drew in a bit, but his lips were quirking upward. This was too perfect.

"It's from 'Seeker,' in the fourth season."

"Oh, right!" Tyrel slapped his steering wheel. "Where they try to harness the energy of an entire star."

"Yes!" She couldn't believe it! A legitimate *Pool of Stars* fan!

On firm ground with their mutual appreciation

for *Pool of Stars*, they chatted all the way to the chapel, Gordon MacRae singing sweetly in the background.

As Tyrel held the chapel door for her, he gave her a discreetly appreciative once-over. She'd gone all out on her simple costume. The garish three-color insignia. A nameplate. A shoulder patch that boasted the *Pool of Stars* motto in Maz: Mer tap sher von! Which loosely translated as, United in right we win.

He sensed her shutting down as they entered the building and joined the crowd. Her smile grew tighter. Her responses became monosyllabic. The little he knew of her began adding up and he led her over to a more or less quiet corner.

"Looks like you were right," he observed, smiling down at her. "They're still setting up the chili." He already missed the woman he'd been comfortably conversing with in the car.

"Large groups of people are always chaotic." Usually, she wound up sitting in a corner by herself. Sometimes, she went out to a foyer where it was even quieter. People were just so…unpredictable.

Tyrel nodded, as much in agreement with himself as with her. He'd called it. And it was something to consider. His feelings about dating her were firmly supported by the promptings he received. Yet he liked people. Liked some chaos in his life. How would that work if he started dating Merry McKinney?

He continued pondering the question as the evening progressed. As she confirmed a movie date with the same honey-blond woman he'd seen her talking to on Sunday; blushed and responded in French to a question that seemed to be about him. Took a long step away from where two teenage girls were discussing music. Flinched away from a few of the people who stopped to talk with him.

Finally, someone announced that it was time for a blessing on the chili. It took a little maneuvering, but he managed to get them and their bowls of chili safely to a table in the back of the cultural hall, as far away from the costume contest as possible. Not that the kids weren't cute or that Merry hadn't pointed out a couple of clever costumes. He simply sensed that she needed some semblance of quiet to regroup in.

"Do you think you'll be able to find a job in mechanical engineering around here?" she asked. Dating. What a weird concept. As was not sitting alone. Or wishing she was sitting alone. Sometimes people came to sit with her because, from their perspective, she looked sad or pathetic or whatever it was that prompted people to think they were the solution to her obvious—to them—problem.

Tyrel stirred his chili. It shouldn't have surprised him to hear her bring up his rejoining the workforce. A five-minute phone call was hardly the ideal circumstance for explaining that he simply didn't *need* to work since licensing his invention to the military. Neither was a trunk-or-treat, in his opinion.

"I meant when you were ready," she hastily restated, coloring slightly.

"I have something going right now," he admitted. "Sort of a follow-up from my last job." He'd had an idea of how to modify his patented air filtration system for other applications.

"A callback?" She straightened in her chair, relieved that he wasn't upset. "That's great."

"It is," he agreed, appreciating her enthusiasm on his behalf. "Now, tell me about this play your friend roped you into." He winked.

She suppressed a laugh and obliged him.

"Wait…" Tyrel wiped his mouth with his napkin and settled both forearms on the table. "What did you say the play was called?"

"*No Time Like the Present.* It was written by some obscure British playwright."

"Okay." He sipped his water. "I'm guessing that the title is some sort of sly pun? The British love their dry humor."

"That's a fact," she agreed. "And yes, it's a play on words. Half of the family gets stuck on the presents instead of remembering the point of Christmas. The dad takes on a ton of overtime so he can get this expensive gift for his wife. The kids make a huge production out of adding to their wish lists. Meanwhile, the mom spends most of the play trying to get them all into the real Christmas spirit—and moving the gifts so the kids can't find them."

He swallowed his last bite of chili. "How does it end?"

The ending itself was pretty obvious, so she focused on the summing up their journey. "The kids start missing their dad, who gets home one night to find that they decorated the Christmas tree without him. He starts helping his kids make presents for their friends. That shifts their perspective as they start getting excited to give instead of get." She smiled. Sometimes clichés were a good thing. "And the mom finally gets her actual Christmas wish, which is to have the whole family together for Christmas Eve. They bake cookies, visit the neighbors, and end with reading the Christmas story from Luke 2."

"Sounds like the ideal Christmas."

"Yes," she agreed. "We talked a little about having him read from 3rd Nephi, too, but we're not sure how it would go over."

"Wow." Tyrel had to think about that one. He'd met some people who argued with him that he wasn't even a Christian once they found out what church he belonged to. Of course, the nickname 'Mormons' could be blamed for some of that. 'The Church of Jesus Christ of Latter-day Saints' might be a mouthful, but it cleared up a lot. Point was, how would someone with a misconception like that react to the idea that the Book of Mormon contained an account of what happened on the American continent the day the Savior was born?

"I think she was going to talk to the Ward Mission Leader about it." Merry's face softened at the thought of her fearless friend. "Odds are pretty good that she'll find a way to work it in."

"That's a great idea," he approved. "And it sounds like a great play. I still can't believe that she put you in charge of designing and creating every single set, though."

Merry laughed at his incredulous tone. "Let's not be dramatic. It's community theater, not Broadway."

"Fair point," he nodded. "But on Broadway, they have an entire team of people working on it. Maybe two teams." He air-shoved the topic away and they both laughed. "I guess what I'm trying to say is, I want to help."

Merry stilled. "Thank you."

Tyrel's breath lodged in his throat. The warmth in her hazel-green eyes was so powerful, it felt like someone had just switched the sun on. It was like nothing he'd ever experienced.

"Merry, there you are." Heidi's abrupt appearance jump-started Tyrel's lungs and he sucked in a deep breath. "Are you okay?" Heidi asked, frowning suspiciously.

"Yeah." He cleared his throat and stood, reaching for Merry's empty bowl. "Can I get you a refill," she was shaking her head, so he switched to, "or dessert? I saw some chocolate chip cookies over there." He watched a funny expression come over her face. If anything, Heidi's eyes narrowed further.

"I…have dessert at home," Merry reminded him, her eyes locked on his. Up till now, she'd made him do all the heavy lifting. Take all the initiative. All the risk. He hadn't scared off, so…she decided it was time to take a chance of her own.

"Right." Tyrel looked down at his hands, having completely forgotten why he was standing there. "Right," he repeated. Flashing her a smile, he turned to take care of their trash and nearly tripped over a trio of short cartoon characters. Ordering himself not to look back to see if Merry noticed his clumsiness, Tyrel pursued his course toward the trash can.

"What was that all about?" Heidi asked, lowering herself into Tyrel's chair.

Merry put her hands in her lap to hide how tightly they were clasped. "I like him."

Heidi had to listen hard to hear her over the dull roar of conversations and happy shrieks of sugared-up kids around them. Stunned, she sat back and stared at Merry. She loved her sister. Her younger sister, who wasn't a kid any longer.

"Are you…" she hesitated. Leaning forward, she touched Merry's knee lightly. "Are you sure he's good enough for you?"

"He…what?" Merry couldn't believe her ears.

What kind of a question was that, anyway?

Was she just trying to be supportive? Or did Heidi know something about him? Frankly, what did Heidi know about *her* anymore? They hadn't discussed anything this important in years. Partly because it was too personal—and partly because Heidi was always busy.

Merry never blamed her. How could she blame someone for bearing and raising other people? For being a fabulous wife and mother? Ludicrous.

However, she had vivid memories of reaching for her phone to call Heidi, then changing her mind because it was Thursday afternoon and the kids had a dentist appointment. Or Friday and they had a big camping trip planned. Heidi's family had simply filled every crack and cranny of her life the way water fills a bottle.

It broke her heart to give up one of her best friends, but it turned out to be good practice. Because every time she made a friend, they got married and left her behind. Again. And again. And…

"Hey." Tyrel had returned unnoticed and had the distinct impression that Merry was close to tears. What had Heidi said while he was gone? "If you're sure you're willing to share your chocolate, I think I could use some." He did his best to act like he hadn't noticed the change.

"Yeah." Merry squeezed Heidi's hand under the table. "I mean, it's technically *your* chocolate, after all."

Tyrel chose not to argue the point. Turned up the volume on the music for the drive back so the silence wasn't awkward.

Merry leaned against the car door, her mind leaping around like a barefoot adult trying to navigate a floor littered with tiny toys. She'd never even considered praying about whether Tyrel was 'good enough.' That sounded so…so arrogant. Vain. Without realizing it, she huffed out a breath. Then why had Heidi, her happily married, level-headed, perfectly normal sister, asked that very question?

Tyrel suppressed his curiosity until they were safely inside her kitchen. "Would you like to talk about it?"

She halted halfway to the freezer. Wrapped her arms around herself. "Are you sure you want to?"

Tyrel's anxiety quotient jumped about a thousand percent, yet he had a funny hunch about this. Rubbing damp palms on his pant legs, he walked to the island and pulled out a set of stools.

"Let's talk."

Merry took the nearer stool. Their knees brushed and she shifted away. This couldn't be happening. Why hadn't she laughed it off? Ignored it? Anything but this.

The way she bit her lip and looked everywhere except at him got under Tyrel's skin pretty quickly. Leaning forward, he took her hands in his.

"I'm pretty sure I'm doing things wrong." He smiled sheepishly. "I should've begged off dessert, then shown up in a couple of days with an expensive bouquet. We would've discussed stuff and things. And, maybe, after a while, we'd tackle a serious subject." He grimaced. It was an all-too-familiar story from his past.

"Sounds like we'd be playing hide and seek," she interjected.

Tyrel straightened on the stool. "Exactly."

"And we don't want to do that," she reminded him of his earlier words.

"*We*," he pointed to himself, "also don't want to move too fast."

She chuckled. "Thank you. But I suppose we might as well get it over with." She took a deep breath and exhaled slowly. "Heidi's worried about me. About us." That was the gist of it, anyhow.

Tyrel didn't like the sound of that. "Did she say why?"

Merry wanted to fidget, but he still had ahold of her hands. "Because we barely know each other." Again, she stuck with the highlights. Whatever her confusion about what Heidi meant, she trusted that her sister meant well.

He nodded and took a moment to examine the notion. "I know how to fix that. Let's spend more time together." His thoughtful response was rewarded by another of her dazzling heart-in-her-eyes-smiles.

"I'd like that," she agreed shyly.

"Wonderful." He looked down at the hands that were holding much too still in his own. Gently released them. "Let's start by doing something we both enjoy."

"Such as?" Merry settled one arm on the table. She'd been so worried about holding hands with him. Afraid was closer. Hugging, holding hands...kissing. She shifted a bit further back on the stool. Resisted the urge to fold her arms across her chest. Definitely wasn't ready for kissing.

"Such as me coming back tomorrow around suppertime. Such as splitting a pizza while we watch some *Pool of Stars*." He watched her carefully while she thought, trying to sort out the signals she was sending.

"Not a western?" she smiled. They'd agreed on a western for their movie night.

"We'll get around to that," he promised.

Merry nodded. "Let's plan on it."

"Great." Tyrel nodded back. Inadvertently looked at her mouth. "Great." Rubbing his hands on his knees, he slid off the stool to one side so that he wasn't towering over her. "Shall we celebrate?"

"You bet." Grinning, she rose also. "What's your pleasure?" His gaze dropped to her mouth for the second time in sixty seconds and she cleared her throat nervously. "We have caramel chocolate ice cream bars, summer dreamsicle pops, dark chocolate mint ice cream…"

"How about one of each?" He winked to let her know he was teasing and she rolled her eyes. A good sign, he thought. When she was tense or upset, she threw up a wall. Closed herself off to the world around her. The night in the hayfield had been a fluke. Too tired or too upset or just plain overwrought, she'd temporarily lost control.

Chapter 11

Every time Merry looked at the clock the next day, another hour or two had disappeared. It was like being in a time warp. She half-expected to look out the window and find that it was spring already. The nervous energy was good for one thing, though. She got the rest of the red teak monkeys carved. And blocked out the remaining pieces.

Around four in the afternoon, she set aside the sharp objects and started pacing. But the workroom was too small. Agitated, she went outside and began walking around her house. Fast-walking, at first. She began praying as she walked, and her pace slowed little by little. As usual, prayer lifted her view from the problem directly in front of her and invited her to look at the whole picture. Tyrel was a genuinely nice person who understood that she had zero experience with dating. She'd live through tonight and everything would be fine.

Hearing gravel crunching under tires, she shot a panicked look at her phone. It was only five! What was he doing here so early?! Pivoting, she sprinted around the building and let herself in through the back door. Started slapping dust off her jeans only to freeze in horror as she remembered the white ash table. Thankfully, it had a good start on its curing and likely wouldn't pick up the little bit of dust she'd carelessly sent flying. Nevertheless, she was trying vainly to wave it away from the table when her doorbell rang.

Okay. The time was now. Grungy and un-showered because she'd saved that for last, she bravely marched herself toward the workshop door.

Where she found Heidi!

Heidi eyed her sister curiously. "It's a little late in the year for flies," she teased. Merry's mouth clicked shut and Heidi nodded. "That's better."

Merry ignored the second remark and looked over Heidi's shoulder. "What's wrong?"

Heidi blinked. "Why should something be wrong?"

Merry looked once more at the empty Toyota parked beside her truck. "Is Brian over at Mom and Dad's?"

"Brian?" Heidi shook her head. "He's over at a friend's working on a project for school. Why do you ask?"

Suddenly recognizing that they were both standing in her doorway, Merry moved back to let Heidi in. "I don't know." She shrugged. "I just expected him to be with you, I guess."

Heidi entered slowly, thrown off from her original mission by Merry's peculiar behavior. Not that Merry was ever anything but peculiar. This just wasn't what she'd prepared for.

"So." Merry tried to figure out what she was

supposed to do under the circumstances. She had a very important guest arriving in approximately fifty-eight minutes and needed to get ready. On the other hand, she didn't want to be rude to her sister. Who hadn't come to see her in…months. Lots and lots of months. As in, so many that she'd lost track. They saw each other all the time. It would've taken a serious amount of determination not to in such a small town with an even smaller church group. This, though. This was different somehow.

"Would you like to come upstairs?" Merry invited eventually.

"Thank you." Heidi started purposefully up the stairs. The formality of the invitation surprised her. Threw her further off-balance.

"Make yourself comfortable." Merry gestured at the couch. "I'm sorry, I've only got a few minutes before I'll have to go shower and change."

"Are you expecting someone?"

Merry lifted an eyebrow at her sister. She wasn't used to explaining herself to anyone and that sounded remarkably like the opening shot of a motherly inquisition. Which…Heidi *was* a mom. Okay. She could make allowances for a couple of decades of habit.

"A friend's coming over for supper."

"On a Thursday?" Heidi saw the eyebrow going up again. Was she coming on too strong? At least she hadn't said 'on a school night?' "I mean," she tried again, "don't they have to work tomorrow?" Merry's eyebrows dipped down in unison this time, worrying her.

"Why are you here?" Merry wasn't angry. She was curious. Heidi obviously hadn't come to check on her sleeping habits.

Heidi blinked, startled. Well. If that was how Merry wanted to do things, it wasn't like they had to stand on formalities. They weren't strangers or anything.

"I wanted to talk with you about Tyrel." Uh-oh. "Don't roll your eyes at me," she ordered without thinking. "Um." She cringed. "Sorry. Reflex," she apologized lamely.

Merry unbent a little and offered a smile. "Occupational hazard for moms, I expect."

"Yeah." Heidi blew out a breath. "Hannah used to roll her eyes at me and I got sort of conditioned, I guess."

"I'm not Hannah," Merry reminded her gently. "I didn't roll my eyes because I think I know more than you do."

"Then…why?" This wasn't going how she planned.

Merry hesitated. "Because it's exasperating to be treated like a child." She said it as kindly as she could. "I know you mean well."

Flabbergasted, Heidi sat quite still for several seconds. "You never told me that before."

Merry shrugged, doubtful that Heidi understood. That anybody could understand in thirty seconds or less the impact of years of being babysat and tended and told how she *should* be doing things by people who had no business interfering in her life. It was almost a relief to be able to tell someone the truth.

"As I said, I get that you know more than I do." She hadn't a modicum of the life experiences of her sister. "And if you're offering to be someone I can call with questions, I appreciate it."

"But?" Heidi prompted when she paused.

"But don't patronize me. Or lecture me. Unless you see me walking off a cliff or something, I'm probably doing okay." Merry listened to herself in amazement. And concern. It wasn't good to get this passionate about things. That was usually when she said things she regretted.

Heidi fidgeted with her purse. Opened her mouth. Closed it and thought some more. "You're right." She sighed. "It won't be easy. You're my little sister, you know."

"I know." Merry stood up and came over, prompting Heidi to rise as well. "I love you, too." She hugged her sister tightly and was delighted to be hugged back.

"And now I better be going." Heidi winked. "Unless you need help doing your makeup?"

Merry resisted the urge to roll her eyes again. "You know I don't wear makeup," she laughed as she walked Heidi to the door. "Strangely enough, he doesn't seem to mind."

"That's a good sign." Heidi smirked. "Darren's gotten to the point that he's surprised when I *do* wear it anymore." She stopped at the head of the stairs to give Merry another hug. "I can see myself out. You go get ready." As she made her way down to the car, she tried to remember the last time she'd put on makeup to stay home. She kept herself neat and tidy always, but getting dressed up specifically for Darren? *Hmm.*

Merry, meanwhile, had dashed up the stairs and into her shower. Heidi had clearly guessed who she was expecting, which was alright. She'd also taken Merry's reproof with good grace, which was fantastic. Merry really did have the most amazing family.

Thirty minutes later, in comfy jeans and a plum-colored blouse, she was down in the kitchen setting up. She hesitated between real dishes and paper, then chose paper for convenience. Put a short stack of napkins on the table by the couch. Smiled when the doorbell rang.

Pressing the button on her intercom, she buzzed him in through the side door. Leaned against the wall while she stepped into a pair of clean, white socks.

Tyrel shook his head as he began ascending the stairs. She was constantly surprising him. The retracting ladder. The lift box, which as yet he'd only heard about. And now being buzzed in as if he was visiting an apartment house? He saw the advantages of it, though. No doubt it saved her countless trips down the stairs.

He was halfway up the stairs when her second story door opened. His heart started doing somersaults that had nothing to do with his recent workout as he looked up and saw his future. He didn't even have a home to ask her to move into, so this was how it would be. As he reached the top, he paused. In the moment he lingered there, his subconscious perception of home changed subtly to revolve around the person he would share it with.

"C'mon in," she invited, stepping aside. The way he looked at her as he did so made her feel like he'd wrapped her in the warmest, snuggliest blanket ever thought of. He took the door from her and closed it, leaving her between him and the wall. It wouldn't have surprised her if he'd kissed her, right then. Somehow, she wasn't even afraid of it.

Instead, he paused to dutifully wipe his shoes. Disappointment pricked her, but it was only skin deep and couldn't touch the contentment that flowed through her as he gently took her hand.

"Hi."

"Hey." Merry's lips twitched at their distinctly un-sparkling dialogue.

"You look beautiful." Tyrel saw the light in her eyes start to dim, so he held her face in his hands until she looked up at him. "I mean it."

Merry's first instinct was to pull away. Make

a snarky comment that would put him firmly back outside her comfort zone. Being honest was a thousand times harder.

"I…am not used to hearing that."

"Let's plan on changing that, too," he suggested huskily. Her skin was warm and soft under his fingertips. She was so close… Kissing her seemed like the natural next step, but there was a wariness in her eyes that warned him off. Funny. A minute ago, he could've sworn that she *wanted* him to kiss her.

She nodded slowly. Took a half step back, freeing her face, and gestured toward the couch. "I thought we could each pick an episode for tonight."

"Not planning to start at the top?" he asked, surprised. Pretending that he hadn't just taken a doozy of a step toward falling in love with her, he began whistling the *Pool of Stars* theme song.

She laughed. "What, you haven't seen it before?"

"Well, I have…" He started to agree, stopped. Grinned. "So just the highlights? That's a great idea," he decided aloud. Resuming his whistling, he headed over to the couch, saw the box of DVDs beside it. The oven opened and shut while he perused the first season's case.

"I'm drawing a blank on some of these episode titles," he admitted, pulling out his phone to do some research. Skimming through the episodes online, he called, "Which one did you pick?"

"'Oddity.' It's one of my all-time favorites."

Skipping ahead to that synopsis, he nodded his agreement. "Yeah, that's a good one. Um…" He scrolled through the episodes. "I guess I'll go with 'Inscrutable' for tonight."

"Now for the tough decision." Merry indicated the cans of soda she'd lined up on the island. "What flavor?"

"Wow!" Pocketing his phone, he came over to study his choices. "We've got grape, orange, root beer, strawberry, cream soda, black cherry cream soda, plain cherry…" He stopped and quirked an eyebrow at her. "Too bad you don't like soda."

Wrinkling her nose at him, she shrugged. "They all make good floats."

He teased her about mixing the different soda flavors with different ice cream flavors until the oven timer went off. Deciding she truly liked all the flavors, he picked a cream soda for himself. When he offered her his hand for prayer, her warm hand slid immediately into his, sending elation shooting through him.

After prayer, Merry sectioned the still-bubbling pizza with her pizza wheel and let him pick first while she popped open her soda. Catching him watching her, she realized she was pouring from a six-inch height into a ten-ounce glass.

"It helps get rid of the fizz," she explained.

"You don't like the carbonation?" Snagging a napkin, he wiped pizza grease off his fingers.

She shook her head. "It stings my throat."

Frowning, he picked up his own can of soda. "Wouldn't it be easier to drink punch or something?"

"I loved punch when I was a kid." She helped herself to the pizza. "Nowadays, all I taste is food coloring."

"Gross," he laughed. Following her over to the couch, he watched her set up for 'Oddity,' which came first in the season. Her entertainment system seemed pretty straightforward compared to some he'd encountered in the past—including a nightmarish assembly of adapters and cables and remotes in a particular colonel's office—but he was glad he'd waited to let her do it.

Merry turned around and found herself face-to-face with a dilemma. Sit right next to him? Or at arm's length? Where would she be more comfortable? Or was it more important to worry about which signal she'd be sending?

Tyrel looked up in time to see her bite her lip. Not knowing what the problem was, he reached for a slice of pizza. "Are you kidding me?" He grinned around the bite he'd just taken, gulped it down without chewing it properly. The lump lodged halfway down his throat, but he kept smiling. "Is this the world's best pizza or what?!"

Merry couldn't help the laugh tickling at her insides and she let it out as she plunked herself down at arm's length. After all, nobody wanted to bump elbows while they were eating the world's best pizza.

The theme song began playing, and they settled back to enjoy the ride. Tyrel watched Merry surreptitiously as the storyline unfolded. The pizza was long gone by the time Faye's heart broke on-screen. A sympathetic tear trickled down Merry's cheek and he reached out to put his hand on hers.

Merry flashed him a watery smile. She'd blubbered all over his shirt before she even knew him. This…this hardly even counted as crying. And, the newness of the experience aside, she thought it was a very sweet gesture.

"I vote for a dessert break before we move on to 'Inscrutable'," Tyrel suggested, reaching out to stack his plate on top of hers.

Merry didn't have to think twice about that. "What's your pleasure?"

His gaze dipped in the direction of her mouth, but he yanked it back up to her eyes. "Surprise me."

Merry gave her heart a moment to finish its impromptu gymnastic performance before starting for the freezer. Halfway into dishing up two bowls of the dark chocolate mint, she realized she hadn't queued up the next episode. And that Tyrel was already on the job. She didn't like that he'd helped himself to her stuff, but he also wasn't hurting anything, so she opted to ignore it.

"I kind of expected you to pick 'Hammered'," she told him as she brought the ice cream over.

"Or maybe 'Mystery Man'."

Tyrel raised his eyebrows and tilted his head slightly as he considered. "I thought about it," he agreed. "It's cool watching Faye discover her completely unexpected ability in 'Hammered'. 'Mystery Man,' though, always struck me as more of a 'gotcha' episode. This one," he nodded at the screen as he waited for her to sit first, "has my favorite tech of the first season."

She giggled as she curled up on one end of the couch. "So, as my niece would say, you're 'jelly' of the Nallo tech?"

"Absolutely." He winked at her despite his disappointment. There wasn't a good way to sit next to her when her stockinged feet would be between them. Still, he casually sat as close to her as he could. "You have no idea how many times over the years I could've used the ability to walk up a wall." Her eyebrow went up and he explained, "It would've made the obstacle course a cinch."

She shuddered. "I can think of so many ways that tech could be misused."

"So you're on Ramo's side?" he squinted at her. The Nallo leader was painfully cautious when it came to sharing any kind of tech.

"Just because he's abrasive, it doesn't mean he's wrong. You wouldn't give a nine-year-old your car keys, would you?"

"Of course not, and how very philosophical of you to put it that way," he teased. Then, more thoughtfully, "You like to err on the side of caution, don't you?" The real surprise for him there was that he hadn't picked up on it sooner. How many flavors of soda did one person usually keep on hand, anyway?

"It makes sense to me," she agreed quietly. Bravely, she searched his face for signs of laughter. He hadn't laughed at her yet, but she wasn't quite ready to let her guard down. It hurt too much to be laughed at to do that.

The intensity of her gaze made him pause. What was she looking for? And was she finding it? He was still asking himself those questions when she picked up the remote and pressed play.

They chatted a little during this episode, pleasantly surprised to find that neither of them minded.

"I hate that they didn't explain the tech better," Tyrel grumbled after Ramo and Martin repaired the spaceship. "I'm serious," he protested when Merry gave him an incredulous look. "What's the point of calling it science-fiction if the science isn't halfway understandable?"

"I think that's the point," she laughed. "It shows how advanced they are—even their simplest explanation doesn't make sense to us. And, maybe," she lifted a taunting eyebrow at him, "this is a good time to stress the 'fiction' aspect of the show?"

"Ohhhh!" He dragged the word out playfully, clasping one hand over his heart as though wounded.

"Anyway, you've completely missed the plot point."

"Which was?" Tyrel was starting to feel a little scolded.

"Ramo's progression! Through the whole episode, he's been watching everyone like a hawk to make sure they don't give away any of their super-duper secrets. Now he decides that he trusts them enough that he's willing to *try* to explain the spaceship propulsion stuff?"

"The spaceship propulsion stuff?" Tyrel echoed. Running his fingers through his hair, he chuckled. "Ramo's change of heart stands out to you that much?"

Sensing that she'd gone overboard, as she had a tendency to do, Merry nodded sheepishly. "That is a pretty lame explanation, though."

Tyrel appreciated her concession. Setting his empty bowl on the table, he held out his hand for hers. Concern flitted across her face, but she relinquished the bowl and he stacked it in his. Next, he took the remote from her and started the episode going again. Last, but not least, he reached out, picked up her hand, and laced his fingers through hers.

Merry's pulse hit a new high—and that was counting the time at girls' camp when she'd found a snake in her sleeping bag.

"Merry." Noella tapped her pencil on the table by Merry's hand. "My friend, are you well?" Over the last few weeks, she'd been watching the quietly developing romance between her friend and the handsome Tyrel with increasing interest. Not to mention the signals Harmony and Grace were giving off—though she hadn't figured out who Harmony was seeing. Still, add her own budding relationship with Danny, and love was getting to be something of an epidemic! Except that Merry had been staring off into space for…too long. Even for Merry.

Merry recoiled from the noise and motion near her hand. "Noella!" she protested. "You scared me half to death!"

"Oh, yes?" Noella sat back in her chair, lips quirking up in mildly sardonic humor. "I should have sent you a text message, perhaps?"

Merry had to laugh at Noella's droll reply. "Sorry, I…I guess I did get a little distracted."

Noella clucked softly, her curls bouncing as she shook her head. "I have seen you distracted, my friend. This, it is different."

Merry puffed out her cheeks and exhaled through her mouth. "I was thinking about Tyrel." In the weeks since Halloween, they'd been spending a lot of time together.

"What?" Noella teased. "Instead of the most

interesting stage designs?" She gestured at the bare stage before them. "This will be your masterpiece!"

"I sure hope not," Merry retorted. Holding up the drawing she'd been working on, she explained, "But, I've read the play and I've measured the stage. All you really need is a couch for the kids to slouch on; a desk for the dad to do too much work at; and a kitchen counter for the mom."

Noella studied the rough outline skeptically. "This rectangle. What is it? The couch or the counter?"

"Both." Merry outlined the items as she spoke. "The couch sits at an angle in the right-hand corner there. Then, when it needs to be the kitchen, we lower a cardboard counter down from the rafters. Once we get the measurements for the couch, I can put the counter together in a few minutes."

Noella bobbed her head from left to right in an 'I still need convincing' motion. "And the Christmas tree?"

"Right." Merry tapped the 'x' she'd drawn toward the back of the stage. "I'm not sure if we'll lower it from the rafters or raise it through the trapdoor, but it's there. I just forgot to mention it."

Noella winked, then touched her lightly on the wrist. "You do not wish to tell me what is troubling you?"

"It's nothing much." Merry shrugged. Nothing she wanted to talk about. With anyone.

"It does not go well with Tyrel?" Noella probed.

"No, things are fine." Merry shifted a little. It was basically the truth. They were halfway through *Pool of Stars* by now. He seemed to enjoy *The Sacketts* when they watched it. Honestly, she'd been thrilled when he brought a movie of his own over—*The Gallant Hours* was sad, but based on actual events from World War II. A firm believer in being able to judge character by what people chose for entertainment, she was impressed with his choice.

And while she knew pride was one of her biggest flaws, yet she couldn't quite bring herself to explain to Noella what *was* bothering her. Getting advice from her sister would be bad enough. As much as she enjoyed Noella's company, discussing her dating life with the much younger woman didn't appeal.

"Good." Noella beamed at her. "You two, you go well together."

Merry smiled shyly and checked her phone for the time. "Hey, I better get going. It's nearly time for auditions to start." Pausing, she looked around the empty room. "Um… Where did you say you put those signs up?"

"Over all the town." Noella's beam brightened still further. "Every store window, every board." She'd almost been too tired to go to the trunk-or-treat afterward.

Merry believed her. The one doubt in her mind was whether or not anyone had seen them. While she personally didn't pay much attention to the various sheets of paper stuck to the windows at Stock's, she'd always assumed she was the exception. Why else would flyers be everyone's go-to?

So…shouldn't there be a line of anxious mothers in here by now? Each one outdoing the other to try to convince Noella that their offspring was perfect for the starring roles? Not that any of the three children's roles could be called the star, exactly, but they wouldn't know that.

"I'll get out of your way." Impulsively, she hugged the younger woman. "Pace yourself. You've still got five weeks of rehearsal, programs to design, tickets to sell…" She slumped as if just thinking about it exhausted her.

"Go, go," Noella laughed. "Before you talk me out of all this fame and glory."

Merry was still chuckling when she stopped at the store on her way home. A…store with no audition flyer in the window? The usual suspects were there—the soup kitchen; handmade items by a local artisan; the ad offering firewood 'cheep.' Wow. She had to squint to read the faded words on the flyer for the summer youth baseball programs. And yet, nothing about the annual charity play.

"Merry!" Judy poked her head out of the store. Leaning back in a little, she hollered to her son, "Josh, you stay with the cart. I'll be right back, I want to talk to Merry."

Strains of one of Helen Montgomery's early covers, "Away in a Manger," wafted out over Judy's shoulders. Having a neon sign abruptly appear over her head might've made Merry more self-conscious. But she sincerely hoped she never got a chance to find out.

"Judy!" She did her best to match the other woman's apparently happy attitude. That was the single best thing she'd learned during her college summer in sales. "What's up?"

Judy's answering squeal drew even more looks, but Merry allowed herself to be yanked into a hug. "The armoire is so perfect, I love it!"

Merry's ear literally rang with the praise and she had to work even harder to maintain her smile. "I'm so glad!"

"So, I did the video thing," Judy chattered on, pulling back so she could look at Merry. "Simply raved about how you fixed it up so I hardly recognized it!"

Reminding herself that word-of-mouth was the single best advertising she could ever hope for, Merry managed a laugh. "Yes, I saw. And I've been meaning to thank you for leaving such an amazing review!" With half the town watching, she couldn't afford to be less than thrilled.

Judy must've seen something through the window, because she waved and yelled, "I'll be right there, sweetie!"

"Hey, Judy." Merry touched the other woman's arm lightly, a thought having occurred to her. "I'm, um, a little surprised you're not over at the community center." Judy's perky face scrunched up questioningly. "For the auditions, I mean." Her stomach tightened. If Judy didn't know about the auditions, *nobody* knew.

"Auditions?" Judy's quizzical expression suddenly cleared. "For the annual play? I thought it didn't…well, I heard something happened and there wasn't going to be one this year." She put one fist on her cocked hip, waiting for Merry to explain.

Taking a deep breath to calm her fury, Merry mentally raced through her options. Telling the whole truth here—as in, pointing the finger at the presumed saboteurs—would only make things worse for Noella in the long run.

"Oh yeah, it's…" Merry began nodding vigorously. Remembering the impromptu audience Judy had gathered for her, she cleared her throat and ramped up her volume a bit. "The charity play is absolutely happening this year. Auditions start today over at the community center. They need three youngsters and two adults. A mom and a dad," she hastily clarified.

"Well." Judy's eyes darted right and left, seeing their audience anew as prospective competition. "Well, Josh and me'll get right over there."

"But Mom!" Josh, tired of waiting, had just stuck his head out to complain. "The ice cream!"

Behind him, Helen Montgomery's clear alto cheerfully harmonized with her soprano for the chorus of "Jingle Bells." Merry felt her cheeks warming, but did her best to focus on Judy, whose face was a study in concentration.

"Cold enough to leave that in the car," she informed him decisively. "Let's go get things rung up."

"That's what I came to tell you," Josh asserted, stepping forward to hold the door for her the way his father had taught him. "Miss Birdie has everything rung up and wanted to know if you was going to be much longer."

"All done," Judy announced. Winking conspiratorially at Merry, she announced, "We've got one more errand today, Josh. We're going to make you a star!"

Her own shopping forgotten, Merry shot a text to Noella, asking her for a digital copy of the flyer. Everyone was great about coming to the show once it was ready, but if people got it in their heads that it wasn't happening, they'd be sunk.

Crossing the street to the nearest print shop, she placed an order for two dozen color copies of the flyer. Spent the next half an hour apologizing to merchants on Main for the mix-up—*No, no typos on this one. See?*—and re-placing the flyers. That was a good start.

Climbing into her truck, she whipped out her phone again. Noella had put her in charge of props, hadn't she? Alright, then. She leveraged that into an excuse to send out texts to half a dozen of the, um…the best-connected people in town. She explained her need for the temporary loan or donation of a couch and a desk, said she looked forward to seeing them at the play, and wished them a happy Thanksgiving.

Thanksgiving. Swallowing her heart, which had leapt up into her chest, Merry put her phone away and turned her truck on. She couldn't ignore it any longer. She needed to talk with Heidi. Who had made a point of letting her know she'd be home today, making pies for Thanksgiving on Thursday.

Twenty minutes later, Merry knocked on her sister's door.

"I'll get it!" Brian's rapidly lowering voice preceded him to the door. "Aunt Merry!" He lunged forward and wrapped his arms around her waist. "Help me. Please!"

Merry ruffled his hair and smiled at his dramatics. Sure, a flower-covered apron could give a teenage boy nightmares, but learning to cook was an important skill. Especially something as delicious as a pie! "Tell you what." She grinned down at him. "You help us finish peeling the apples, and then I'll talk your mom into letting you off the hook. Deal?"

"Deal!" Relief radiated from him as he stepped back to let her in, then abruptly his eyebrows drew in. "How'd you know we were making apple pies?"

Merry tried to look mysterious, but ended up laughing as she held up a piece of apple peeling that he'd transferred to her shirt when he hugged her.

"Sorry about that," he muttered, turning red even as he half-grinned back at her.

"C'mon, handsome." Draping an arm around his shoulders, she guided him back to the kitchen where Heidi sat peeling apples to Christmas music. Pausing in the doorway, she raised one arm dramatically. "The cavalry is here!"

"Huh?"

Merry and Heidi both chuckled at Brian's confusion.

"You know," Merry nudged him, then set her keys on the table. "Like in the old westerns." Pumping some soap onto her hands, she started scrubbing.

"The ones Grandpa likes to watch?" Heidi prompted, handing him another apple. "The good guys are down to the last few bullets and everyone's bravely saying goodbye." She struck a tragic pose.

"When suddenly they hear a bugle!" Merry shut off the water and dried her hands. "It's the cavalry, come to save the day!"

Brian nodded like he remembered, but kept giving them strange—and what he probably thought were discreet—looks.

"In the homestretch now!" Merry announced as she dropped the last apple core in the trash and high-fived Brian.

"Alright, buddy." Taking the hint, Heidi smiled at her long-suffering son. "You've put in your time. Now scram. Go do something fun."

He grinned at Merry. Said, "Yes, ma'am!" And was gone.

"Why can't he ever move that fast when I ask him to take the trash out?" Heidi mock-complained.

"I'm pretty sure that would be a violation of nature's laws," hooted Merry.

Heidi snickered and shook a crumb topping over the final apple pie. McKinney tradition was that the host provided the meat while the guests provided sides and dessert. Since her family was keen on apple pie, she always made a couple extra to save at home. Not that she'd have to do it for much longer. Even Brian was growing up. He hadn't complained once that morning. Shoot, he'd be getting his driver's license in…seventeen months.

"Silent night. Holy night."

Merry stared in shock at the speaker on Heidi's counter. Her sister listened to Helen Montgomery, too? Since when?? She suppressed a shiver. This was getting spooky. Was her alter ego stalking her?

"What do you think?" Heidi asked, jerking her chin in the direction of the speaker.

"About what?" Merry blinked at her.

"The singer, Helen Montgomery." Heidi's face scrunched up as she struggled to get the terms right. "She's some independent artist that's hugely popular with the girls at church right now."

"Really?" Merry hadn't known that. Which wasn't too shocking, given that she wasn't serving in the young women's program and Heidi was. "That's a little odd, don't you think?"

Heidi chuckled. "Hey, in today's world, I'm just glad they picked a singer-songwriter who keeps it clean."

"Yeah, that's great." Merry idly picked at something she'd gotten on her shirt. "Is that all you like about her?" She probably shouldn't have pushed the issue. Heidi's casual disinterest just happened to be driving her crazy.

"Well, I haven't listened to all of her stuff yet. I guess she's got about fifty songs out." She shrugged. "Some covers, some originals. Her originals are just a little melancholy for me, I guess."

"Oh." Merry was sorry she asked. Ha. *Merry* was melancholy, apparently. "Are those for the pumpkin pies?" she asked, nodding at a stack of empty tins.

"Yeah." Heidi popped the pie into her counter oven and dropped onto a chair. "I think I'm getting old."

"Nah." Merry shook her head. Started opening the cans of pumpkin. "You've just learned to pace yourself. The holidays have barely begun, y'know."

Heidi huffed out a, "True." Taking a gulp of her ice water, she tugged at her collar. The condensation was at half-mast on all the kitchen windows, but she was burning up thanks to the activity and the heat from the stoves. "I think I'll do all my Christmas shopping online this year."

"Sure," Merry agreed glibly. A few years ago she'd cleverly redesigned family movie nights to her own purposes and now sent a parent-approved movie to each of her siblings' families for Christmas. Plus snacks, of course.

"Sure," Heidi echoed. Getting up, she went over to check on the rest of the pie dough. Great-Grandma Edwards' recipe claimed to make two pumpkin pies, but she always wound up with three. Not that she was complaining… "So. What brings you here?"

Merry sighed. "I need to talk to someone."

Heidi waited. As long as she could. "I heard the front door slam, so we've got the place to ourselves for at least an hour."

Merry barked a laugh. "That almost makes it easier."

Heidi's eyes narrowed slightly. She took another drink of water to give herself time to try to figure out how to encourage her sister. "I remember my first serious boyfriend," she said at last.

"Oh?" Merry wasn't convinced she wanted to hear it, but it was marginally better than having to face her problem.

"Like it was yesterday."

Merry looked up, surprised at the dreamy note in her sister's voice.

"He was the best basketball player in my college ward. Had this deep, husky voice and the deepest brown eyes I've ever seen. It was like looking into a mug of dark, dark, hot cocoa."

"Darren?" Merry interrupted, recognizing the description as Heidi's husband. "*Darren* was your first serious boyfriend?"

Heidi nodded, mildly amused at the startled lift to Merry's eyebrows. "I mean, I dated in high school. I even had a few dates in college before Darren noticed me."

"How long had you been dating before you introduced him to the family?" Merry asked as casually as she could.

"Oh, now you want me to do math!" Heidi scowled and took another sip of water. Was that what was bothering Merry? Technically, Tyrel had already met everyone local when he came to dinner back around Halloween. Nearly a *month* ago. Of course, things had progressed since then. They even sat together at church last Sunday.

"Yes, please," Merry agreed quickly. Teasing her sister helped keep things light. "The precise number of hours between making Darren's acquaintance and introducing him to Dad."

Heidi snorted. "In whole numbers or with the remainder?"

"Whole numbers will suffice." Merry snickered when Heidi stuck her tongue out at her. She hadn't had this much fun with Heidi in a long time. And while talking about an awkward subject, no less! She offered a prayer of gratitude as she began rolling out the pie crust.

"It wasn't that long," Heidi admitted. "Less than two months, I think." Holding the cold glass to her warm cheek, she smiled. "It's a whole new level of anxiety, introducing the man you hope to marry to your father. I got all hypersensitive, y'know? I noticed things about Dad that hadn't annoyed me in years. And Darren, oh." Without realizing it, she put her hand over her stomach like she was feeling ill. "I overanalyzed everything that man did for the entire visit."

"You wanted Dad to like him." Merry barely heard herself, but Heidi nodded slowly.

"I didn't know it was possible to want something that badly." Heidi checked herself. "Of course, we already knew. We…" She gestured vaguely as she tried not to lecture. "We were on the same page about what we wanted."

Merry got it. Darren and Heidi 'had an understanding,' as Mom would say.

Heidi leaned forward, her excitement growing by leaps and bounds the longer Merry remained silent. "Merrrrry?" she prompted.

Merry blushed. "Yes." Lifting her eyes from the pie dough, she shyly confirmed, "We have had some conversations." Their discussion over lasagna the other night had gone as far as talking about whether or not there would be room in the barn for a nursery and additional bedrooms. He hadn't produced a ring, thankfully. Talking hypothetically about becoming a mother was heart-wrenching enough. One more shock that night might've done her in.

"Merry!" Squealing, Heidi leapt to her feet and wrapped her arms around her sister. "This is so exciting! We…we've got so much to do. Do you know what your colors are? Have you decided which temple…?"

"Ohhhhkay." Merry grabbed Heidi's arms and shook her lightly. "Earth to Heidi!" Her sister blinked and mercifully stopped talking. "I said we talked. I didn't say he proposed."

"Okay." Heidi nodded jerkily, stuck between the conclusion she'd jumped to and the now-massive question of exactly *what* they'd talked about. "But…these are things you're going to need to decide. If not today, then pretty soon."

Merry decided it was time to change the subject—before the spaghetti monster transmogrified into a linguine casserole. "How did you do it?" Merry dropped her hands from where they were still holding onto Heidi. "I feel sick to my stomach every other time that I see

Tyrel—in a good way, I mean—and if," she covered her own abdomen. "I mean, if he's on…on trial at Thanksgiving dinner, I don't know…"

Heidi jumped to her feet and hauled a white-faced Merry over to a chair. "Don't you dare pass out!" she ordered. Grabbing a glass out of the rack, she filled it with ice and water. "Sip this slowly, okay?" She brushed a strand of hair out of Merry's face. "Savor the cold. Feel it traveling down your esophagus. All the way down to your stomach."

She didn't actually know what she was doing, beyond getting Merry's laser-focused mind off a subject that was making her physically ill. It seemed to be working. At least, a little color was coming back into Merry's cheeks.

"Better?"

Merry nodded weakly. "I knew I didn't want to talk about this," she half-joked.

Heidi squeezed her hand sympathetically. "I wish I could make it better." Shoot, where did those tears come from? Big help she was. "I mean, it's gonna be fine. We just, you and I, we worry about things. We chase every trail marked 'how it could go wrong.'"

Merry laughed and nodded. "Yeah, we do. All in the name of being prepared." She'd forgotten that about her sister. Heidi was mellower, but they did both tend to entertain worst-case scenarios.

"Right," Heidi laughed. "Let's look on the bright side. We know Mom approves." They exchanged wry looks. While Elaine might start wailing the stereotypical 'my baby's getting married' song eventually, at the moment she was all for it. "Chad thinks he's hilarious."

"Yeah, that's a tad concerning," Merry interjected, prompting a snicker from Heidi. They both loved their brother. He just had an offbeat sense of humor.

Since there were no teenagers present to witness the forbidden behavior, Heidi rolled her eyes. "You two find plenty to laugh at together, don't you?"

"That's true," Merry admitted. They were averaging two *Pool of Stars*-or-movie nights a week—barring Fridays, of course, since she refused to become the stereotypical absent friend—and typically, they laughed at the same things. "Voila," "Downloads," and "Season of Change" had proven special favorites for them both.

"Brian likes him, too." Heidi grinned. "I guess he overheard Brian and his classmates discussing their science project and volunteered to help."

Merry's eyebrows knit together. "That's going to be the first high school rocket to achieve escape velocity," she predicted. "Mister Wallace will be fit to be tied." She had no difficulty in picturing the white-haired Mister Wallace, who threatened to retire, staring slack-jawed as a colorful rocket vanished into the sky.

Heidi must've been thinking along the same lines because she laughed so hard that she snorted. That cracked them both up and they laughed until they cried. It was amazing.

Chapter 13

The next night, Merry joined the others at Noella's again—had it really been a month already?—for the second installment of the *Murder at the Opera* series, *D Flat Aria.*

"This is so good!" Harmony closed her eyes in the bliss of savoring her third gingerbread man. "Is this an old family recipe or something?"

Noella laughed and shook her head. "I found it in a book at the library."

"No way!" Harmony's eyes popped open. "In that case, maybe I could get a picture of it? I'm taking treats to my clients next week and this beats anything else I've got."

"Of course!" Beckoning for Harmony to follow her the few steps into the kitchen, she brought out her recipe card system and they quickly became absorbed in it.

"Sounds like our Noella put her own spin on things." Grace chuckled as she listened to them discussing ingredients.

"As always." Merry swallowed a bite of gingerbread, shot a glance at the others, then remarked in a lowered voice, "I'm worried about this year's Christmas play."

"What?" Grace's forehead furrowed. "Why?"

"Because the theater committee is sabotaging her at every turn." Hastily, Merry explained the debacle with the flyers.

"So the flyers I've seen around town, those are the ones you put up?" Grace's frown deepened at Merry's nod. "Taking the first set down was a dirty trick."

"It gets worse." Checking again to make sure Noella was suitably distracted, Merry continued, "I practically had to twist arms to get the loan of one couch and one desk. And forget about a stage crew. Everyone's 'too busy.'"

Grace's lips quirked up. "I think I know where to find a stage crew."

Merry couldn't believe her ears.

"One of the…guests at the Rockin' R is majoring in theater. I don't know how much experience she's had with being boss, but I do know that she's got the entire male population of the ranch wound around her finger." Grace blushed a little at Merry's inquisitively raised eyebrow. Alec, the ranch's foreman, had finally noticed her at the trunk-or-treat this year, as Merry well knew. She was the first person Grace had told. "Almost the entire population," she corrected herself, giving Merry a friendly shoulder shove.

"But if she's only going to be there over Thanksgiving break," Merry was thinking of her niece's schedule, "she won't be here for the play. Poof, no more stage crew." She savored a bite of the gingerbread.

"Noooo." Grace hesitated. As a country vet, Grace heard a variety of tales of woe and made it a solemn policy not to share them. The 'guest' she'd been speaking of was none other than Edna 'Eddie' Brooke—the youngest child of Mister Collin Brooke, owner of the Rockin' R. "That's not it." Because Eddie had been expelled from yet another Ivy League college. Wait a second. What was she wishing on her friends here? A solution? Or an even bigger problem?

"Okay." Merry hesitated, not sure she liked the way Grace was rubbing her left palm on her jeans, an old nervous habit. "I guess it's worth a try—if she'll be around for the play."

"Let me ask her," Grace suggested abruptly. "I'll ask her the next time I see her."

"Ask who what?" Harmony asked, handing them each a plate of re-heated gingerbread men.

"I was telling Grace about our stage crew problem." Merry nodded at Noella to include her in the conversation. "She knows someone she can ask to help out." She shrugged diffidently as she spoke, not wanting to get Noella's hopes up too high.

"Magnificent!" Noella tried to clap her hands for joy and nearly spilled milk everywhere. "We have the theater. Most of the cast." She angled a sidelong glance at Harmony, who had eyes only for the serving tray of gingerbread cookies. "And maybe the stage crew. Yes. Very good!"

"Sounds like things are going great." Merry heaved a sigh of relief.

"Oui, but for one thing." Noella paused for a dramatic moment. "We have no draw." She'd found that word through an online translation system and now anxiously watched her friends' faces to see if she'd used it correctly.

"Draw? Like, a big name to draw in the crowds?" Grace clarified, eyes narrowing quizzically.

"Exactly." Noella handed over the glasses of milk and plopped into her seat. "I hear the talk. Because Mrs. Arnold's children did not make the cast, the people will not come."

Merry toyed with the idea of throwing something. "Of all the two-faced, double-dealing monsters," she growled. She took a calming breath and smiled tightly at Grace and Harmony, who'd turned wide-eye toward her. "Mrs. Arnold is the committee chairwoman who sandbagged Noella at that meeting. Now she's upset that her 'little starlets,'" as the woman had often been heard to call her offspring, "didn't get three out of the five roles in the whole show?"

Grace rolled her eyes. "Sounds like her." She had her own experiences with the woman.

"I'll say," Harmony huffed. "Cadmia's queen bee strikes again." Mrs. Arnold had a long history of playing the town like a fiddle. Thanks to her vendetta against this play, not a single adult had auditioned. Which was why Noella wanted Harmony and Grant to play the mom and dad, complete with a 'kiss and make-up' scene at the end.

"It was one thing for her to turn the town against the idea of rezoning Fleischer's pasture for a mall," Grace remarked quietly. Privately, she was grateful for that bit of interference. "But the proceeds from the charity play go to paying for food, fuel, clothes, and even Christmas presents for some of the families around here."

"Maybe we need to remind people of that," Merry grumbled.

"How?" Noella stuck out her bottom lip. "The merchants, they have agreed to set up tables to sell tickets, but nobody buys them. I went to the newspaper to beg them to write a story and they say it is old news. The churches, well, they buy a few tickets." She hesitated, her fingers fluttering. "That is where I hear about Mrs. Arnold."

"The play's only a couple of weeks away." Harmony bit her lip.

"But what draw is there that would counteract Mrs. Arnold?" Merry asked. "It's not like there's room in the play for," she waved vaguely.

"Helen Montgomery."

Merry jerked, nearly turning her remaining gingerbread men into base jumpers. "What?"

"Helen Montgomery." Grace repeated uncertainly. "From what I can tell, she's all the rage right now."

"Yeah, she's popular." Harmony frowned. "But do you really think an indie singer is, well, spectacular enough to overcome the bee?"

"If we can get her to come, the teenagers will

spend their own money to buy these tickets." At least, Grace knew of a few of them who would.

"This may be true." Noella's fingers fluttered descriptively as she added, "Everywhere I go, I hear the voice of this singer."

"The grocery store, the beauty salon, even the family-run restaurants are all playing her," Harmony agreed thoughtfully. "If you could get her, and that's a pretty big 'if,' she might put the play over."

"Wonder how much she'd charge?"

Merry frowned at Grace's question. "Who says she'll charge anything?" She hadn't meant to sound so irritated, but her discomfort level was rising.

"Oh, I dunno." Grace shrugged. "She's a performer. I just assumed she would want some kind of compensation."

"We can always ask," Harmony pointed out. "Tell her it's a charity play, sort of a last minute emergency, and see what she says."

"Last minute is right," Merry grumbled to cover her increasing panic. She couldn't say no if they asked. Grace was right about the local needs. Okay, so people should take care of each other without expecting to get something—like a play— in return. Since that didn't exactly happen, and since it was better to have the town involved in taking care of its own than not, they had a charity play. "She probably has big plans with family by now." Her eyes fastened on Harmony, who was typing on her phone. "What're you doing?"

"Asking Helen Montgomery to sing in our play." Harmony hit send. She didn't want to play the mom in this show any more than she wanted to eat liver and onions, a personal hate of hers, but she could send an email.

Merry's phone dinged. Aaaand suddenly all eyes were on her. "What?" she squeaked.

Grace's eyes narrowed, but mercifully she kept quiet. Of all those present, she was the most likely to recognize Helen's alto as Merry's once she started thinking about it.

"Nothing…" Harmony frowned. "That was some weird timing, though." Her left eyebrow went up as if to ask, *Wasn't it?*

Noella clapped her hands. "This is wonderful! Helen will say yes. The play, it will be a success. And everyone will have a merry Christmas." She hit play on the remote before anyone could contradict her.

Under the cover of the movie's opening scene, Merry winced. She'd always hated having a name she could find in a dictionary. Especially one with a definition that didn't fit her. Of course, that was the least of her worries. While the screen lit up with sisterly banter and romantic tension between Molly and *two* of Barber Lake's most eligible bachelors, Merry was busy wrestling with the problem of what to do about Helen.

Sure, she knew the basic answer. There was a real need, so she'd be there. Feeling stupid in glasses, a red wig, and full-on makeup. Scared to death. Would she even be able to squeak a note out past the fear in her throat? Questions and doubts peppered her from all angles until she wanted nothing more than to get out. Get out of the room, away from the noise of the movie, and pace.

"Okay." Harmony mock-swooned as the end credits rolled. "*That* was a kiss." Her quip was rewarded with a round of laughter.

Even Merry laughed. She'd conditioned herself to blend in so long as she had the strength.

Rather than joining in on the discussion that followed, Merry hopped up and began collecting dishes. She hadn't been so distracted that she'd missed the climactic kiss. Unfortunately. Now a whole new, secondary string of questions began marching through her brain. Tyrel's face sprang to mind and her own face heated. He'd taken to complimenting her whenever he came over. *Wow, that color brings out your eyes.* Or, *I love it when you wear your hair down.* And then there were the times that he didn't say anything.

"That's a lovely shade of pink you're wearing," Grace whispered, coming up beside her. Since when did Merry blush?

Merry flicked a glance at where Noella and Harmony were talking animatedly about the auction scene from the movie.

"Wow. Tyrel must be doing something right," Grace teased.

Merry's eyes narrowed. Two could play that game. "How're things with Alec?" Score! Grace's fair skin betrayed her instantly. It never ceased to amaze her how easily her redheaded friend's cheeks crimsoned. "This is good, right?" she asked, careful to keep her voice down. Grace's crush on Alec began at about sixteen, the instant she first saw the widower. She'd looked right past everyone else and fallen for him. Only to have him look through her and everyone else as he mourned his wife.

"It's something." Grace blew out a breath. "Complicated. Yeah, that's it." What else could it be after seventeen years of being first invisible, then a colleague? "Enough about me. You better answer Harmony's email."

Merry froze in place. Before she could get her voice working again, Harmony called to them.

"Hey, what do you two think?"

"What do we think about what?" Grace laughed. Squeezing Merry's arm, she dragged her back over to where the others still sat.

"We were talking about working Helen into the story," Harmony explained. "There's no room for another character, so I think she should play the mom." That sounded plausible, right? She'd already tried and failed to convince Noella to do it. Opposite her boyfriend Danny, of course.

"Ridiculous." Noella flapped a hand at her. "You wish only to avoid the role for yourself."

"Which means you have a different plan,"

Grace interpreted.

"Helen will sing the Christmas music." Noella beamed at them, terribly pleased with herself. "The mother listens to music while she works. They all listen to music at the end. Voila. It is perfect."

"I don't know," Merry objected without thinking. Obviously, she didn't want to find herself kissing Harmony's boyfriend, Grant—or anybody else, come to think of it. But the other idea didn't sound so great, either. "It's a two hour-long play. You want her to, what, stand stock still on stage all that time?"

Noella's brows knit together. "No, that would not do. We will have to give her a chair. She can stand each time she is to sing. With a spotlight."

"Then fade into the background again when the spotlight switches to the others." Grace shrugged. "That might work."

"Yeah," Merry agreed halfheartedly. They were closing the loopholes almost faster than she could find them.

"Okay," Grace wrapped Noella in a hug, "enough plotting for one night." Straightening, she smiled at her hostess. "Thanks for having us over."

"Yes." Merry followed suit, hugging first Noella, then Harmony, who'd risen to hug Grace. "And the delicious gingerbread."

"I better go, too." Harmony collected a hug

from Noella. "My place for a musical next time!" They skipped movie nights on weeks with major holidays, so that meant she was free until December sixth. Hmm. Maybe it was time for another getaway?

"Can't wait," Grace assured her.

In the confusion of sorting out coats, scarves, and so forth, Merry made eye contact with Grace, who responded with a barely discernible nod.

"Night!" Merry headed out to her truck. "Breathe," she muttered to herself after her third failure to insert the key into the ignition. "Breathe."

She almost forgot to watch for Harmony's car to start. Almost turned down the wrong road on her way to Blinky's. Almost turned her truck around and went home instead of parking. *How* had Grace figured out her best-kept secret? She stared hard at the diner's front window, through which she could see Grace sitting at the counter, chatting with the owner's daughter.

Best way to find out was to ask.

Climbing out of her truck, she pushed open the glass door. The combined odors of onion and grease, along with about a thousand years of black coffee and sticky maple syrup, washed over her. Blinky's hadn't changed much since their teenage days, but once the vinyl-covered stools got to be more duct tape than vinyl, they'd given in and replaced them. Word was they were now fighting public opinion on re-covering the booth seating, but Merry planned to risk it.

As she took her first step on the vintage linoleum, she heard Grace say, "I think we'll probably stick with hot chocolate tonight."

"You got it." Susan patted Grace's hand, waved to Merry, and meandered toward the back. Nobody came to Blinky's strictly for the hot chocolate. What these two were really after was a private conversation.

Merry didn't know if the diner was actually ninety degrees or if it was her nerves, but it was irritating. The scrape of a fork on a plate set her teeth on edge. Even the crumbs on the table at the empty booth she'd chosen made her angry. Or maybe it was that her favorite booth, way in the back corner, was already occupied.

Closing her eyes in prayer, she waited for Grace to join her. *No one was supposed to know. And I can't talk to her while I feel this way.* Yell, maybe. Talk? Ha. She kept praying even after the booth shifted with Grace's slight weight.

"Here's your hot chocolate," Susan announced, plunking the mugs onto the table. Waved a can of whipped cream at them. "Any takers?"

Grace cheerfully held out her mug for a heaping helping and Merry did her best not to cringe away from hoarse hissing noise the can made.

Merry shook her head when Susan cocked an eyebrow at her. Even if she liked whipped cream, it wasn't worth the sensory aggravation tonight.

As soon as Susan was out of earshot, Grace set her mug down and took Merry's cold hands in hers. "You know I won't tell anyone."

Merry took a deep breath and focused on the warmth of Grace's hands. Worked her way up to the determined set of Grace's mouth, then the warmth coming from her eyes.

"I know," she said when she truly believed it. The anger was gone. "I…I don't like…" She struggled to put her frustration into words. Would that even help?

"You always liked your secrets," Grace observed gently. "I'm sorry I teased you at Noella's."

Merry felt her irritation draining away in the face of Grace's apology. "Thanks."

"Of course."

"How did you know?"

"I'm not sure." Grace cocked her head to one side. "The way you react whenever she comes on or gets brought up. All the years we spent singing while we pulled weeds and hauled wood. I guess I just know you."

Merry groaned. "If it's that's all it takes, I'm in serious trouble."

Grace laughed softly. "No, I don't think so." Faced with Merry's confused scowl, she shrugged. "I was also in the right place at the right time tonight."

"What you're saying is," Merry's shoulders slumped, "I could've played dumb and gotten with it.”

“Pretty much.” Giving her hands a light squeeze, Grace released them and reached for her mug again. “Susan preps this to coffee temps,” she warned.

Merry managed half a chuckle. “I always forget that.” Wrapping her fingers around the mug, she stared at it. Invested all of her attention for a moment on the heat coming from it into her chilled digits. Blocked out the sounds and smells until it was just her, the mug, and Grace. Now that the shock was wearing off—and the idea that others would figure it out seemed a lot less imminent—she could admit that she was grateful to have someone to talk this over with. “I can’t do what they want me to.”

“Not even with help?” Grace offered. Merry’s eyes met hers for an instant, then dropped back to the mug. “What would you need to pull this off?”

Merry shook her head, then shrugged so Grace wouldn’t misinterpret that as a ‘no.’

“Does anyone know what, um…?” Grace glanced around casually, but no one was paying attention to them. “What she looks like?”

“There’s a picture on her website.” Merry blew on the hot chocolate and tried a cautious sip. Nope, still hot enough to melt her teeth.

“Okay, let’s see.” Grace tugged out her phone and ran a search. “Whoa.”

Merry tried not to squirm as Grace studied

her, then the picture, then her again.

"If I didn't know this was you…" Grace pursed her lips. "This could work."

Merry perked. "What're you thinking?" Hope pierced the bubble of anxiety, letting some light in.

"First, let's see the email." Grace put her phone away and Merry got hers out.

Together, they skimmed the email and Merry frowned. "There's hardly any information in this."

"Yeah, I don't think Harmony expects *her* to say yes," Grace agreed.

Merry composed a short, non-committal response asking for more details, had Grace read it over to make sure she hadn't given anything away, and then they spent an hour quietly scheming how to bring Helen to life for the charity play performances.

Susan's curiosity eventually got the better of her and she brought over a second round of hot chocolate—on the house—but Grace glibly switched the conversation to a story of a heifer currently staying at her practice and Susan went away as mystified as before.

Merry's phone buzzed in the middle of the tale and now she slid it over so Grace could see it, too.

"Okay, that's better." Grace nodded as she read. "Dates, times, and how 'bout that, an address for the community center."

They muddled through an answer that was politely interested but made no promises, because Grace felt like a complete stranger would need a minute to think about it.

"And maybe we should sleep on it?" Merry teased as Grace's face nearly split with a yawn.

"Sound idea." Grace nodded, winking. "Let's do it."

Giggling, they paid their tab and left, agreeing to let each other know if they heard anything from Harmony or Noella on the subject of the 'guest star.'

Shockingly, Merry fell asleep as soon as her head hit the pillow. She couldn't eat a mouthful of breakfast the next morning, though.

A few hours of hard work finished the chess set, which she lovingly packed and shipped off to receive a hard wax polish. The matching chessboard was ready for its second coat, which polished off the morning. And left her with hours to fill before she had to be at Tyrel's.

A frigid shower later, she sat down at her roll-top desk, nerves still jumping every time she thought about the play. Not to mention when she thought about telling Tyrel. She hadn't known if she would until this morning.

They were friends. Who held hands. Watched movies. Talked about the gospel. The other night they'd gotten so involved in swapping mission stories that they never got around to *Pool of Stars*. She didn't understand how someone as kind and clever and handsome as he was could ever be interested in her. And yet, every time she prayed about their relationship, the Spirit nudged her forward. 1 Thessalonians 5:21 *Prove all things; hold fast that which is good* was starting to make sense.

Which brought her back around to telling him about Helen. She'd known she would as soon as she opened her eyes that morning. Something about waking up to a cold, gray light filtering in through her windows had aroused a near certainty in her that she would be discovered at the play.

So. She smoothed a piece of paper. Twiddled her pen around her thumb. She needed to write before her inner turmoil and anxiety ate her alive.

It starts so small.
A flicker of hope.
And through it all,
I'm never quite sure.
But I will dare!!!

Chapter 14

"You can do this." Her whisper hung in the silent car. She'd told herself that once for every heartbeat as she drove over, but still hadn't convinced herself. "*I* can do this." Her death-grip on the steering wheel didn't relax. Good grief, what would it take to get her…

Tyrel's door opened and his head poked out. No, he wasn't just planning to holler at her from his door, he was coming out. Step by step he drew closer, her heart rate increasing exponentially until it threatened to phase right through her rib cage.

"Merry?" His voice, muffled by a scarf and the closed window, reached her. He tried the door to her car. It was locked. "Are you okay?"

She glanced up at him. Forced a smile. "No." Above his scarf, she could see his cheek muscles pulling up in a small smile.

"Want to come in and talk about it?"

His gentle invitation broke the spell. Her fingers uncurled from the steering wheel. She took a great big breath and nodded. Unlocking the door, she shivered at the blast of cold that curled around her ankles, nose, and investigated the gap between her scarf and her neck.

"Is that a guitar?" he asked, catching her elbow to steady her as she climbed out.

"Yeah." She hefted the case a little as if to let

him get a better look and was only mildly surprised when he offered to carry it for her. She could get used to his understated, gentlemanly ways.

"I didn't know you played." His hand still on her elbow, he hurried her up the walk to his door. "I'll say this for the property manager here," he closed the door between them and the cold, "he keeps the walks clear!"

She nodded. "That'll be important as the winter progresses." She grinned a little as the sound of Gordon MacRae singing "Silver Bells" reached her.

"Right." Looking to her for permission, he put the guitar by the couch. Noticed one end of his weight bar sticking out from under the couch and nudged it back into place with his toe.

She watched as he returned, shedding his heavy coat, scarf, and hat as he came, bringing the scent of soap with him as if he was freshly showered. Maybe he'd just finished working out? Whatever the explanation, half of his damp hair stayed down where it properly belonged. The other half rose with his hat and stood more or less at attention.

"What?" His eyes narrowed at her giggle. "It's my hair isn't it?"

He didn't reach up to smooth it and she wondered why. Was he just going to leave it that way? Maybe he needed a mirror? She'd never been there long enough to use the bathroom, but she assumed there was one in there. She glanced down the hall to confirm that there wasn't another door past the kitchen. Great. If she ever *did* have to use the bathroom here, she'd have to go through his bedroom to get there.

"Is it bad?"

The husky timbre of his voice jerked her gaze back to his. Oh no. He was leaning slightly toward her, one hand in his front pocket. Almost as if he was waiting for her to smooth it. Her hand began to lift of its own volition. She'd been diligently not thinking about just such a moment since they met. Now here she was, her fingers slipping into his hair. Soft…so soft. It was like running her fingers through individual strands of silk.

The tips of her fingers trailed down his cheek. Strange. His skin was smoother than her father's, with just a hint of stubble. He hadn't shaved a second time today for their date. She stopped short of touching his lips. Curled her fingers into her palm and brought her hand back to her body.

"There." How could she sound so calm? Her hormones were zinging around inside her like sugared-up kids in a bouncy house.

"Thanks." Tyrel took the hint and straightened away. A kiss would be nice, but he didn't want to push her. "I looked up homemade fettuccine alfredo online."

Her jaw dropped. "You—you made fettuccine alfredo?"

He shrugged, pleased to have surprised her. "I not only made it, it's what we're having for supper.

I'm hoping," he linked his fingers through hers and began leading her into the kitchen, "it will convince you to give me your recipe."

She laughed at his pleading puppy eyes. "You can't be serious. You made this," she inhaled a deep breath of the fragrant dish on his counter, "and you still want my recipe."

"Oh, I'm very serious." Grinning, he handed her a plate. "After you." Christmas music kept playing in the background as they settled themselves in the front room.

After the prayer, she praised the pasta with each bite, along with his garlic bread, but refused to give up her recipe. Truthfully, his was so creamy, so perfectly flavored that she couldn't imagine why he still wanted hers!

"Alright, I'll make you a deal." He pulled a popular game from under the coffee table and showed it to her. "If I win, you give me your recipe."

"That's a pretty big prize." She bit the inside of her cheek, thoroughly embarrassed to admit that hers was a bag-and-can recipe.

"If you win, I'll give you a kiss." Stunned, Tyrel froze. Had he just said that out loud? Judging by the way her face had drained of color, yeah, he had. "To be claimed at the place and time of your choice." The words rushed out of him like air escaping out of a balloon. He couldn't seem to inhale after that. He was just stuck there, waiting for her response. An agonizing ten or twenty seconds later, she shifted slightly. Gave the tiniest of nods.

"Alright."

Tyrel took a deep breath. "You set it up. I'll get the brownies." Watching Faye spit out Garten food during the *Pool of Stars* episode "Unexpected Triumph" had prompted a lengthy discussion about food, which naturally included desserts. She liked just about anything with chocolate, but brownies were what he knew best, so double-chocolate-mint brownies graced the plate he set before her.

He'd gotten the idea to play this game with her from seeing it on her shelves. Much to his surprise, though, her playing was erratic at best. On one move, she'd earn a whopping thirty-eight points. On another, she'd overlook an obvious choice and leave herself wide open to attack.

Perhaps it had something to do with why her eyes kept straying to her guitar case as she continued trying to play?

"Hey." He gently touched her wrist as she stared at the board. "Would it be alright if we finished this some other time?"

"Are you sure?" Merry hoped he was, because she couldn't concentrate.

The relief in her voice settled it. "I'm sure." Kissing the back of her hand, he dumped the pieces from both their trays into the bag, stacked the cards and stowed it all haphazardly in the box. "Truth is, there's something important that I need to talk to you about."

"I…there is?" Merry didn't think she liked the sound of that. She couldn't take any more news or serious conversations right now. Could she?

With an effort, she forced her attention away from her own problems. He'd retained one of the game pieces and was rotating it between his fingers and thumb. Come to think of it…he'd done an awful lot of mouth-wiping during the meal. As though he was nervous about something. And now he was reaching for his laptop.

"Here," he patted the cushion beside him. "We both need to see this."

Curious, she slid closer. He'd opened his laptop and the monitor lit up to reveal… "Are you moving?" Her eyes flicked over the screen until they settled on the location indicator. Whew. At least he was looking at houses near Cadmia.

"My lease is up in December," he explained, scrolling down to the next listing.

"Wow. These are…quite the upgrade." Huge was the word. Five bedrooms, a three-car garage, and who knew what surprises the backyard held?

He chuckled. "One of the reasons I moved here was to see if I could live a normal life. This," he gestured at his apartment in general, "is bigger than the studios I used to sleep in."

"Sleep in?" Unconsciously, she drew a little closer to him. Her time in rentals had never been quite so bleak that she thought of them only as places to sleep.

"If I wasn't at work or the gym, I was usually sleeping." He shrugged and went back to the top of the page. Adjusted the settings for two-bedroom houses. "I'm going a little stir-crazy here, by myself, to be honest."

"In this little nest?" she asked without thinking.

His lips twisted wryly. "I'm sure it wouldn't seem so big if two people were sharing it. Or three."

Merry dropped her eyes. She hadn't thought of that. What did it mean that he was?

"I could extend my lease here for a while." He wished she'd look at him again.

"That might be best." She risked a glance at him through the curtain of her lashes. "At least until you get steady work." His eyes sparkled with humor, puzzling her.

"Merry, I need to tell you the truth about my—" his fingers lightly tapped the sides of his laptop as he hunted for the right phrase, "—financial situation."

"The truth?"

Closing his laptop, Tyrel set it on the table and shifted so that his arm was on the back of the couch between them. "Merry, I'm retired."

She blinked. "From the military."

"Yes." He leaned forward. "And from…work in general. I licensed some of my patents to the military. I'm not a multi-millionaire or anything, but it'll be a long time before I need to work for a living again." He hesitated, not sure how to interpret her tightly folded hands. "I thought you had a right to know I wasn't just taking a break."

"Wow. That's...amazing." Merry nodded once.

Tyrel had a funny, let-down feeling. It was sort of like when he'd told his grandparents. They heartily approved of his decision to try to find a life while there was still some time for one, but neither of them was overly excited by his account balance.

"You must be pretty brilliant." She didn't understand that startled look he gave her. "Well, you did invent something that nobody else has, didn't you?"

"Yeah. I guess I did." Funny that he'd never thought of it quite that way. Anyway, the smile she gave him meant more to him than the military's paycheck ever could.

"I'm glad you told me. It makes what I have to tell you easier. Sort of." He straightened away and she wondered what he thought she was leading up to. Or maybe he was disappointed in her response? "I'm not doing this very well, am I?"

Tyrel put his hand on hers, stilling them. "Something tells me you've got a big announcement of your own." He tried to cup her hands in his own, but she resisted.

"I sort of need these. So I can play the guitar," she explained haltingly. How was she ever going to sing? "Could I have a glass of water?"

It took a moment for him to catch up with the change of topic. "Won't be a second," he promised.

She'd be able to see him the whole time, but Merry smiled anyway as she reached for her case.

Tyrel heard a strum or two over the sound of water rushing into the glass, then individual strings being plucked and tuned. Deciding she might need time more than the drink, he turned the water off and straightened a few things before returning.

"Thanks." Merry accepted the glass and took a sip.

Not knowing what else to do, Tyrel reseated himself.

Merry willed her hands to stop shaking as she set the glass on the table. "It's been a while since I've played in front of anyone," she confessed.

He nodded at the instrument, hoping to take the pressure off of her. "Did you make that?"

"No." She shook her head, a faraway smile curving her lips softly as she stroked the rosewood headstock with her thumb. "My great-grandad did. He taught my grandad to play on it."

"And he taught you," Tyrel surmised, awed by the legacy.

"He did," she nodded. Sensing a profound respect in his words, she played the opening chords of her latest song, "I Will Dare."

He watched her eyes half-close. Saw her shoulders rise with a deep breath. Sat stunned as her rich, clear voice sang about risk and consequence.

At church, her lovely, reverent alto blended with the rest of the congregation. Now, she sounded different, somehow. More confident, more… The word eluded him.

Merry lingered over the last refrain.

It's okay to fall.
It's worse to never try.
So spread your wings…
And soar!

She let the notes fade before she looked at Tyrel. "I write and record songs for sale under the name of Helen Montgomery." The thud of her heartbeat was deafening in the ensuing silence. His mouth moved, but no sound came out.

"You…" He blinked and tried again. "*You're* Helen Montgomery? The singer the entire town's raving about?"

She flushed, thoroughly uncomfortable. Nodded.

"That's…amazing. I knew you had a nice voice, but wow, I never put it together."

"Well, you weren't supposed to, so that's a good thing." She focused on setting her guitar in the case to give him a minute to process.

"A good thing." He pinched the bridge of his nose. "That means you don't want anyone to know." Of course she didn't. This was Merry, anxiety and reserve personified in a very potent mix.

"Absolutely no one." Embarrassed at how quickly, and decisively, she'd snapped the answer, Merry clasped her hands tightly in her lap. She wanted to run away, but that wasn't an option. No, she'd trusted him with the truth and she had to see it through.

Sliding closer, he took her white-knuckled hands in his. Gently pried them apart and positioned both of their right hands over his heart.

"I will tell absolutely no one," he promised solemnly.

Her shoulders sagged in relief. Then…

"That my girlfriend is incredibly creative, talented, and has a voice worthy of Carnegie Hall."

"Tyrel, I…" She had no words. Nothing flowery, anyway. "Thank you."

Smiling, he kissed the backs of her hands and returned them to her.

"Thank you for telling me."

"I sort of had to." She felt heat rising in her cheeks. "I've, um, Helen has been invited to perform at the Christmas play and if something goes wrong," she didn't elaborate, the thought was the stuff of nightmares for her, "well, I didn't want you to find out that way."

"That's, that's quite an honor." That also put a different light on the situation. Yes, she was everything he'd said, but it boiled down to the fact that she was a celebrity. *He* was dating a celebrity!

He was thinking of marrying a celebrity. Which meant…what, exactly?

He got up. Walked to the far wall—a full five steps—and walked back.

"I pace, too." Rising, Merry set her guitar in its case. "Sometimes I even go for a walk." Relief flooded through her when he held out his hand. Tucking hers inside his, she went with him to the closet.

Once they were bundled up against the cold, they stepped out onto the street. Hand in hand, they made their way to the end of the block. At first, Tyrel's longer legs carried him along so swiftly that Merry almost had to run to keep up. Then, as he noticed, he adjusted his pace so that they were striding at the same speed.

"I guess I always had a traditional view of marriage," he said after a few blocks. "If he's at all able, the husband holds the responsibility for providing food and shelter."

Confused, Merry slipped her hand into the crook of his arm and slowed still further. "I guess

I have a traditional view too, then."

Tyrel looked sideways at her. "I'm struggling to see how I can hope to support you."

"Tyrel, wait." She stopped walking, waited for him to face her. "Do you think I'm rich or something?"

He tried running his fingers through his hair, but the gloves made it awkward. The hat made it impossible. Giving up he asked, "Aren't you?"

"Not like that." She turned toward his apartment. "C'mon. Let's go finish this conversation inside."

"Let's talk while we walk," he countered, smiling faintly. "Because I'm really confused."

"Okay. It's a good thing you live in town, y'know." She grinned up at his puzzled expression. "Sidewalks make things a lot easier." The walk, combined with the release of having told him about Helen, had loosened the gears of her brain again. "Now. Do you seriously want to buy a house?"

"What?" Startled to be back on that subject, he took half a block to respond. "No, not especially. That was my way of telling you… Of trying to tell you a couple of things."

She couldn't help the sigh that escaped. "I was afraid of that." He looked at her sharply and she lifted her free hand to ward off any negative misinterpretations of her statement. "I don't always do subtle. Ask any of my siblings." His eyebrows slowly returned to their 'at rest' position and she relaxed a little. "You were talking about buying a house, so I thought that was what you planned to do."

He laughed, his breath crystallizing in the cold. "Remember the bit about providing shelter? I didn't want you to worry that you were dating an out-of-work man who'd want to move in with you after the wedding."

She missed a step and he had to catch her. *Wedding* rang in her ears like the fire alarms from her college dorm hall.

Shifting his grip slightly, Tyrel held her in his arms. His nose was so cold it was starting to run and unless she was just pale from shock, her lips were starting to turn blue. Not a stellar setting for a first kiss.

"I probably could've waited to tell you that until we were inside," he half-laughed. The corners of her lips quirked up obediently, but her eyes never changed. They continued searching his as if the secrets of the universe were inside him somewhere. "I think you need some chocolate."

"Yeah." Strength was coming back to her legs and she carefully straightened away. "Hot chocolate, I hope."

"Good idea," he agreed.

They shivered the rest of the way to his apartment, where he hung up their coats and took her in his arms again.

"I'm not trying to rush you," he promised. "I just thought you deserved to know I'm not hopelessly impoverished." Sniffling, he drew back.

"And I wanted to be the one to tell you about my alter ego. But she's not rich by any stretch of the imagination." Was the tingling in her toes from the heat in his apartment? Or his proximity? Her gaze dropped to his mouth—and was arrested by the mucus trailing down his upper lip. Pulling a packet of tissues out of her pocket, she helped herself to one, then offered them to him. Maybe there were some perks to being herself after all. Sure, thawing noses spoiled romantic moments. Other than that, though, she didn't care.

"Thanks." Regretfully, he took one and wiped his nose. He tried to recapture the romantic feeling as they washed their hands at the kitchen sink, but when she squirted him with the faucet, he knew it was long gone.

"I wouldn't mind," she said, offering him the towel she'd just dried her hands on. "What you said. I'd rather stay where I am than move, so…" The answering light in his eyes sent her scurrying into the front room. "I better put my guitar away."

While he dried his hands, Tyrel pondered her reaction to him. Every time kissing her crossed his mind, he reminded himself that even holding hands was new to her. Trouble was, he was past ready to move on to kissing. Asking for patience as their relationship progressed at her speed had become part of his daily prayers. And it was worth it.

Chapter 15

The sun rose slowly Thanksgiving morning. Grudgingly, as if it wanted to sleep in like everyone else. Thick clouds absorbed most of the warmth, leaving the world bitter cold and gray. Even the sun's golden rays couldn't have done much to help today, though. As was often the case, it was a brown Thanksgiving. Here and there a tree still sported various shades of orange, but most of them had surrendered their leaves and now looked like strange works of modern art, their bare limbs stretching out every-which-way against the slowly brightening sky.

Eventually, Merry got up, folded the couch blanket, and trudged upstairs for a shower. Her room still smelled of lavender from her attempts to sleep the night before. It didn't help the knots in her spaghetti monster now, either. Tyrel had agreed to keep her alter ego a secret—even from her family. She trusted him, but she was still getting used to having other people in on her secret.

More family than just Chad and Heidi would be at the late Thanksgiving lunch. Hannah was home from college for a few days. Gwen and her family were driving over from Fire Clay. Granted, it could've been worse. The entire tribe would've turned out if they had any idea she was bringing her boyfriend.

Boyfriend. The thought simultaneously evoked a goofy grin and new knots in her phantom spaghetti monster.

The smile faded as she hesitated between her dresser and her closet. Boyfriends were great, especially the kind that planned to mature into a husband, but they sure complicated life. Last year she'd simply worn the t-shirt she found on top in her drawer. Couldn't even remember which one it was. This year?

Choosing two button-ups, Merry walked back into the bathroom and held them up. First one at a time. Then one on each side, overlapping, as she tried to pick one. They were both nice. She thought Tyrel would like either of them.

Except… Pickled beets and brown gravy were uniquely suited to creating permanent stains. And then there was the home-bottled grape juice to think about. It wouldn't take much of an *oops* to find herself wearing any of the three. Or all three at the same time. Then what? Her clothes usually followed a simple path from brand new to comfy-grungy to shop rags. Button-ups made terrible pajamas, in her experience. And she'd hate to have to tear up practically new clothes just because of a few stains.

Sighing, she hung them back up and dug into her t-shirt drawer. Down near the bottom she found a shirt she'd forgotten she owned. A shirt that she hoped was the perfect compromise in heather-gray, with three-quarter sleeves, white cuffs, and a white collar. Three imitation pearl buttons completed the look. Dressy, but not over the top.

Ready at long last, she carried her socks downstairs to the kitchen, where she dropped to her knees by the couch. She prayed around her fears for quite a while before she was able to put them into words. She was afraid that 'they' (her family) wouldn't like Tyrel. She was afraid that Tyrel wouldn't like the ones he met for the first time. Afraid that her fears would reach critical mass and cause an emotional implosion before dessert was served. Half-afraid that she was going to scuttle back upstairs and hide in the recording booth where nobody could find her.

Rising, she pulled out her phone. Opened her Sunday playlist. The opening strains of "I Stand All Amazed" poured into the room, soothing her soul like grape juice on a sore throat.

I stand all amazed at the love Jesus offers me,
Confused at the grace that so fully he proffers me.
I tremble to know that for me he was crucified,
That for me, a sinner, he suffered, he bled and died.

Setting her phone on the island, she slipped an apron over her carefully selected outfit and began setting up. Pre-cooked bacon wouldn't take long to reheat, and scrambled eggs didn't need much tending, so she pulled out her waffle irons. Once she had them both up and running, she puttered around the kitchen until Tyrel rang the doorbell promptly at ten. Buzzing him in, she switched off the music and hung up her apron. Nervously smoothed her shirt.

"It is *so* cold out there!" Tyrel announced as he let himself in. "I thought I was going to turn into a popsicle before I could make it from my car to your door." Hanging up his jacket, he shivered his way over to her and engulfed her in a bear hug. "Mmm. That's better." He meant it as a joke, but she surprised him by wrapping her arms around his waist and burying her face in his neck. Instinctively, he tightened his hold on her. Rested his cheek against her hair and prayed to know what to do next. Almost of its own volition, one hand began tracing circles on the small of her back.

She clung to him, drawing strength from his solidness. From the incredible feeling of safety that she found in his arms. She didn't want to let go.

"Merry?"

She felt his voice rumble in his chest and smiled.

"Merry…darling?" Smoothing his hand down her hair, he eased her head back. "Darling, look at me."

With an effort, she complied. Saw the worry wrinkles on his forehead. "Morning." It came out huskier than she expected.

"Morning," he returned, not sure whether to be relieved or more concerned. Maybe he'd misread the situation. The way she'd relaxed against him as though she planned to stay there. As though she belonged there. As always, being that close to her affected him. She fit so perfectly in his arms. So soft and warm.

Noticing his focus drifting down to her mouth, Merry blushed and drew back. "You're right on time," she observed breathlessly. She was much closer to being ready for a kiss than she'd ever believed possible. Just not before breakfast.

Tyrel forced a smile as he watched her walk away from him. "You promised me food," he reminded as lightly as he could. They finally finished off the last of the frozen food from Fresh last Saturday and she insisted it was her turn to cook that morning.

"And it's almost ready." She picked up a stack of freshly made waffles and a bowl of scrambled eggs. "Oh." She blinked in disbelief at the place settings. "I forgot the plates."

"I'll get them," he volunteered. Retrieving the gallon of milk he'd deposited on the far end of the island, he relocated it to near their place settings, then went to the cupboard. By the time he'd made it back around to what had officially become his place at the island, she'd added containers of bacon, butter, and syrup to the spread.

"You sure know how to set a table," he complimented her as he took his seat.

"Well, naturally," she teased, feeling more relaxed than she had in the last forty-eight hours. "The way to a man's heart is through his stomach, after all." Automatically, she offered him her hand.

As his hand closed over hers, memories of the stiffness of their first few interactions sprang to mind. They'd come a long way in a relatively short period of time. He spoke of that in the prayer that he offered, asking for guidance as they moved forward.

After he closed the prayer, Merry left her hand in his for several awe-filled seconds. Watched as he brought it up to his mouth and kissed the back of it lightly.

"I love you, Merry." It wasn't how he'd planned to tell her. It just…felt right to say it. Like finding the missing piece of the puzzle after scouring the house for it.

She'd waited a lifetime to hear those words and now, once again, the entertainment industry was proven wrong. No fireworks. No bolt of lightning running the length of her body. Instead, an overwhelming sense of the rightness of the moment settled over her. A joy welled up from the depths of her soul and lit up her whole world.

She wasn't even afraid to say, "I love you, too, Tyrel."

A slow smile spread across his face. "I hope your father feels the same way."

Her stomach shuddered, then became curiously quiet. "I'm sure he will." Hadn't he just prayed for things to go well? Talking with her father was definitely moving things forward.

He leaned forward and bumped his plate, which hit his glass.

Giggling, Merry reached out to steady it. "Good thing that wasn't full of milk."

Tyrel took a moment to mourn the loss of an opportunity, then released her hand and reached for the gallon jug. "It will be in a sec," he laughed. He filled both their glasses while he was at it, then dished up moderate portions of waffles, eggs, and bacon. The one downside he'd noticed to falling in love was that he'd started gaining weight.

"I hope your recipe for Belgian waffles isn't a secret," he told her later as he finished his milk. "Those were better than any restaurant I've eaten at."

"No secret." She toyed with the idea of telling him the truth about her chicken fettuccine, but she was still having fun with that. "Start with a mix and serve fresh."

"You make it sound so simple," he laughed. He reached for her plate, but she stopped him.

"I'll load the dishwasher later. C'mon, it's almost time for the annual Sawyer's Thanksgiving Day parade to start." Thank goodness none of her local nieces and nephews were in marching band. She'd much rather stay inside where it was comfortable and enjoy the festivities on her TV.

"Right." He helped collect the refrigerator items. "My first Sawyer's parade."

"I can't believe you've never seen one of these before." Merry curled up next to him, resting her head on his shoulder and wrapping her hands around his bicep. What did he work out with that he had biceps like a four by four hardwood post?

He wasn't sure he'd be watching this one, with his attention so thoroughly taken by the woman beside him. "How'd this tradition get started?" he asked dutifully, pressing a light kiss to the top of her head.

"I have no idea." Merry lifted her free shoulder in a shrug. "Mom just always called us in for it. We'd scatter out on the floor in front of the TV," she gestured descriptively, "and ooh and aww over the balloons and the floats." She frowned. "The performances used to be a lot classier, come to think of it."

He didn't have to wait long for an example of what she meant. "Hmm." He shifted so that he was turned mostly toward her instead of the screen full of half-frozen, skimpily clad females. "What would you like to talk about?"

Delighted, she laughed at his direct approach to ignoring the inappropriate routine and kissed his cheek before she realized what she was doing. Pressing her cheek against his shoulder, she held perfectly still as he bent closer.

He jerked back and slapped at his jean's pocket.

Recognizing the ringtone, he muttered, "I…have to take this."

Wide-eyed, Merry watched him simultaneously apologize to her and fish his phone out. Felt his lips on her forehead and heard him whisper, "Saved by the cell," before he winked and strode into the kitchen.

"Grandma, hi! And, happy Thanksgiving!" He chuckled at something she said, then shook his head. "No, sweetheart, remember? I told you I was going to spend Thanksgiving with," his gaze landed on Merry and he swallowed, "friends."

Merry wished for the first time in her life that she kept pillows on her couch. She could've used something to hold onto right then. Her head was spinning from two near misses—or should that be kisses?—in one morning. Suddenly, the change in Tyrel's tone of voice caught her undivided attention. Was something wrong?

"You what?" Tyrel pushed his fingers through his hair, trying not to panic. "No. What? No way," he laughed. "I'm ecstatic. I always love to see you guys."

The couch squeaked in protest when Merry, who'd half-risen to go to him, abruptly sat back down. Hard. Her lungs locked up and peace fled. She was *not* ready for this.

"Merry." Ending the call, Tyrel dropped to the floor in front of her, throwing his phone on the couch to take her face in his hands. "Merry!

Breathe!"

Something inside her responded to his touch and she obeyed, sucking in a huge, shuddering lungful of air.

"That's right." He held her gaze until she began breathing in rhythm with him. "You scared me out of ten years of my life, do you know that?" he asked, stroking her cheek with his thumb. "I look over and you're not breathing?"

"Sssorry," she choked.

"Oh, honey, that's…" Rising onto his knees, Tyrel wrapped her in a hug. "Don't apologize. That's not what I meant." Kissing her forehead, her eyes, her cheeks, and stopping just short of her lips, he murmured softly, "You're not in this alone."

The words swirled around in her mind like glitter snow in car headlights, reminding her that she never had been alone. As a daughter of heavenly parents, she'd never been left to face life alone. But this…hearing Tyrel's deep, warm, wonderful voice affirm that she had him, too…

Tyrel's world tilted as she shyly pressed her lips to his. For a heartbeat, he felt like a rocket breaking loose from earth's gravitational pull. He hit the ground with a thud when she pulled back, her lovely face an adorable shade of pink.

"So." Hazel-green eyes blinked at him. "Your grandparents decided to surprise you?"

Breathe. Tyrel nodded. "I guess they forgot I had plans." Moving carefully, he got to his feet, then seated himself a discreet distance away from her. Men might not do butterflies, but he had an entire squadron of C-5 Galaxy planes loaded with things he wanted to say to her doing loop de loops and barrel rolls in his stomach. And none of it was about his grandparents. "I told them I'd have to check with you before I could make plans with them."

Merry shut off the TV. "Let's go get them."

He blinked. "Shouldn't we ask your mom first?"

"I'll call her on the way over," she agreed as she got up. Held out her hand. "She always has leftovers for a week after Thanksgiving. So unless your grandparents have special dietary needs, she'll just want a heads up on how many plates to add to the table."

"And if they do have special diets?" he asked, standing and taking her by the waist.

Her breath hitched as her hands came up to grip his forearms. Had he always been this tall? "We'll figure something out."

Touching his lips to hers, he savored the moment. She smelled of soap, bacon, and syrup, and that ever-present shampoo. He ached to pull her closer, but denied himself.

Merry eased away from him. "You better call your grandparents," she suggested breathlessly.

Less than five minutes later, they were on their way to his apartment. Merry completed her call to her mother before they reached the first stop sign, leaving her with the rest of the ride to worry in. Which wouldn't solve anything.

"How…do things work from here? With us and kissing and…" Her voice trailed off. Unpredictability was not her strong suit—particularly where things that left her weak in the knees were concerned.

He covered her hand with his and answered firmly, "We both have to want it."

"Does kissing ever get to be like holding hands?" She turned hers so that they were palm to palm, and laced her fingers through his. "Ordinary?"

He squeezed her hand. "Yes, it can. After people have been together for a while, they sometimes take kissing for granted."

"That's what I thought." Leaning back against the seat, she rode in silence for a few blocks. "You've been so patient with me. I hate to ask for more." She inhaled shakily, uncomfortably aware of the heat creeping up her cheeks. "I'm just not ready for, um, public displays of affection."

"There's no hurry," he agreed. Smiling, he gently rubbed his thumb along her knuckles. "What size ring do you wear?"

Her heart lodged in her throat and she shook her head. "I don't know. I hardly ever wear jewelry."

"About that." He shot her a sidelong glance. They were nearly at his place and he needed to know a lot more than a ring size for what he had in mind, so changing the subject wasn't a terrible idea. He might even learn something that'd help him pick out a Christmas present for her. "Is that for safety reasons? Because you're worried it'll get caught on something in the shop?"

"That's a valid consideration, but I don't think that's it." Her forehead creased slightly as she pondered the question. "I think I used to want to wear jewelry. I remember having a small jewelry box as a teenager."

"What happened?"

She shrugged. "I guess I stopped wearing it. Got completely out of any semblance of the habit. Then, I realized I had a box of things I didn't want."

"You gave it away?" he inferred, amazed.

"Most of it. I kept a few of my grandmother's things." She bit her lip. "I feel kind of guilty about that. Jewelry, it's sort of art, isn't it? Has to be seen to be appreciated or enjoyed. Here I've got half a dozen pieces sitting in the back of a drawer, going to waste."

"I've never thought of it that way." He squeezed her hand. "But it's okay for you to keep those memories. It's okay for them to be *your* memories, too. That's not a waste." Spotting a strange car in front of his duplex, he shot her a grin. "Now, if we were talking about a cake or something. The kind with huge buttercream roses? Keeping one of those in the back of a drawer, that would be a tragedy."

And so it was that Merry had a huge grin on her face the first time she saw his grandparents.

Chapter 16

"Merry," Tyrel helped her out of the car, "I'd like you to meet my grandmother, Joan Anderson."

"Hello Sister Anderson." Merry offered her hand. And was enveloped in a warm hug by a woman a good four inches shorter than she was.

"Call me Joan," a pleasant voice invited. "All of my friends do."

Released from the hug, Merry looked down into the sparkling blue eyes of a pleasantly plump woman. "I will, thank you."

"And you can call me Jared."

Merry looked up and up into the tanned, weathered face of Tyrel's grandfather. "Yes, sir." Automatically, she offered her hand and it was swallowed up in his massive paw.

"Sir Jared. Hmm." He stroked his chin with his free hand, then winked at her. "Has a nice ring to it."

Merry laughed out loud. "I'm so glad to meet you both."

"Not half as glad as we are to meet you," Joan assured her, winking cheekily at Tyrel. "Now, why don't we ride in the back so we can talk?" She arched an eyebrow at Merry.

Tyrel put his hand on Merry's shoulder, ready to jump in if she needed rescuing, but found that she was smiling.

"Alright," Merry agreed. "How was your trip?"

Joan shuddered. "Don't get me started!" She threw up her hands and marched to the back passenger door, which Tyrel immediately opened for her.

"She doesn't like flying," Tyrel murmured to Merry as he shut one door and opened the next for his grandfather.

"Good to know," Merry murmured back. She almost made it to the other door before he reached it.

Intent on eavesdropping, Tyrel took his time settling himself into the driver's seat and buckling up. His grandfather's hand gripped his shoulder, the familiar contact taking him back decades to their early morning driving lessons.

"How're you liking your new home, Ty?"

Turning the key in the ignition and catching a glimpse of Merry in the rearview mirror, he smiled. "I love it, Grandpa." Luckily, the roads were even emptier than usual, as he divided his attention between keeping an ear on the conversation behind him and answering his grandfather's questions about Cadmia.

To her intense delight, Merry found that Joan was one of those rare people who talked enough to take the pressure off, without going over the edge into a monologue.

Yes, it was true Joan didn't like flying, but frankly, she preferred a few hours of crowded, questionable transportation to a day and a half on the road. Oh, Merry liked to fly? Wonderful! Flying opened the world to travelers. So many places Joan would've liked to see—if only she could walk there!

"And here we are!" Merry gestured to where her home was filling the windshield.

"This is where you live?" Joan gasped.

"And work," Merry clarified. "The bottom floor is my workshop."

"Really?" Jared stared wistfully at the building. "I'd love to see that."

"Tyrel can show you around while Joan and I get things together," suggested Merry.

"Sure," Tyrel agreed, shutting the car off. "You won't believe the project she's working on right now." In the rearview mirror, he saw Merry's mouth open and snap shut. "We'll have to be careful not to touch it," he added, remembering the way she'd reacted to his attempt at helping her move it.

"Never disturb someone else's project," Jared's baritone approved.

"Joan," Merry returned her attention to her guest. "How do you feel about elevators?" She'd intentionally purchased a lift mechanism that would handle twice her own weight.

After Jared made a point of inspecting the lift box and asking a few questions, Joan agreed to ride up to the verandah in it.

"I don't do so well with stairs anymore," she admitted as she stepped aboard. Holding onto the waist-high wall on one side, she nodded to indicate that she was ready.

"Transfer to the verandah once the box stops," Merry instructed. "I'll join you in a minute." Joan called out to Jared all the things she could see from her new perch while the box came back down, giving Merry a chance to whisper to Tyrel, "I'm sorry I overreacted about the secretary."

"What?" Tyrel frowned, puzzled.

"That night. Halloween. When you tried to help me with the…desk." Merry bit her lip. "You were just trying to help."

Reading sincere contrition in her eyes over something he'd considered resolved, Tyrel took her hands in his. "You barely knew me, Merry. Our personalities bumped, that's all."

"Bumped?" She wrinkled her nose at him. "Don't you mean clashed?"

"Nah." He squeezed her fingers and helped her into the box. "That's for when people can't or won't get past things."

She was tempted to tell him again that she loved him, but just then Joan called down.

"There's a car just pulling into the house next door. It's nice to see families getting together for Thanksgiving."

A micro-shudder passed through Merry, who nudged Tyrel back and switched the lift on. "We'll be at least twenty minutes," she told him. "I'll buzz you two in first."

"My goodness, you have an enormous kitchen!" Joan watched wide-eyed as Merry shifted into gear. Leery of interfering in another woman's kitchen, she wisely asked, "How can I help?"

Merry immediately put her to work setting up microwaveable bowls on the island while she went to the freezer. Returning loaded down with bags of green beans, broccoli and cauliflower mix, and corn on the cob, she armed Joan with scissors then retrieved a second, smaller but powerful microwave from her appliance closet.

Leaving Joan to run the microwaves, she filled a pot with water and set it to heat. In the pantry she lifted down a canister of dried potato flakes.

"This is unbelievable," Joan remarked for the third time as Merry lined a cardboard box with towels.

"If you say so." She flashed a grin at the remark because, to her, it was a somewhat typical mad dash. Organization and a little planning went a long way in semi-emergencies like this.

As Joan lidded the bowls of piping hot vegetables and stored them in the box where they could keep each other warm, Merry scraped the mashed potatoes into another bowl. Handing it to Joan for lidding, she hurried over to the intercom and gave a two-minute warning to the men.

"You go down first," Merry insisted to Joan a moment later. "I'll handle the box." It was so cold out that she added a final towel to the top of the box before heading out onto the verandah.

"Okay, let's buckle up," Tyrel suggested to his grandparents when he read the tension in Merry's body as she rode the lift down. "We're just going next door, but I'd hate to explain that to a curious policeman."

Diverted by his lame joke, Joan and Jared did as he asked, which put them all in the car and ready at about the same time. Somehow, Merry ended up in the front seat this time.

"We're almost there," Tyrel assured her softly, taking her near hand in his. Her slight squeeze in return told him he'd interpreted her tension correctly.

Merry's seatbelt got wrapped around the box somehow when she tried to get out, so she was still in her seat by the time Tyrel opened the door for her. On the other side of the car, his grandfather was performing the same service for Joan. Merry's appreciation for Tyrel's gentlemanly gesture went up a couple of notches as she realized it was a family tradition.

"There you are!" Elaine stood in the open front door, drying her hands on a dishrag. "Merry, I declare. The kids were all getting hopeful that they wouldn't have any vegetables this year."

Merry laughed and shook her head, knowing that wasn't true. Her contribution was a drop in the proverbial bucket when it came to

Thanksgiving preparations.

"I'm Merry's mother," Elaine introduced herself as Joan and Jared came up the steps. "I hope you'll pardon the chaos."

Merry surrendered the box to Tyrel, who headed for the serving table where Heidi was already rearranging something.

"Mom," she looked over her mother's shoulder to where her father had appeared, "Dad. These are Tyrel's grandparents, Joan and Jared Anderson." Mental snapshots of the moment burned into her memory. The giddy expression on her mother's face as she reached out to hug Joan. The serious way the two men sized each other up while shaking hands. The concern in her father's eyes when he thought nobody was looking. The looks on her siblings' faces as they began to get curious.

"Sister McKinney." Tyrel popped up at Merry's elbow. "I'm sure Joan has already thanked you, but we truly appreciate you making room for us all today."

"Oh, no." Elaine tittered. "It's our pleasure!"

"Brother McKinney." Tyrel held out his hand and it was seized in a vice-like grip. "Thank you for having us." He met the older man's searching gaze directly, not in challenge, but with a soul-deep certainty that he was looking at his future father-in-law.

Andy McKinney released Tyrel's hand. "Folks,

if you'll join us?" he invited a shade awkwardly, motioning for Jared and Joan to follow him into the dining room.

As if by some coded signal, parents and older children began rounding up the rest of the crew, bringing them in toward the tables. Toddlers were pacified with hugs and promises of food, and in short order, a reverent silence had descended on the group.

"Andrew," Brother McKinney looked at the grandson who'd been named for him. "Would you offer the prayer, please?"

Andrew squared his seventeen-year-old shoulders and nodded. Closed his eyes before he could give in to the temptation to look at the visitors again.

Tyrel held Merry's hand during the humble prayer and smiled at her after the 'amen.' Under the cover of the instant orderly disorder as the lines formed around the serving table, he leaned in and asked quietly, "What do you want first? A boy or a girl?"

Her reflexive embarrassment was overridden by the emotions the prayer had evoked in her. "Yes." Thank goodness they'd already discussed having children or the question might have sent her running for cover.

The sparkle in her eyes stole his breath. This was a Merry he'd never seen before, ten times more beautiful than he already knew she was.

"Here." Merry's nine-year-old nephew, Mark,

shoved paper plates into their hands. "Utensils and napkins at your places, okay?" He relayed the information in a disinterested monotone, oblivious to the spell he'd just broken.

"Thank you, Mark," Merry responded hastily. She didn't get to see Gwen's family often and tried to make a point of calling her six children by the correct names.

"How do you remember all their names?" Tyrel asked once the boy was out of earshot. There were well over two dozen children in the room. And this wasn't even the whole family!

She laughed. "A lot of practice." Noticing Chad heading their way, she grabbed Tyrel's arm and tugged him into line behind Joan and Jared, who were cheerfully chatting with Andrew. "I think they're onto us."

"Onto us?" Tyrel glanced around until he accidentally made eye contact with Chad. "Oh. Do you mind?"

The question brought her up short. The type of person who kept important things to herself, yes, absolutely she minded opening herself up to other people's uninvited opinions and interference. On the other hand, after years of living because she hadn't died yet, she was embarking on a whole new path, mined with tough decisions and well-meaning intrusions. Yet what choice did she have? It was too late not to love Tyrel.

Rapidly reaching the conclusion that forward was the only direction open to her, she lifted her chin. Put her hand in his. "Scared to death," she murmured even as she shifted to face Chad.

"That makes two of us," he concurred, mimicking her motion and squeezing her hand.

"Hey, Ty." Chad punched him lightly on the shoulder. "We'll be playing a little football after lunch. Want to join us?"

Ty hadn't survived war games in the military to get suckered into a football game with overprotective brothers. "No, thanks." He shook his head. "Football's not my thing."

Chad stared at him in disbelief. "What is your *thing*?"

"Martial arts." If that didn't make Chad back off, he was going to have to scrounge up a tank from somewhere.

"You…"

"The line's moving." Merry cut Chad off and pulled Tyrel along with her. "Are you serious?" she whispered.

"Don't you believe me?"

"I…" Merry let the question spin in her mind briefly. That didn't fully explain his physique, but it certainly removed a lot of question marks. "I guess I do."

He smiled, pleased. "You should. I've been studying Kajukenbo for two decades."

"Kah-joo…what?"

"Kajukenbo," he pronounced it more slowly. "It's a composite of several disciplines."

"Ohhhkay." She moved forward with the

line. "How did you get started?"

He told her the short version as they finished making their way through the line, then let the topic shift to flow with the conversations going on around them at the table.

Throughout the meal, Tyrel felt eyes on him. Twice he caught Heidi and Gwen exchanging glances. Meanwhile, Chad and Merry's brothers-in-law, Matt and Darren, were in conference over what was left of the pie. What worried him, though, was the way Brother McKinney was pushing his food around on his plate. He'd counted on the meal to put him in a good mood. Maybe it would be better to wait?

"Cleanup time!" Heidi clapped her hands. "Hurry scurry!"

Startled, Tyrel watched the kids jump to their feet. "What's this?" he asked Merry.

"Redrock Bears," she laughed. "I'll show you the cartoon sometime. We're a little more organized than they are, though. Recycling to the right. Burnables to the left." Stacking her paper plate on top of his, she passed them along accordingly. Plastic utensils went to the right and grandkids showed up at the ends of the tables to collect it all.

"Keep your glass," she advised. A moment later, a magic marker came down and she labeled their plastic cups.

"Okay, this is impressive," he acknowledged. The older grandkids surrounded the serving table, where they were dividing and conquering the leftovers.

"Hours to make the meal, minutes to eat it, and, done this way, minutes to clean up afterward." She gestured toward the kitchen. "Thank goodness for dishwashers."

"Electric or two-handed?" he quipped.

"Some of both," she laughed.

Tyrel stiffened as a hand settled on his shoulder. Oh great. Here it was. The do-or-die football moment.

"Do you mind if I borrow Tyrel for a few minutes?" Brother McKinney smiled down at his youngest.

Tyrel felt his mind twist in a vain attempt to catch up with what was happening. Brother McKinney wanted to talk to him? He made eye contact with his grandfather, who had shifted to the edge of his seat. A subtle shake of his head was the best he could do under the circumstances.

As he rose, he forgot to let go of Merry's hand, accidentally revealing to anyone who was looking—and it felt like everyone over fifteen was—that they'd been holding hands under the table.

Merry left her hand in his, surprised to find that she didn't mind. Her reflexes were so tuned to keeping secrets that if she'd thought of this scenario last night, she would've had a beaut of a nightmare about it. Now it felt as natural as breathing.

He gave her hand a squeeze before releasing it. Followed her father…out the back door? Not into a room where they could shut a door and talk privately?

"Have a seat." Andy gestured at the twin padded rockers. Watched his grandchildren frolicking across the brown yard. "How long have you and Merry been dating?"

"Four weeks."

Andy nodded. "Exclusively?"

Tyrel pondered the question a moment, considering for the first time that Merry's parents might not be aware of their daughter's emotional distress on the subject. She'd only shared it with him under considerable pressure. Remembering that she hadn't even told them about her singing only served to strengthen his resolve to keep her confidences.

"Yes sir."

Andy's head swiveled around, his gaze piercing. "Why is that?"

"Because I intend to marry her."

Andy blinked. "Do you."

"Yes, but I'm not making any unilateral plans Brother McKinney." Tyrel sent up a prayer of thanks for every single officer who'd ever put him on the spot as he steadily returned his future father-in-law's gaze. "Merry's got a mind of her own."

Andy grunted and resumed watching his

grandchildren. "That's her biggest problem." From the corner of his eye, he saw Tyrel's jaw sag. "Or hadn't you noticed that she doesn't fit in anywhere?" A sigh escaped him. "Even in her own family."

Tyrel sat back in his chair and tried to absorb what he'd just heard. "I noticed." Today seemed a little better than the Sunday he'd come over for dinner. Perhaps because there was no longer a life-sized secret between them.

"That's not going to be a problem for you?" Wise old eyes assessed him from under graying brows.

Out in the yard, the 'Mother, May I?' game progressed from one end of the row of participants to the other while Tyrel studied on the question. And the man asking it. A man who left church as soon as it was over, just like his daughter did. A man who rarely spoke in class at church, just like his daughter. A man who stood alone in a crowd—just like his daughter.

"I asked myself that same question on our first date." Tyrel rocked his chair thoughtfully. "We went to the trunk-or-treat together. She only warmed up to a few people."

Andy nodded. "Like I said, she's different. Does things her own way. Spent her life paying the price."

"The price?" Again, Tyrel's mind went back to the night in the hayfield. Brother McKinney might not know the precise nature of Merry's torment, but his words and tone of voice made it plain that he was no stranger to suffering.

"The more time you spend around people who can't figure you out, the more you wonder what's wrong with you. Because there are lots of them and they all get along fine. They're normal, so you're *ab*normal." Andy's hands formed into fists. "Gets mighty lonely. Lonely like the bitter winter wind that sucks the heat right out of you. Seeps into your soul, starves you..."

"Andy?" Elaine came out onto the porch. Put her hand on her husband's shoulder. "Andy, it's too cold for you to be out here without a coat on."

"We're almost done," Tyrel intervened, rising respectfully.   His understanding of Sister McKinney had just broadened by about a thousand percent. On the surface, she was the polar opposite of her reserved husband. Those who took the time to scratch that surface, though, just might realize that she was, as the scriptures said, "an help meet for him." She was exactly what he needed, made ever more so over their years of loving each other. It was inspiring really. And incredibly humbling. "He needed to ask my intentions regarding your daughter."

Chapter 17

Tyrel grinned happily to himself as he parked his car at Merry's and climbed out. It was just over a week since Thanksgiving and he had a brilliant idea.

She must've been watching for him, because the door to her shop opened immediately.

"Alright," she called, voice muffled by her scarf as she crunched through last night's snow. "What's the big mystery?" As she got closer, she saw that he was holding a cane and her anxiety spiked. Was he alright? Should she try to coax him inside, suggest a less strenuous activity?

Um…wait. She didn't know what they were doing.

Nevertheless, questions and concerns started building inside her, nearly choking her and she gripped her keys tightly. Reminded herself of prayers she'd offered that morning and felt a sweet peace wash over her. Other thoughts came, including one rather obvious one—Tyrel knew what he could handle.

"You'll see." He laughed out loud and hugged her instead of answering. Waited for her to react to his cane, but though he could tell she had noticed it, she didn't mention it.

"You're going to have to tell me soon," she insisted, sacrificing the warmth of her pocket to hold hands with him on the way to her truck. His laughter was a good sign. Right? "I *am* driving." She almost added, *At your request.*

"Well." He solicitously helped her into the truck, where she promptly put the key in and started the engine. "We're going shopping."

"You want to go shopping for family home evening?" she asked incredulously. Her family had done a lot of different things growing up, everything from service projects to playing basketball, but she couldn't remember ever considering shopping to be a bonding or growing experience.

"Yep." Closing the door, he grinned at her exasperated expression and walked carefully around to get in on the other side. Snow wasn't quite as hard for him to walk in as sand, but it still wasn't easy.

She threw the truck into gear and headed for the road as soon as he was buckled in. "Okay, boss. Which way?"

"Left."

She kept trying to guess where they were going as he guided her first toward, then past the church building. Frowned when he directed her to turn onto a narrow track that led into the woods. Eyed the prominently placed 'No Trespassing' sign with trepidation. What in the world did Tyrel want to buy? And from whom? Sasquatch? The snow ahead was untouched, so they were the first ones to drive here since last night's snowfall, and maybe longer.

"We're nearly there," he promised when she slowed way down.

"Great," she muttered, eyes and mind on the deceptive snow buildup. A rock would most likely still be visible, but a deep rut or pothole could easily hide under the drift, and she didn't want to hit one at full speed.

As the truck crept along, he wondered uneasily if he should've told her what he had in mind. Sure it would've spoiled the surprise. On the other hand, he'd noticed that she didn't really like surprises and should've taken that into account.

"What is this place, anyway?" She cringed at her grumpy tone. "I mean, I've never been back here." That sounded better.

"I guess I can tell you now." He almost heaved a sigh of relief when Alec's cabin came into view. "We're picking out a Christmas tree."

She looked at him, brow furrowed, and parked.

"Why?"

Startled, he stared at her. "Why?"

"Why are we getting a tree?" She asked the whole question this time.

"Why are we getting a tree?" Great, he sounded like a two-year old, repeating everything she said.

She folded her arms across her chest and waited.

"Because it's fun?" He smiled weakly. Definitely should've told her what he was planning.

"You think so?" She didn't, but if he did... She'd go along with it to be nice.

"Yes?" The word came out hesitantly, as though he wasn't sure it was the right answer.

"If that's what you want." She wasn't going to ruin her afternoon with him just because she didn't see the point in getting a Christmas tree. "I didn't bring my chainsaw, though."

"Ah!" Unbuckling, he pointed at the small shed by the cabin. "Alec said we could use his."

"Alec?" She studied the cabin with renewed interest. This must be the place Grace had told her about.

"There's, um, just one little difficulty." He tapped his left knee. "The snow makes it hard for me to walk with my prosthetic."

Surprised, she sat up and looked at the snow-covered ground that surrounded him. "He's probably got a snow shovel around here somewhere," she thought aloud.

Tyrel forced his eyebrows to go back down. That...would never have occurred to him.

"Probably." He fidgeted with his cane and her eyes settled on it. "This actually helps a lot. I only mentioned it because I was hoping you wouldn't mind walking ahead of me." He waited as patiently as he could for her to answer, the tilt of her head telling him she was thinking it over. It was a simple request. What was there to think about?

"If I go first, then you can walk in my steps.

Is that it?"

"Exactly."   Smiling at her, he mentally smacked himself for being impatient. This was all still new to her.

At the shed, she found Alec's chainsaw and everything they needed to get it ready.

"Okay, let's," she swallowed 'get this over with' and substituted, "do this."

His excited smile melted her heart, but did nothing for her chilled digits. She plowed ahead, wishing for his arm around her, as he rambled on and on about the great memories he had of Christmas trees as a kid. Lucky him.

Periodically he'd point out a landmark and make a course correction, and she took comfort in the fact that he had a specific destination in mind.

"And here we are."   Alec's directions were perfect and Tyrel made a mental note to thank him. However, Merry hadn't said a word since leaving the shed, which couldn't be a good sign.

She caught her breath as they stopped in front of a small stand of snow-covered pines. Various shades of green stood out like promises of spring and renewal in the drab brown and white world. The sunlight on the snowy branches made the trees sparkle as if they were strung with diamonds.

For an instant, she was too caught up in the beauty to notice the cold.

Tyrel studied the trees with a practiced eye.

He didn't have to worry about ceiling height this time, but they probably should get one short enough to fit in the bed of Merry's truck. Which…was quite a ways behind them. And he couldn't see a way to get the truck in there.

"How about that one?" He pointed at a medium-sized tree on their right.

"Hmm?" She followed his finger and frowned. "Isn't that too big for your apartment?"

He opened his mouth to spring the rest of the surprise and stopped to rub the back of his neck. Oh yeah. He *definitely* should've discussed this with her first.

"It'll look great at your place," he suggested tentatively.

"My place?" She shook her head. "No thanks, I never have a Christmas tree." Stepping away from him, she assessed the trees from a different angle. From the corner of her eye, she could see him gaping at her.

"Didn't you have a tree when you were a kid, though?" He couldn't hide his shock.

"Yeah, we had one every year." She blew into one cold hand, shifted the chainsaw over and blew into her other hand. "Everybody put their presents in a huge pile under the tree. By the time 'Santa'," she used air quotes, "came and went, we had a small mountain."

"That sounds awesome." Even more puzzled that she didn't want a tree he asked, "Where do you put your presents now?"

"On top of the end table." She shrugged. "There aren't that many."

The bitterness lacing her words tore at his heart. He knew, if only from what her father had said, that she often felt like an outsider, even at gatherings where only her own family was present. It never would've occurred to him, though, to see only the empty spaces under a Christmas tree.

Then she stated firmly, "Trees are way more trouble than they're worth."

His jaw sagged as he listened to her list the things she hated about Christmas trees. They had pokey pine needles, which fell off and took months to finally finish vacuuming up. And the sap! Ugh. Getting rid of the sap—once you found it—was a chore she did *not* enjoy. Putting the lights on. Taking the lights off.

"They're just a hassle from start to finish." She grimaced. All of this talk about Christmas trees just underlined the painful reality that the worst thing about them was how they magnified her aloneness.

She didn't mind that he wanted one, of course. In fact...

Prepared to suggest a modestly-sized tree on the far side of the group. He was staring off into the forest, lips tightly compressed. "Tyrel? What's wrong?" She had a pretty good idea. She'd been too honest again. That never worked well for her.

"Nothing, I…" He leaned on his cane, thinking hard, more worried about the barely-hidden fear in her question than the Christmas tree. He'd never encountered anyone who felt this way and had no idea what to do with what she'd just told him. "I mean, um." Seeing her shoulders start to slump stung him into action and he started across the clearing, intent on taking her in his arms.

She hung back a moment, immersed in her own feelings, until he stumbled.

"Tyrel!" Lunging forward, she got there in time to stand awkwardly in front of him.

"It's okay." Poking his cane into the snow, he left it standing there and cupped her face in his hands.

She started to hug him, then remembered she was holding the chainsaw. "One sec." She carried the chainsaw over to a dry stump and set it down. Walked shyly back over to him and was grateful when he seamlessly picked up right where he'd left off, his arms reaching for her waist.

"I'm sorry." He rested his cold cheek against her knit cap. "I thought we'd have a great time today. I thought…well, I only saw things from my perspective. I…"

She cut him off with a kiss that warmed them both. Her eyes remained closed as he kissed the tip of her nose, followed the curve of her cheek, then cradled her close.

"So," he whispered huskily. "What would you like to do for family home evening?"

"Let's discuss that over a late lunch at Blinky's, okay?" She squeezed him once then stepped away. Caught his hand and tried to tug him along with her.

"Hang on." Turning back to the trees, he pulled out his phone and took a few pictures. "There." He flashed her a grin. "At least we sort of got a Christmas tree."

"I love you." Her cheeks heated despite the cold and she shuffled her feet, suddenly shy. "For trying to understand." Tears stung her eyes and she couldn't look at him as she sniffled. "For not making me feel stupid or inferior for feeling this way. For…"

He softly pressed a kiss to her lips. "I love you, too." He knew he was interrupting, but sometimes that was okay. He wasn't about to let her go on demeaning herself, however indirectly.

"If I walk beside my steps from before," she asked suddenly, "could I walk beside you, too?"

A slow smile spread across his face and he wrapped his free arm around her in answer.

She snuggled close all the way to her truck, where they were reluctantly parted by seatbelts. Blinky's wasn't far and, thankfully, was only sparsely occupied at this time of day.

Tyrel drew her to a booth and put his arm around her, keeping her close to him as they studied the menu and placed their order. He even went so far as to wink at an openly curious Susan, who gave him a shocked look and nearly ran into the edge of the counter she'd worked behind for twenty years.

"Do you really want a tree?"

"I'd like one, yes." He'd considered saying no. But—she'd been honest with him. "To me, they represent years of memories of time spent with my grandparents. Laughing. Talking." He couldn't help smiling. "A lot of important things happen around Christmas trees."

Sighing, she leaned her head against his shoulder. "We always gathered around the tree as kids on Christmas eve so Dad could read the Christmas story to us."

She missed that. She'd tried reading it to herself a few times and it made her so sad and lonely that she'd stopped. That was the worst part about going from a large family while growing up to a big, empty house as an adult. And since her experimental Christmas party turned her into a hermit for two weeks afterward, she hadn't known what else to do but go on being lonely.

"I'm glad your memories of them aren't all bad." He kissed the top of her head, his eyes closing in a silent prayer of gratitude for their open communication.

"Sorry to interrupt, guys." A teenager bustled up to the table and plunked their plates down. "I'll be right back with your drinks."

They chuckled and joined hands as they blessed the food.

"I want you to have a tree." She drew circles on the tabletop with her finger. "And I think I know how we can both be happy about it."

"You do?" He caught himself before his enthusiasm carried him away. He could imagine her telling herself she was happy because he was—whether she was actually happy or not. "You're sure?" She nodded. "Absolutely positive?"

Laughing, she bumped him with her shoulder. "Yes."

"What's your plan?"

She outlined it as they ate and he was grinning from ear to ear by the time they finished.

"Darling, you're brilliant." He kissed her forehead. "Ready?"

"Let's go." Merry surprised herself by waving to a gaping Susan as they left. "Want to drive?"

"Sure!" He drove them to Beryl, the next town, and followed her directions to Nordson's Christmas tree lot. "Lucky we're shopping early." Catching her hand, he held it firmly. "These probably go quickly."

They didn't have to go far to find the rows of live Christmas trees.

"Which one?" she asked, perfectly willing to let him pick.

"Mmm, that depends." He winked roguishly at her. "On which one you like."

"If this was a lumberyard, you can bet I'd have an opinion. But since Christmas trees are your area of expertise," she poked him lightly in the side, "I think you should decide."

They went back and forth briefly, their moods improving as they enjoyed each other's company. Eventually, they settled on a friendly-looking little guy and Tyrel took the tag to the office where he paid for it. Returning with one of the workers, they rolled it onto a dolly and loaded it onto Merry's tailgate lift.

"Will it be safe back there?" She frowned uncertainly as the lift raised it. "I don't want it to go rolling around or anything."

"I could ride with it," he suggested.

"Ha." She wasn't amused. "Ha." Climbing into the back of her truck, she rearranged things so that she could strap the tree into one corner.

Getting the small tree into her house was as easy as reversing the process using her dolly and the lift box to her balcony. And then it hit him.

"Oh nuts." He smoothed the old sheet she'd brought out to put under the pot. "We didn't get any decorations."

She bit her lip and looked out at the rapidly darkening landscape. "Guess we'll just have to use what I've already got."

Startled, he followed her up the stairs to the attic, where she loaded him down with boxes of more ornaments and lights and baubles than their little tree could possibly hold. But oh what fun they had putting them on!

"Not that way." She giggled when he 'accidentally' wrapped the lights around her wrist, then tried to steal a kiss. Since she was still recovering from his kisses in the clearing, she quickly turned her head and held up the shoebox of ornaments. "What do you think? Red Christmas birds? Or white ones?"

Taking the hint, he released her wrist. "Both."

"Both?" She eyed the tree skeptically. "I don't think there's enough room!"

"Tada!" He plugged in the antique lights, which he'd inspected carefully as he'd untangled them, and the tree glowed with the festive colors. "I can't believe how big these bulbs are," he marveled. "I've seen smaller walnuts!"

"They belonged to my grandparents. All of this did." Gesturing at the piles of boxes at their feet, she hung a bird, then a bauble. "Those lights are at least as old as I am." She bit her lip, instantly regretting her reference to her age.

With any other woman, Tyrel might've tried a quip or a compliment such as, *So not a day over eighteen, right?*

Tonight, however, he moved behind her and slipped his arms around her waist. "The kids are going to love them."

"I hope so," she said in a small voice.

"Hey, you know what's missing?" He snapped his fingers. "Music! Christmas music!"

Turning to get his phone from where he'd left it on the counter, his foot struck a shoebox, knocking the cover off. "Wow."

"What? Did you find something?"

"Just gold, that's all." Squatting, he examined the cassette tapes, most of which had handwritten labels—including one marked simply 'Radio.' He looked up at her, one eyebrow raised. "Radio?"

"You remember radios," she teased. "That big box that used to sit in the window with a silver collapsible rod sticking out of it?"

"And a smart aleck DJ inside it?" He rolled his eyes as he got to his feet, holding the dilapidated box carefully.

"Bingo." She snickered. "My grandparents recorded hours of Christmas music off the radio."

"Hours?" He checked the box. Most of the cassettes were in professionally-designed cases. "So there's another box of these around somewhere?"

"Maybe even two." She brushed a thumb across a salt dough ornament with 1986 written on the back in a childish scrawl. The whole family had made those that year, but she thought she remembered making this sad little snowman personally. That is, his expression was cheerful enough. She'd drawn his smile almost from one side of his hat-line to the other. But there were permanent indents from her unskilled fingers in the lopsided figure.

"I don't see any more down here." He finished his quick search of the other boxes. "Alright if I go check upstairs?"

"Hmm? Oh, sure." She called after him, "You better look around for something to play them with while you're up there!"

"Will do!" At the top of the stairs, he opened the attic door and flipped the light on. Passing dozens of interesting things, including an old trunk with travel labels from as far away as Madagascar, he reached the spot where they'd gotten the ornaments.

Hmm. One tidy stack of plastic totes was further out from the wall than the others. Moving it, he mentally cheered at the sight of a leaning tower of ancient shoeboxes.

Stooping to get them, he spotted something else. Something about an inch thick and green under the dust.

Overcome with a curiosity he couldn't explain, he worked the plank of wood free. Leaned it against the wall and tried not to sneeze. Even if he could've ignored the shape, the tiny bulbs poking out of one side clinched it.

This stubby little thing was a Christmas tree. *Her Christmas tree?* Yes, he could imagine it perched on the end table in her living room, a handful of presents stacked at its base.

Rubbing the back of his neck, he took a deep breath. And sneezed. Each sneeze stirred up more dust, provoking another sneeze, until finally he sneezed so hard he thought he was going to fly up and hit the ceiling like a cartoon character.

"Are you okay up there?"

"Fine!" Jerking the front of his shirt up over his nose, Tyrel pinched off the next two sneezes. His ears ached now, but so did his nose and throat, so he figured he'd won in the long run.

Leaning against a stack, he waited until his breathing had returned to normal, then wiped tears from his eyes. Putting the 'tree' back where he'd found it, he scooped up the boxes of cassettes, mindful of the split corners. Spotted a radio in one corner and retrieved it.

He paused at the door to glance back at the hidden tree, a lump in his throat. He knew he couldn't fix a lifetime of hurt in a single holiday. And her outlook, which experience had distorted into an expectation of the worst, might never change. Even so, he looked forward to helping her create new and fun memories at every opportunity.

Chapter 18

"I love her lyrics," Grace gushed. "She writes the most meaningful songs!"

"You're not wrong," Tyrel chimed in. "But for me, it's all about her voice. Soft, a little husky." He expressed the rest of his thought via a wolf whistle.

"Enough." Merry got up and walked away from them. Circled the kitchen island twice, then returned to her living room. Even the Christmas tree twinkling in the corner couldn't cheer her up. "I can't do this." They both opened their mouths and she threw up her hands. "Look at me! Tell me I'm not beet red."

Grace chuckled. "I wouldn't say *beet* red. More magenta." She slanted a look at Tyrel. "Although, when he whistled, I think I saw a hint of scarlet…"

Merry buried her face in her hands. "This isn't going to work."

Rising, Tyrel wrapped his arms around her and pressed a discreet kiss to her temple. In the two weeks since Thanksgiving, he'd made amazing progress in their interactions. Finesse was the key. Letting her decide.

"Why don't you go upstairs and put on your disguise?" he suggested rather than announcing that he thought she needed a break. "I'll prep the chicken pasta and Grace can finish the salad while you're gone."

Merry felt the tension falling away as she nodded. "Okay." Telling him the secret of her 'secret' chicken fettuccine recipe had been a cinch compared with prepping for her command performance as Helen Montgomery. Shoot, she didn't even mind his teasing wink.

Anxious to prolong her reprieve, she moseyed up the stairs and into the attic where she stored the glasses and wig she'd used for her artist photo. Bizarrely, she'd inherited both items from her grandparents along with their house, land, and the barn she now lived in.

The makeup she planned to wear wasn't quite that old. She didn't have much use for it since retiring from a life of 'business casual,' but she'd never gotten around to throwing it out. A light dusting of face powder. Shimmering cherry gloss for her lips—hmmm, when had they gotten so chapped? Brown mascara to reveal the full length of her lashes. Too bad there wasn't something in her kit for trembling fingers.

She appreciated everything Grace and Tyrel were doing to help her prepare for next week. Truly. She just wasn't sure how much more of it she could stand. Did they honestly think people were going to want autographs? Her stomach lurched.

"Come in," she answered the light rap on her door.

"Tyrel kicked me out of the kitchen," Grace

announced glibly as she wandered into the bathroom where Merry was. And all she'd done was to ask when he planned to propose. Insufferable man. "So I thought I'd see how you were doing." With the familiarity born of decades of mutually acknowledged friendship, she examined Merry's face critically. "Hmm."

"What?" Merry's heart was pounding like an angry blacksmith. "Am I breaking out?" Wouldn't surprise her with the amount of stress she was under.

"Pfft, no," Grace laughed. "I was thinking about the lighting. Your look is perfect for a casual date night, but I'm afraid you're going to disappear on stage." Thankfully, Eddie had agreed to boss the stage crew, including the lighting, prop management, and… "Oh, have a heart," she groaned, suddenly realizing how Merry had perked up at the idea of disappearing. "It's for charity, remember? The audience will expect to be able to see you."

"Fine." Merry endured the accompanying shoulder bump from Grace with a resigned dignity. "But I don't have to like it." She glared darkly at Grace, who gave in to peals of laughter at that.

"Wow." Grace inhaled deeply and fanned her eyes. She hadn't laughed that hard for a long time. "Let's head back downstairs before he comes up after us."

Tyrel heard them before he saw them. "Just

in time, ladies." Pulling out two stools with a flourish, he went to smile at them and couldn't take his eyes off her. "Wow," escaped him in a gasp.

"Is that my phone?" It wasn't, but Grace needed an excuse to give them a moment of privacy.

"You look amazing," he murmured, moving closer. On second thought, he put the stools away and shot Grace a look. Her back was to them as she hunched over her phone.

"It's just a little makeup." Merry tried to laugh it off, but she couldn't get enough air in her lungs. "Ty, I don't know how I'm supposed to do this." She gestured in frustration. "Every time we have one of these sessions," she gulped when he caught her hands in his, "I can't seem to breathe. How can I sing if I can't breathe?"

He rubbed her icy hands gently, trying to warm them. "We can spend all day at the center tomorrow if that will help," he promised. "I'll chase everyone out and let you sing until that stage feels like home."

"Thank you." His words—and the look in his eyes—warmed her from the inside out.

"Sorry guys, I'll be right there. I've gotta…" Grace's voice trailed off.

Tyrel got the hint. Dipping down, he kissed Merry lightly on the lips. Led her over to the stools and seated her just in time for Grace to join them.

"Everything alright at work?" Merry asked her, striving for a casual tone.

"Everything's fine," Grace assured her. Surprisingly, she'd actually found a message waiting for her. "*White Christmas* is playing on Saturday and Alec wants to go. It'll be his first time seeing it in theater!"

Merry nodded. That explained the light pink in her friend's complexion. "Isn't that your favorite Christmas movie?"

"It's pretty high on my list," Grace agreed.

Tyrel offered the prayer, remembering Merry. Smiled as he passed around the garlic bread. Noticed that Merry didn't take a piece.

"I still cannot believe you're eating this stuff again," Grace laughed as she served herself some of the pasta. "I *know* you swore off it after college."

"I love it," Tyrel interjected sincerely.

"Oh, okay." Grace winked at them both. "I get it."

Tyrel touched Merry's knee under the table, then dropped a wink of his own at her. She could explain about the 'secret recipe' if she really wanted to, but it was okay to have a story that belonged solely to them, too.

"Before I forget again," Grace looked up from where she was buttering a slice of warm garlic bread, "what're you planning to wear to the play?"

Merry shrugged and shifted her pasta around,

hoping it would look like she was eating. "Clothes?"

Grace choked on the garlic bread, so much so that Tyrel leaned over to thump her on the back. She lifted a hand to prevent more well-intentioned first aid and coughed her way to a clear throat.

"Are you okay?" Merry frowned.

"Sure." Grace downed half a glass of strawberry soda, cleared her throat, and nodded. "Fine. I just thought I heard you say your disguise," she motioned to include the wig and glasses, "included jeans and a tee."

"What's wrong with that?" Merry couldn't help the touch of indignation in her tone. She loved casual clothes.

"That might make you easier to identify," Tyrel observed. Taking a sip of his own water, he assessed Merry with some concern. Was she losing weight?

"Exactly." Grace drummed her fingers on the counter, her food forgotten.

"What're you planning?" Merry eyed her friend suspiciously.

"I'm not sure yet." Grace eyed her right back. "We don't have much time to get you an outfit that half the town won't recognize."

Merry shrugged. "I can order something tonight. Should get here in plenty of time."

"Yeah, you could." Grace twirled her fork through the pasta. Took a bite, chewed and swallowed. "But I've got a better idea."

Against her better judgment, Merry responded, "I'm listening." Catching Tyrel's eyes on her, she put half a forkful of pasta in her mouth and chewed.

"The other day Eddie told me that her mom is in an organizing frenzy right now. Cleaning out clutter with a vengeance." She gestured broadly.

"And?" Merry started to take a drink, then slowly set her glass back down. The more excited Grace got, the less likely it was that Merry should be eating or drinking.

"And she just started on her closets." Grace leaned forward. "Her 'this is so last season in Paris' closets! Chock full of stuff that nobody in town has ever seen."

"Except Eddie," Merry snorted. "And isn't she a size two or something?" Remembering that Tyrel was listening, she avoided mentioning her own size twenty-if-you-bought-the-right-brand body. "Besides which, Paris fashion isn't exactly synonymous with modesty."

"Hear me out." Grace held up her hands. "Eddie hasn't spent any real time with her parents since she started kindergarten. Sad as that is, it takes care of the problem of Eddie recognizing your outfit. Objection number two." She held up two fingers. "She's a size eight when she isn't starving herself. Objection number three." She grinned. "Alterations."

Merry still had her doubts. Size eight was a

long way from size twenty. If they found an outfit that could magically be altered to her size, what would be left over to cover her back, shoulders, or whatever else the fashion gurus thought was okay to show off?

"We can try."

"Great!" Grace squealed. "This is going to be so much fun!"

Tyrel jumped in with, "I'll rent the limo."

"What?" both women asked in unison.

"The limo," he repeated, glad to have taken the spotlight off Merry. "Helen should arrive in a vehicle at least as fancy as her outfit."

"Perfect!" Grace agreed.

"I've never ridden in a limo," Merry admitted. It was on her list of wishes that she wasn't allowed to acknowledge because they hurt too much. The idea of riding in a limo didn't hurt. Doing it alone—like she'd had to do so many other things—*that* was what hurt.

"You'll have to pick it up outside of town," Grace cautioned. "Like, waaaay outside of town."

"No problem," Tyrel laughed. "I've been wanting to take Merry somewhere a little fancier than Blinky's."

"Good old grapevine," Merry muttered. She'd already agreed to Harmony's request to take pictures on opening night, and the last thing she needed was to have someone connect the dots long after she'd stopped holding her breath.

At least it sounded like she'd get some time with Tyrel out of the charade.

"Grapevines are old-fashioned," Grace snickered. "This town went wireless a decade ago."

Merry rolled her eyes. "We'll have to do the same for any alterations. If we go to Sew Cut," she grimaced as she mispronounced 'cut' to sound like 'cute,' which was how the owner insisted on doing it, "MaeBell will tell everyone she knows before I get a chance to try the dress on."

"Already have that figured out." Finished eating, Grace hopped up and added her things to the dishwasher. "Be ready to go at seven-thirty tomorrow, okay?"

"Isn't that a little early?" Merry protested. She was never going to get the Wooton refurbished at this rate.

"We'll need every minute." Grace hugged Merry, nodded at Tyrel, and let herself out.

"She's quite a whirlwind, isn't she?" Rising, Tyrel reached for her plate. Her mostly full plate.

"Hang on." Smiling, she put her hand on his wrist to stop him. "You cooked. I'll clean up."

"At least let me help," he protested, but she was already moving. He watched her fluid motions as she took care of the plates and retrieved a handful of lids. "You have the most efficient setup in here." Sliding the stools in, he stole some lids from her before she could stop him.

"What do you want to watch tonight?" Merry asked, stacking the containers nearest her.

"Oh. Sorry, I can't stay." Tyrel opened the fridge and stacked his containers on the ones she'd just added. He wished he could stay. He was worried about her. "I'm also sorry if we've been pushing you."

"It's okay." Merry exhaled slowly. "It's great, actually. Thanks to your help, I might make it all the way to the stage before I pass out."

"Hey." He took her hands in his to make her hold still. "You didn't eat much tonight."

"I, um… No, I didn't." She started to put her hand over her stomach, then remembered both of her hands were occupied. "I can't eat when I'm this nervous."

"Oh, honey. I'm sorry. We really have been pushing, haven't we? I should've seen this sooner. I…" He freed one hand and snapped his fingers. "I can get you something special. Anything. Chinese? Mexican? Indian? Name it."

Merry couldn't help laughing a little. "Indian?" she echoed at the end. "Do you know how far you have to go to find a decent Indian restaurant around here?" Little Persia in Springfield sprang to mind, most likely because that was where Alec took Grace recently.

"So?" Taking her in his arms, he did a couple of dance steps. He'd pulled her along with him during a swing number in an old musical the other night and they'd both been pleasantly surprised.

She let him twirl her, then shook her head. "So I still wouldn't be able to eat it. It means a lot to me that you're offering, but for now I better stick with protein shakes."

"Alright." Tyrel couldn't lie and say he was happy about it. And no matter how hard he thought, he couldn't come up with a way to fix it.

"You're sure you can't stay?" She smiled as she realized she didn't mind letting him know that she really wished he could.

"Talking my grandparents into staying through Christmas was a great idea, except..." He carefully invaded her space. "As it turns out, they expect to see me occasionally."

"Do they?" Merry held her ground even though her pulse had doubled.

Placing his hands on the counter behind her so that she was loosely hemmed in, he smiled down at her. "Silly, isn't it?" Her lips glistened in the light coming from behind him.

"Isn't... What?" She'd completely lost the conversational thread.

"Yeah." Gathering her close, he covered her mouth with his. The wig shifted when he slid one hand around the back of her neck, gently tilting her head back. Her lips moved tentatively beneath his. Forgetting her inexperience for a moment, he kissed her the way he'd so often wished he could.

Startled, Merry turned her face away. Hid it against his chest, making the glasses dig into her skin.

Still holding her tightly, Tyrel bowed his head. He was sorry he'd made her uncomfortable, but he'd enjoyed those few seconds immensely.

"Hey." Lifting his head, he brushed a loose strand of red hair back from her face. "Merry?" One eye peeked at him, but she stayed glued to him. "Please tell me you liked that."

Her response, though muffled, sounded like, "Why?"

"Because married people should like kissing." Her eye closed again and he thought he'd blown it.

To his complete surprise, she exhaled and move out of his arms, leaving him feeling strangely empty.

"You'd better go." She didn't want him to go. She needed him to go. Otherwise she was never going to sort herself out. Her emotions were racing around inside her like cars at a demolition derby, crashing into each other with such force that she could barely tell elation from fear from a powerful urge to have him kiss her that way again.

Tyrel miserably complied. *I've wrecked everything!* he despaired. Six weeks of growing closer and he'd just shoved a wedge between them. She followed him over to the door and he had a mental image of her locking it behind him for good. It was too much.

Turning, he started to plead his case, "Merry, I…"

Reaching out, she pressed her finger to his lips, effectively silencing him. "I'll kiss you like that after we're married." Her stomach flipped, but it felt so good to say it!

Stunned, he allowed her to nudge him out onto the landing. Somehow made it out to his car where it finished sinking in and he let out a whoop of joy. And, coming to himself, offered a humble prayer of gratitude that he hadn't managed to ruin the most important relationship in his life.

Too restless to watch anything, Merry shut off the kitchen lights and went upstairs to take her disguise off. It took a few minutes to repair the wig after that kiss. She just wished it was as easy to undo the surge of emotion it had caused. Were her feelings more or less potent after years of lying dormant? Or just average?

That question and others like it circled in her mind as she stared at her peaked ceiling for the next couple of hours. At last, bleary-eyed, she dragged herself out of bed and over to her roll-top, where she wrote the words that refused to let her sleep.

I thought I was all the 'me' I'd ever be until we met.
Now I'm learning and changing,
My world's re-arranging…

She was still there, dozing over her paper when her phone buzzed with a five-minute warning from Grace.

"Oh, no!" Shooting to her feet, she scrambled to the bathroom. She changed clothes and brushed her teeth so fast that she had to stop at her bedroom door to take her toothbrush back to the bathroom.

Finally, socks in hand, she hustled downstairs. Saw Grace's truck pull up and was grateful when she sent another text instead of honking. Dropped two slices of bread in the toaster before answering it.

[Be right down.] She texted back.

Poured milk into a travel glass and smeared peanut butter on the toast, which she wrapped inside a paper towel.

"Shoes." Setting her breakfast down, she stuffed her feet into her socks and shoes, then hurried out to where Grace was waiting.

"Good grief, girl," Grace laughed. "Haven't you had breakfast yet? How late were you up last night?"

Merry buckled herself in, offered a prayer, then put her head against the headrest. "I went to bed early. Couldn't sleep, though." Sitting with her head back eased the pain in her neck and shoulders a bit.

"Aww, I'm sorry. Well," Grace shifted into reverse, "you can nap after you have your breakfast. We've got a long drive ahead of us."

"Are you sure?" Merry dutifully unwrapped her toast. Grace's interior had stood the test of chickens, planting soil, stray dogs, and whatever else she'd voluntarily stuffed inside her cab during her last eight years as a country vet. Some crumbs or peanut butter wouldn't even faze it.

"Yeah, go ahead. I'll wake you when we get close." Thoroughly amused that Merry was patently oblivious to the back seat full of dressing bags, Grace turned north and settled in for the drive.

It was nearly ten before Grace roused her. "Hey, sleepyhead. C'mon, wake up."

"Are we there already?" Merry rubbed the heel of her palm against her eyes.

"Yep." Grace turned down a rutted dirt road. "Already."

"Whoa, okay!" Merry's hands slammed onto the dash to brace herself as the truck listed to one side. "I'm awake, I'm awake!" Tuning in to the rustling noises coming from behind her, she turned to look.

"I told you she had lots of clothes," Grace reminded her smugly.

"You didn't tell me there was enough for a small village!" Merry frowned. "We have to carry all of those inside…" She glanced around at the empty pastures slipping past on either side of them. "Wherever it is that we're going?"

"No, Moira and I already did a preliminary sorting. The ones behind me are our best bet."

"Moira? Mrs. Brooke? She just…gave these to you?"

"Moira is her personal maid," Grace corrected. "And I'm doing her a favor by taking these to a thrift store. We're just temporarily rerouting one of them."

"Thrift store?" Merry touched one of the dressing bags, noting the hand-stitching and expensive material. "They're not going to know what hit them."

"I know, right?" Grace burst out laughing as she pulled into a driveway. "Now, here's the deal. You're going to a fancy Christmas event. And Tammy is the best seamstress in the four states. Once she has the dress and your measurements, all you have to do is write the check."

"Sounds too good to be true," Merry muttered. The truck stopped and she took off her seat belt. "Better let me decide which ones we take in," she suggested. "I can tell from here that the leopard print isn't what we're looking for."

Chapter 19

Tyrel stopped twice on their way out of town next Friday. First stop, the grocery store.

"Hey, you two."

Merry almost jumped out of her grandad's leather jacket when Heidi rounded a corner and came up beside them. "Hhhey." Noting the pile of cans in her sister's cart, she abruptly remembered that the grocery store was running an early sale on Christmas candy. Rotten luck that Heidi happened to be cashing in on it right there, right then.

"Getting ready for movie night?" Heidi grinned, nodding at the basket of deli sandwiches and chips Tyrel was carrying.

"No…" Merry started shaking her head and couldn't stop until Ty's arm slipped around her shoulders.

"Going for a drive," he said nonchalantly. "Thought we'd save a few pennies by getting stuff here."

"You'll be back for the play, won't you?" Heidi asked. She stifled the urge to suggest that they stop to change first. The play wasn't black tie or anything, but worn jeans and beat-up tees might dampen the festive mood.

"We wouldn't miss it," Tyrel answered easily.

"Great!" Heidi brightened. "We'll save seats for you."

"Oh no." Merry bit her lip to keep the rest of the words from spilling out.

"I'm bringing my grandparents," Tyrel inserted. "I'm not sure where they'll need to sit."

"Oh." Heidi glanced back and forth between them, her forehead creasing slightly. "Yeah, sure."

"See you later." Tyrel flashed her a grin and used his light hold on Merry's shoulders to steer her toward a checkout lane that had just opened up.

Merry kept her hands in the pockets of her grandfather's worn leather jacket during the checkout, hoping to hide the manicure Grace had given her the night before. Grace hadn't done much more than smooth her nails and trim her cuticles, but a packet of fake, press-on nails was waiting for her in the car.

"What's that?" Tyrel leaned closer as he waited for the cashier to hand his card back.

"Um…" She cleared her throat. "I was just saying that this takes 'going a country mile' to help out to a whole new level."

He chuckled about that all the way to their second stop at a gas station on the far side of town.

She made an unnecessary trip to the restroom, then bought a package of gum to ensure that she was seen. Setting up an alibi for their trip out of town seemed like overkill to her, but Tyrel was having enough fun for them both.

"Anybody spot you on the inside?" he asked in his best tough-guy voice as she fastened her seatbelt.

"You're a nut," was her only response.

At her suggestion, they listened to some episodes of Lux Theater, an old program that adapted popular movies to the radio. Tyrel snickered through the comedy, *What a Woman*, and listened intently to *The Story of Louis Pasteur*.

"Can you imagine what the world would be like without men like him?" Tyrel shook his head as he parked beside a low-slung muscle car.

She shuddered. "I try not to think about it."

Tyrel carried her garment bag into the hotel, which left her with a small black rolling bag that kept banging her in the ankle whenever she turned.

Just get through this and you can ride in a limo, she told herself. Repeatedly. All the way to room four-oh-three, where Tyrel opened the door and hung her garment bag for her before returning to the hall. He winked at her, then crossed the hall to the room where he would change into something a little classier.

"I can't believe I'm doing this," she grumbled. A spaghetti monster would've been a comfort compared to the nest of reptiles currently writhing in the pit of her stomach.

A tear slipped down her cheek as she went over to kneel by the bed. Somehow, around the scents of commercial cleanser and fabric softener, she managed to thank Heavenly Father for the gift of her voice. For the opportunity to serve her community by participating in the play. For friends like Grace and Tyrel who were going out of their way to help keep her secret.

Calmed by the prayer, she whisked through a shower, using honeysuckle-scented body wash, a luxury she wouldn't ordinarily indulge in. Then, it was time.

Yards of soft, silky fabric spilled out of the garment bag as she opened it. The top layer of the skirt flopped up it as she fluffed the layers of tulle, then slid back down her arm, a river of dark chocolate with bursts of icy white that trailed down from the bodice. The gown originally had a bow-train-monstrosity on the back, and Tammy assured her that it would provide more than enough material for the necessary alterations.

She held her breath as she stepped into it. Watched the fabric pull tighter as she zipped it. Straightened the filmy white sleeves. Smoothed the bodice. Risked a shallow breath. Chanced a deeper breath. Tammy's altered seams didn't rip. She twirled just for the fun of it next, enjoying the whisper of silk and tulle as the skirt flared.

Giggling, she resumed watching her reflection. Filled her lungs and ran through some warmups, her volume gradually increasing. Unbelievable. In fact. It was shockingly comfortable. She definitely needed to send Tammy a bonus.

Satisfied on that subject, she got back to business. Pulling her hair into a low, severe bun, she added the hairnet and pinned it in place. Placing hand towels on her shoulders and bodice to catch any errant makeup, she decorated her face. Then took the wig out of her rolling bag, touched it up, and slipped it on. Winced as she added enough hairpins to hold the wig in place. Settled the glasses on her nose.

Shivered. "Hello, Helen." Even knowing the transformation was coming, it was still spooky to see her eyes staring at her out of a stranger's face.

Her phone buzzed with a text from Tyrel.

[Ride's here.]

"Okay." She hoped her voice wasn't that shaky on stage. "Time for that limo ride." Maybe if she didn't let herself think about where the limo was going, she wouldn't be petrified by the time they got to the community center.

The elevator doors opened with a business-like *ding* and she stepped hesitantly out onto the first floor. Her skin crawled as she felt people staring.

Then she saw Tyrel.

He straightened slowly from where he'd been lounging against a chair. His entire posture changing as he looked her over, working his way up from the floor-length hemline to her eyes. She could tell from the heat in her cheeks that she was blushing, but she wouldn't have traded a second of his admiring perusal for a dozen limo rides.

Not to mention it gave her a chance to appreciate how he looked. His long-sleeved, burnt orange button-up accentuated his muscles while making his eyes bluer than she'd thought possible. Navy blue slacks gave the impression of added height, and she toyed with the idea of going up for a kiss, just to check.

In the end, though, she was too overwhelmed to risk it. Her mind was already working double-time to keep up with things, and too much was changing too quickly. Her clothes, her face, even the temperature when they stepped out into a frigid wind.

She gratefully accepted his coat when he draped it over her shoulders. She did her best to hold her skirt up for the short distance to the limo, where…the door opened from the inside?

"Climb in before you catch your death!" a friendly voice invited.

Merry stopped. Looked at Tyrel. "Is this the right limo?" She blinked. Wow. That was a question she'd never expected to ask. Hang on. Why was he smiling so big that he looked like a kid wearing his grandad's dentures?

"Better climb in," he encouraged.

Merry took a final long look into his clear blue eyes, then ducked into the limo as directed. Where she found herself sitting across from none other than Adina Cohen. A music star. She blinked. Shook her head to see if that would make the mirage vanish.

"Hello, Helen." The mirage spoke.

"You're…" Merry sucked in a gulp of breath. "You're… You sang "It's My Day" in *Carla*." *Along with every other song written for the title character. Good Merry, good. Now tell her something else she already knows.* Her hand, which didn't really seem to belong to her, reached out and touched the other woman's knee. "You're real." Squeezing her eyes shut, she leaned back against the seat, willing herself not to be ill.

"Uh-oh," rumbled a deep voice. "Looks like you have a fan."

"Looks like you fellas had better give us a moment."

"What?" both men asked at the same time.

"Honey, it's cold outside," protested the man that Merry realized had to be Adina's husband, Brett Warren.

"Bitter cold," Tyrel concurred anxiously.

"Wait inside the hotel, then," Adina answered evenly.

"There's no arguing with that tone," Brett announced.

Merry's skirt moved as he brushed past, then the door closed, cutting off the chilling breeze from around Merry's ankles.

"Alright," Adina's voice said gently. "It's just the two of us now. Think you can catch your breath?"

Merry's stomach was still reeling from shock, but she didn't want to disappoint her favorite celebrity, so— "I…I think so."

"Good." She patted Merry's knee.

Merry bit her lip, tasted makeup, and made a face. "I don't understand why you're here, though."

"Your fella." Another kind of knowing smile played across Adina's lips. "He thought you could use some moral support."

"So he just called you and asked you for a favor?" Disbelief colored Merry's tone.

"Not exactly." Shifting over so that she was sitting beside Merry, she explained, "Tyrel knows Brett from their time in the military."

"What did…he tell you about me?" Merry asked out of sheer curiosity.

"Not much." Adina was just as curious about her. "Just that you needed a friendly face tonight."

"And that's you?" Merry squeezed her eyes shut. Counted to ten and opened her eyes. "Let me rephrase that. Meeting you is a dream I never thought would come true. But meeting you tonight, when I'm already a basket case?" She stopped there, figuring they'd all get her drift.

Adina squeezed her cold fingers in genuine sympathy. "I'm sorry we surprised you."

"I guess it had to be that way." Merry laughed feebly. "I'd never have left the hotel if I'd known." On top of the stress of singing at the play, she now had to not do or say anything in front of Adina that she'd regret. For ever and ever and…

Adina smiled knowingly. "I'll never forget meeting my favorite Broadway diva for the first time. I was minding my own business, singing in the chorus of my first big show, when I came around a corner and there she was." She snickered at the memory. "I was so star struck that I got my own name wrong when I introduced myself."

Despite herself, Merry smiled at the story.

"It happens to all of us is what I'm saying," Adina assured her kindly.

"Thank you."

Smiling, Adina reached over and lowered the window an inch. Sure enough, they were standing right outside the door, walking and swinging their arms to stay warm. "Climb back in, I think we're ready to go."

As he climbed in and sat across from his wife, Brett stole a kiss.

Tyrel grinned mischievously at Merry and leaned forward too, though he paused with an inch to spare and let her come the rest of the way.

Brett used the intercom to let the driver know they were ready, and they were underway.

"I hear you're quite the singer." Adina smiled encouragingly at her.

"Oh." Merry smiled back wanly. Gesturing toward Tyrel, she observed, "He's not exactly a reliable judge."

Tyrel caught her eye. "I think what she means is," he flicked a look at the phone in Adina's hands, "*she* hears it."

Sure enough, Adina's phone began playing Merry's cover of "Silver Bells." Adina was about to mention Helen's gift for singing from the heart when she noticed the faint green tinge on the younger woman's face.

"Ohhhkay." Merry ducked her head. Thank goodness she hadn't actually eaten much of her half of the sandwich.

Adina stopped the music and motioned for Tyrel to open the window on their side.

Merry all but shoved her face out the window, taking in huge breaths of cold air to lower her temperature and force her stomach to settle again.

At that point, Adina was starting to get worried. There was no way this kid was going to make it through a performance if she couldn't even listen to a recording of her own voice without getting queasy. Maybe it was time for a different approach.

"So, how'd you get started? Singing, I mean."

Merry took a final breath and pulled her head back in. Snatched off her instantly-fogged glasses. "Started? Um…" She looked longing at the window Tyrel was closing. Logically she knew she couldn't ride the two hours to Cadmia with her head out the window and still expect to sing when they arrived, but ohhhh, it was tempting to try. "Music has always been part of my life."

Adina smiled and raised both eyebrows encouragingly.

"There was music class in grade school, of course. And I joined the church choir in college so I could practice the different parts." Her eyes dropped to where her hands were folded tightly in her lap. "But mostly we sang while we worked as kids. I was pretty terrible."

Adina's forehead puckered at that. A performer needed a certain minimum amount of self-confidence to really make good.

"Anyhow, after I finished renovating the barn where I live, I finally had a space of my own. Started singing again." Looking up through her strangely thick and dark eyelashes, she checked the faces of those around her. No one tried to fill the silence of her pause, so she continued. "There's this musician online who does all of his own accompaniment. Gave me the idea to do the same thing. One thing led to another and now I've got a tiny recording booth where I can work as Helen." She hesitated. "But my real name is Merry." The words came out in a rush that left her limp as a wet noodle.

Tyrel twitched involuntarily, but otherwise, the world rolled right along in its proper order. She hadn't exactly expected a photographer to pop out of the glovebox, yet it was still something of a surprise to have Adina and Brett simply smile at her.

"Merry. What a nice name." Adina's lips

curved up. "What's your last name, Merry?"

"McKinney," she answered automatically.

"Merry McKinney." Adina nodded. "That's a nice alliteration, has sort of a sing-song quality to it." Cocking her head to the side she remarked, "I'm a little surprised you don't use it professionally."

"Oh, no. No, I couldn't do that." Merry read the question in Adina's eyes and answered it the best way she knew how. "I'm not *you*. I'm…me. Just me. No one would…pay to hear *me* sing. Worse, what if… Oh, I can imagine what people in town would say if they ever figure out…"

Adina took Merry's hands and gripped them firmly. As she'd hoped, the contact seemed to refocus the younger woman, stemming her rising anxiety. Maintaining eye contact, she inhaled slowly, deliberately. Exhaled. Repeated the process until Merry was breathing with her. Merry was off to a good start as a singer, but she had a world-class case of stage fright waiting to ambush her.

"All kinds of reasons to use a stage name," she said firmly. "One young man told me that every time someone mispronounced his name he thought they were announcing the daily special. Of course, he was working a lot of international restaurants at the time." Her efforts were rewarded with a wobbly smile, which she decided to count as progress. Inspiration struck and she leaned forward. "In general, we artists are a strange lot. Why, I know one who barricades himself in his room and turns on whale noises when he writes."

Her anxiety fading, Merry giggled. "Wow, that's pretty intense."

"Oh come now." Sensing his wife's intent, Brett jumped easily into the conversation. "You probably do something unique yourself."

"I…don't think so." Merry shrugged a little. "If a tune or the words won't leave me alone, I stop to write them down." Wondering if that sounded arrogant, she amended, "Then I have to work out the other half of the song. It's a lot easier to start with the words than the music."

While they all chuckled with her, Adina discreetly checked the time on her phone. They were over an hour out. Good. Plenty of time.

"How did you get started?" Merry asked.

Adina grinned and settled into the story. Somehow, by the time they crossed the county line, she had them all singing carols, Merry included.

"Just the girls this time," Brett said after the last chorus of "Deck the Halls."

"Oh, what shall we sing?" Merry asked, thoroughly caught up in doing something she enjoyed with people she liked.

"How about "Silent Night"?" Adina handed her another of the small, bottled waters from the limo's beverage console. They both stopped to drink and she privately admired the glow emanating from her sweet young friend.

"That's my personal favorite," Merry agreed huskily. Twisting the lid back onto the bottle, she took a deep breath. "Silent night," she sang.

Adina hummed along for the first verse, then joined in on the second.

Merry's ears registered the perfect mixing of their voices as they faced each other and sang the ancient carol. Adina's soulful, polished voice was the perfect contrast to Merry's simple, honest vocalizations.

Panic tried to close in on her as Merry realized that the limo was slowing. Looking out through the limo's one-way window, she saw that they were pulling up to the community center. From the way they were inching forward, she guessed that the driver was trying to get past the crosswalk to drop them off. Remembering her wig for the first time in an hour, she double-checked it with trembling fingers. Shut off her phone and held it out.

"I'll stay in the car until it's safely away," Tyrel explained as he accepted her phone. "My grandparents are going to meet me at the parking lot a couple of blocks away. You're somewhere backstage, helping with the play, or wherever we're not. Okay?"

"I'm still not comfortable with all this deception."

"Deception is for amateurs." Adina winked.

"Tonight you're not only the magician, you are your own finest illusion."

Merry clung to those words as she accepted Brett's help in exiting the limo to oohs, aahs, and even a few squeals. Each sound was like a fork squeaking on a plate until she realized at least half of it was for Adina, who'd come to stand beside her.

"Alright now. Keep waving and let's get inside before we freeze our vocal cords."

Merry obeyed, startled that she hadn't felt the chill at all this time. The elbow-length white gloves she wore provided some protection, as did the layers of tulle in her skirt, but her ears and nose were in danger of freezing solid.

Chapter 20

Merry clung to Adina's arm shamelessly while Tony—yep, the same fella who'd spent hours teaching her how to pose for her website video—circled them with a camera. Behind him, another two rows of teenage and middle-age fans were busily working their cellphone cameras. Merry had more pictures taken of her in those two minutes than she had in her entire life.

"You are here!" Noella burst onto the scene like a firecracker, startling Merry so badly that she jumped. "I am Noella Cormier." She shook hands with them both. "Thank you for coming, we are so excited to have you." Glancing past them at the swelling crowds, she invited, "Will you come with me, please?"

Merry watched Adina sweep into the community center after her, skirt slightly raised so that she wouldn't trip on it. Merry came along behind them at a more sedate pace, cautious of the heels she'd let Grace talk her into. Something about how they'd change her height and her gait and make her harder to recognize. Yeah, well, if she tripped and face-planted, they were also going to change her face in a way that nobody could miss.

The lobby was empty except for a few strategically-stationed volunteers. And the funky odor that was the domain of buildings used for everything from sporting events to cooking classes.

She offered up yet another silent prayer as they entered the theater area, then looked over and saw none other than Mrs. Arnold. The woman who was arguably responsible for the whole mess. Who was, in fact, mid-argument at that moment.

"Enough of this nonsense." Mrs. Arnold's speech was clipped and her shoulders rigid with irritation. "We've got crowds and crowds of people out there, in the cold, waiting for this…this, this *person* who hasn't shown up and simply isn't going to." She clapped her hands sharply. "My little starlets have been practicing like mad all month and are ready to perform this evening, but the entire stage will need to be rearranged. Quickly now!"

The group she'd been addressing—or perhaps holding captive was a better term?—looked over her shoulder at the new arrivals, grinned, and got back to work.

For Eddie, that meant coming right over to where they were standing.

"Ms. Montgomery, my name is Eddie Brooke. Welcome to Cadmia." Eddie gave her a firm handshake. Turned to Adina, Broadway diva extraordinaire. "Mrs. Cohen. I've had the great pleasure of attending several of your performances. I'm…so honored to meet you."

"My, how sweet of you to say." Adina's

sincere smile kept the words from sounding trite. It helped that she believed the girl, who looked like she had a lot more to say but was quite properly restraining herself.

"We were only expecting one singer," blurted John, Eddie's assistant. And promptly withered under Eddie's reproving look.

"What he's trying to say," Eddie smoothly translated his words to her own satisfaction, "is that we were about to run a sound check. And though we're not sure if you'll be joining Ms. Montgomery on the stage, Mrs. Cohen, we will be happy to make the necessary arrangements if you'd like to." She hadn't spent her formative years around society's smoothest for nothing.

"We've only got six mics!" protested John, who clearly hadn't learned his lesson the first time.

"John." Eddie put her hand on his shoulder and spun him around in a one-eighty. "I just remembered that I haven't seen the cardboard turkey since this morning. Would you go find it for me, please?"

Merry watched the mini-drama playing out before her with genuine amusement. Mrs. Arnold had collapsed onto a chair like a kite whose string was just cut. Noella was already distracted by a handful of minor emergencies, and Eddie was laser-focused on Adina.

"I wouldn't dream of intruding on Helen's performance," Adina demurred, taking Brett's arm. "We're just here to support a worthy cause."

"Oh, Adina, please." Merry stepped forward earnestly. "I…" She gulped as all eyes settled on her. "I know I should've asked you sooner." Seriously, why hadn't she? "But I would love to sing with you tonight."

"If you're sure?" Adina reached out and took her hand. She'd never believed in sink-or-swim and especially not in this case. If Merry felt like a flop tonight, she'd probably pick up and move. Or literally die from embarrassment.

Merry smiled. "I'm sure."

"Alright." Eddie nodded, her mind racing through options. "In that case," she spun on her heel and projected her voice to the stage crew, "I need another stationary mic and a second chair, pronto!" Luckily, though John was right about their limited wireless mics, the center had acquired a handful of stationary mics over the years.

Merry mouthed, 'Thank you!' to Adina, who waved it off with a smile and a wink. She made a mental note to thank Tyrel later. Apparently he knew her better than she knew herself, because a friendly face—standing beside her on stage—was exactly what she needed tonight.

They ascended the stairs together, their skirts swishing softly as they moved over to the stationary mic that the crew was scrambling to set up.

"This is where you'll sit during most of the play." Eddie indicated two relatively comfortable-looking chairs.

Adina gave the no-frills set-up a glance, then asked, "Could we get some water bottles?"

"Absolutely." Eddie hand-signaled for them. Turned back to the singers. "The prompter will cue you when to start and when to stop. He'll be standing there." She pointed at a large red 'x' taped to the back wall, pleased that she'd finally found the perfect job for last year's stage manager. To Helen she said, "I understand you have a list of songs prepared?"

"A playlist, yes." Merry chuckled, surprising herself, and handed over the CD she'd brought. "They're all Christmas carols except the last one," she told Adina. "Harmony, um," she realized Eddie was still there, listening, and fumbled, "Wells, asked me if I could do a special number."

"Special night," Adina bumped her shoulder in old-friend fashion. "Unveiling a new song."

Merry's cheeks paled, but Eddie was nodding in agreement.

"And we're ready for a sound check," Eddie announced, switching gears seamlessly at a wave from the sound booth.

"After you," Adina deferred to Merry.

Merry smiled weakly and stepped up to her mic. Noticed that it was the same brand as the one she used in her recording booth. Retreated a bit due to her experience with the brand. Ran a scale. Eddie was using her hands to talk to the sound booth, but Merry barely noticed. Somehow, standing up there with the lights and the bustle and the mic, "I Will Dare" bubbled up out of her.

To her astonishment, Adina joined in on the second verse with a beautiful harmony.

"If I have dirt on my face and hands, it's because I have fallen. But again I stand! And again I will dare!"

They soared through the rest of the song with the energy it called forth from their souls. The room was dead silent after the last echo faded away. Then someone whooped and everyone began to clap. Adina included.

Merry was glad when someone called for everyone to take their places. "When did you memorize my song?" she asked Adina in astonishment as they took their seats.

"Oh, I couldn't help it. It's just so poignant, I've hardly been able to get it out of my head since the first time I heard it!"

"Thank you." Merry felt her blush deepening. Noticing the gathering audience, she sucked in a breath. "Look! My parents." They whispered softly as the seats filled, Merry describing her relatives and friends as they entered.

"Quite a cheering section," Adina noted as an entire row went to Merry's family.

"Except they don't know I'm me." Merry sighed. "I'm not…I'm not ready for them to know."

"I understand." Adina waved to a group of particularly excited fans in the near seats. "Now tell me, what've I gotten myself into?" She grinned to take any sting from her words. It was a full house tonight and she didn't really want Merry to think about that.

Merry laughed. "It's a Christmas play, so I just chose some of my favorite carols. You'll be able to recognize them from the first few bars."

The doors closed and the house lights went down. A short burst of Christmas music signaled the play was starting. Three warmly-wrapped tweens stumbled onto the stage, pretending to stomp snow off their boots as they hollered to let 'Mom' know they were home.

Adina genuinely enjoyed the play, clapping her hands and laughing with everyone else at the clever dialogue. At the signal for them to sing, she took care not to overshadow Merry. However, as the play went on, as Merry sang the familiar songs, she seemed to gain confidence, leaving Adina in the enviable position of joining in whole-heartedly in the delight of singing of their Lord and King.

Despite their best intentions, they stopped the show twice due to applause from the audience. The cast didn't know what else to do, so they politely joined in until Merry stepped forward, holding up her hands for silence. The audience complied, and she motioned for the play to resume.

"Well done," Adina whispered, squeezing her arm.

The first hour whisked by faster than Merry would've believed possible. The intermission was only bearable because of Adina's support.

And then, all at once, it was nearly over. She swallowed. Nearly time for her solo. This song was different from the others. Harmony and Grant, who had somehow ended up as the parents despite Harmony's best efforts, were on stage 'cleaning up' after a late Christmas breakfast and Merry's song was essentially mood music.

Stepping up to the mic, she hummed along with the opening strains of her first official love song. "It happens every time." She shifted slightly so she could watch the happy couple. "Every time that I remember life before you. My heart cracks a little—till you take me in your arms."

Grant complied, sweeping Harmony into an embrace that brought a gasp from the audience.

"And promise me again your hopes, your fears. Your smiles, your tears. Are all mine. Mine to share."

Grant lowered his head for the happy ending and Merry smiled as Harmony rose ever so slightly to meet him.

"I am yours and I'll be there. Every time. For

all time." She continued to the second verse, her volume decreasing as the stage lights dimmed. "For," she held the final notes, "all time."

The world erupted into chaos after that. Autographs. Selfies. Fans. Compliments that made her face flame as red as her wig. And Adina stood by her through the entire ordeal until Noella came to rescue them.

"It's getting late," Noella called over the din at last. "The community center is closing and I'm sure Ms. Montgomery and Mrs. Cohen need to be going."

The disappointed groans tore at Merry, but she'd passed exhausted about thirty autographs ago. Where had all these people come from, anyway? Had the town population doubled overnight? Maybe they'd bused people in? For some insane reason. Yeah, she was so tired, she…

"I'll…be here again tomorrow." She cringed away from the boisterous response.

Adina's arm tucked around her waist and Merry found herself whisked away toward one of the community center's many exits.

"Psst." Grace beckoned and Merry hastily led Adina into the women's locker room.

The door had barely closed behind them when they heard some giggling fans pass by.

"Whew." Grace locked the door. "Your clothes are over there. Put your dresses in these bags and I'll smuggle them out later. And your truck," she gave her the keys, "is parked two blocks down by the post office."

Merry was relieved to see that a bag waited for Adina as well. Her tired mind decided that Tyrel must've passed along their plans and she rolled with it, gladly swapping her heels for sneakers. Once they were both in tees, Merry with her wig off and Adina's riotous black locks tamed into a braid, they ventured into the hallways.

"Easy does it." Adina linked her arm through Merry's as they left the community center. "We're just a couple of people headed home from the play."

"Oh!" Merry stopped at the crosswalk. "Br...I mean..." She shook her head to clear it, something the frigid air had somehow failed to do. She'd almost mentioned Brett by name. "Will *he* know where to meet us?"

Adina gestured with her phone toward the crosswalk, where the policeman who was directing traffic was signaling for the crowd to cross. "Yes, I've texted him."

"Wonderful." Merry yawned so hard her jaw popped. "Wow. Um, where can I drop you?"

"Tyrel has a rental car waiting for us," Adina answered. "And then we're heading to the airport, I'm afraid."

"The airport?" Merry couldn't hide her disappointment.

"Yes, unfortunately." Adina wrinkled her nose.

"Some bigwig is hosting a huge Christmas party and we simply have to go." She simpered the last few words, making Merry laugh. Brett passed them just then, but Adina had done enough fan-dodging in the past that they knew better than to acknowledge each other.

"Will you come back?" Merry bit her lip, embarrassed that she'd asked. Adina was an insanely busy person.

"I'd like to." Adina smiled at her quaint surroundings and squeezed the arm of her new friend. "Or maybe you could come visit me."

"Wow." Merry blinked. "Yeah, I guess. I mean, if you're sure…"

Adina laughed. "I promise, I don't invite people to come visit me unless I actually want to see them."

They chatted companionably all the way to Merry's truck, where Brett was already waiting in the rental car conveniently parked beside it. Hugged. Adina wiped away Merry's tear. Hugged her again.

Merry waved goodbye as they pulled away.

"Hey, lady." Tyrel stepped down from the sidewalk. "Give a guy a lift?"

Merry buried herself in his arms, breathing him in. "Thank you. Thank you so much for scaring me to death by introducing me to a complete stranger that I was dying to meet."

If Tyrel hadn't had both arms wrapped tightly around her, he would've scratched his head in confusion. "So…we're okay?"

"We're wonderful."

"You're wonderful." Tyrel's arms tightened as she relaxed the rest of the way, so that she seemed almost boneless. He chuckled and kissed her hair. "C'mon, let's get on the road."

Tucking her into the passenger seat, he set the bag with her wig in it carefully inside before backing out and starting toward her home. Waved at people he recognized as he drove. Waited until traffic had thinned out, then turned around and drove to a highway that would take them to the hotel. Merry was still asleep when they arrived, and he seriously considered trying to carry her in. Deciding that would draw too much attention, he shook her arm instead.

"Up and at 'em, gorgeous."

"Hmm?" She stirred. Her eyes fluttered. "Hmm? What…?"

To take his mind off how adorably kissable she looked, he cleared his throat and reached into the back seat. "I'll get the bags."

"Tyrel! What are…?" She tried to sit up and found herself restrained by…a seatbelt? Reaching down to unclick it, she snagged one of her fake nails. "Ouch!"

"And she's awake." Tyrel smiled as he helped her with the seatbelt. "We're at the hotel."

"Oh." She groaned and slumped back in the chair. "I have to do that whole performance again tomorrow."

Coming around to open her door, Tyrel helped her down. "We're almost there. Two snug, warm beds where we don't have to get up until we're ready. Hot breakfast in the morning." He kissed her temple as he guided her into the lobby.

She snuggled against him as they rode the elevator to the fourth floor. When he found the hall empty, he scooped her up and carried her to her room. Swiped her card, slipped it into her hand, and pressed a light kiss to her lips.

"Goodnight, gorgeous."

Merry smiled sleepily. Tripped on the gripper strip as she started through the door. Caught herself on the doorjamb and decided that she should probably throw the deadbolt as long as she was still in the general vicinity of the door. Shuffling over to the bed, she flopped down face-first.

Eventually the cold and discomfort got to her, forcing her up long enough to kick off her shoes. It took several tries to get her phone plugged in, and then her mouth tasted so bad that she picked up her bag and went into the bathroom. One thing led to another, so that when she crawled into bed again—under the nice, warm covers—she was in a pair of new, comfy pajamas that she'd ordered especially for the occasion.

The drops of lavender she'd put on the pajama shirt collar did the trick, and she was sawing logs in no time.

Tyrel, on the other hand, spent most of the night praying and pacing. As they were leaving the play, his grandmother had grumpily asked why Merry hadn't joined them.

Much to his surprise, his grandfather had jumped into the conversation. Wrapped an arm around Tyrel's shoulders, and admonished him quietly, "She's a special woman. Don't you do anything foolish like letting her get away."

The jewelry box Tyrel had unpacked and brought along was proof enough for him that he wasn't making a snap decision to make his grandparents happy. On the other hand, a successful proposal took *two*. Was Merry ready? He'd officially gotten the go-ahead from her father before church last Sunday.

So what? So her parents liked the idea. So his grandparents liked the idea. So he...loved the idea. So he prayed.

He was still on his knees the next morning when his cell phone trilled with a message from Merry.

[Hey! You promised me food.]

Remembering when he'd said the same thing to her, he laughed.

[Twenty minutes?] he texted back.

Pain lanced through his legs when he tried to stand. "Ooof." Rolling onto his hip, he rubbed both legs and wished he'd asked for thirty minutes. Laughed and shook his head. He was getting old. Pushing past it, he hauled himself to his feet and into a cold shower. Dressed quickly and exited his room.

"About time," Merry teased from where she was leaning against her door, arms folded across her chest.

"Note to self," he grinned, tucking his room card into his jean pocket. "Don't keep Merry hungry."

Holding hands and giggling like children, they left the hotel and went out to breakfast. Then to a theater where he'd arranged a surprise.

"Okay, I give up," she laughed after guessing wrong about a dozen times. "What are we watching?"

The lights went down just then, saving him from having to answer. He shifted the popcorn tub so that they could both reach it, then slipped his arm around her shoulders. He *really* hoped she liked this movie as much as her mother thought she did.

Merry gasped and covered her mouth with her hands as the opening credits began to roll. "No way!" Turning to him, she impulsively kissed his cheek. "You're amazing! How in the world did you make this happen?"

Laughing, he squeezed her shoulders. "If you don't mind, I'm trying to watch a movie."

She clapped her hands as the action started. It took Tyrel a little while to get past the period costumes, but in the end, the movie wasn't half bad. Who could argue with a story where the underdog got the girl and beat the slimy, conniving fop in a life-or-death sword fight? Sure, the princess was temperamental. But she'd met her match in the gentleman-soldier she eventually married.

As the lights came on, Tyrel took Merry's hand. Laced his fingers through hers. "I think I know why you like this one."

"Of course you do," she laughed. "It's a good movie."

"Yeah, I'd watch it again." Grinning, he rose and tugged her to her feet. "I kind of feel like he got off easy, though."

"What? How?" It was on the tip of her tongue to recite the list of trials the main character had endured, but she wanted to be sure she knew what Tyrel was talking about first.

"I didn't see him propose." Tyrel stopped and looked down at her as he spoke.

"Oh." Surprised, she dropped her eyes and tried to tell the butterflies in her stomach to calm down. They were a huge improvement over the old spaghetti monster, so she couldn't really complain, but…

"She sort of proposed on the boat, I guess," he hedged. "But I'm going to get down on one knee," he suited action to word, glad they'd moved onto the carpeted section, "and make the requisite speech." Looking up at her, with her hair framing her face, the red glints catching every ray of light so that she appeared to be wearing a halo… He swallowed hard.

"I've been looking for you for a long time, Merry McKinney. And when I started to get to know you, I'll be honest. I was intimidated. You're not only a capable, intelligent, beautiful woman, you had absolutely no experience," he saw her shoulders start to stiffen, "with flawed men." He wanted to get up and tuck her into a hug, then kiss away the hurt look on her face, but he stayed where he was. It would be fine. He just had to finish. "I'm no match for heroes from books or movies." He began to relax when she did. "I started worrying that you wouldn't be happy with a man who didn't save the world once a week."

"Twice on Saturdays," she quipped breathlessly, referencing old-time movie theater schedules.

His lips curved up in a slow smile to match the shaky one she was offering him. "I'm going to make mistakes. I'll forget important dates or buy the wrong size or something equally imperfect. But I'll always love you." Lifting the ring from his shirt pocket, he asked, "Knowing all of that, will you marry me?"

She couldn't help the fearful hesitation that sent her eyes darting back and forth between the ring and his face, his eyes. A perfect round diamond the size of the tip of her pinky finger nestled in the center of rounded golden prongs.

Smaller diamonds encrusted every other prong and ran halfway down the band on both sides. *Was this real?* Was that exquisite ring being offered to her by the most wonderful man she knew?

"I'll never be able to wear this in the shop." She clapped her hands over her mouth, mortified.

Tyrel came swiftly to his feet, well inside her personal space. "Is that a yes?"

Slowly, her hands moved to rest on his chest. "It is."

Lifting the ring from the box, he slid it onto her finger. Kissed the palm of her hand. Kissed her forehead, and cradled her close, keeping just enough distance that he could watch the wonder on her face as she held the ring up to the light. Moved her hand, setting the diamonds twinkling.

Merry could feel the ring's temperature changing to match her own. What had been cold metal moments before was now forever a part of her. Taking care of it would mean setting it someplace safe at times, but in her heart she would always wear the commitment she'd just made. For time and all eternity.

Slipping her arms around his neck, she kissed Tyrel warmly.

Thank you for reading <u>A Country Mile</u>, I hope you enjoyed it!

To learn more about Grace, Noella, and Harmony, read the rest of the "Gifts of the Heart" series.

Visit me at
leacarterwrites.wixsite.com/flinch-free-fiction

More titles by Lea Carter

<u>*Contemporary Romance*</u>
"Gifts of the Heart"
Four single Latter-day Saint women find love in the tiny, fictional town of Cadmia.
A Country Mile
In Due Season
Food For Thought
Home Free

<u>Fantasy</u>
"Silver Sagas"
The ongoing adventures of the royal fairy families.
Silver Princess
Silver Majesty
Silver Verity
Troubled Skies
Dress Blues
The Seeker's Storm
Heartwood
Wedgewood
Fission – coming soon
Fusion (2021)

"Coddiwomple"
Three high-flying adventures in the fictional world of Jattori.
Dragon Sparks
Dragon Fugue
Dragon Thunder